The World Comes to Mercy Creek
A Morrissey Family Novel

Jason L. Queen

This is a work of fiction. Names, characters, organizations, places, events, and incidents are either products of the author's imagination or are used fictitiously. Any resemblance to actual persons, living or dead, or actual events is purely coincidental.

Copyright © 2021 by Jason L. Queen.

All rights reserved. . No part of this book may be reproduced in any manner whatsoever, or transmitted by any means electronic or mechanical, without express written permission of the publisher.

FIRST EDITION

Cover and layout design by Chloe Renee Tobin

Marketing and Distribution by Independent Literature Brewing Company, Winchester, Virginia

For more information please visit www.bookbrewers.com or email jasonlqueen@bookbrewers.com

Printed in the United States of America

ISBN 978-1-7360070-1-3

The World Comes to Mercy Creek

To My Mom and Dad

You Taught Me How To Be A Husband, Father, and Provider

Part 1

Chapter 1

Whenever cars crossed the Mercy Creek bridge, the tires of the car and the old boards of the bridge would join together to produce a loud, rhythmic thumping sound. Those not familiar with crossing the bridge would immediately pull to the side of the road and prepare to change whichever tire had gone flat. Upon realizing there was no flat tire to change, the driver would look back at the small covered bridge and turn their head to one side or the other in a quizzical manner as they tried to figure out what had made that troubling thumping sound.

Locals had long since grown used to the thumping and either paid it no mind or found some sort of solace in the constancy of it - not only of the rhythm but in its continuing existence. The newest generation of drivers remembered that sound as a child in the back seat of their family's vehicle. Others claimed to remember it when the rhythm joined the cadence of the hooves of horses pulling a wagon or cart.

Younger locals approached the bridge with a different mindset - and often at a higher speed. The more reckless teenage drivers discovered that the faster they drove, the faster the thumping, and at some point the thumping would become chattering. Along with the chattering, another phenomenon would sometimes occur for the most skilled of the reckless teenagers. As their car emerged from the bridge, a plume of road dust and exhaust would swirl into one and follow the vehicle off of the bridge and into the open air, giving the brief impression of a cyclone chasing after the emerging automobile. One such skilled, yet reckless, teenager was Virgil Morrissey, Jr. He was known by his family as Little Virgil, but his friends all called him Virgy. Virgy Morrissey was able to produce a sound no one else had been able to. The combination of his light car - an Austin 7 he had salvaged from the Kaiser's Estate - and a dangerously high rate of speed, produced not a thumping, and not a chattering, but a humming sound. And a rumor, which quickly became legend, was that Virgy Morrissey had once produced not just one, but two cyclones.

On this particular day, the youngest Morrissey son was driving his mother back from a quick meeting she had attended at her friend's house up the river. Out of respect for his passenger, he created a slow thumping sound as he passed through the Mercy Creek covered bridge. As they crossed the bridge, Little Virgil's mother, Nellie Morrissey, was silently thankful that the bridge was covered, because the creek below it was frozen over and she had, for seven years, successfully avoided looking at the creek when it was frozen.

After crossing the bridge, Little Virgil made a right onto a gravel road that led straight up the mountain. Little Virgil accelerated and his tires spun for a moment, throwing gravel in a shower behind them. Nellie laughed unexpectedly and immediately felt embarrassed. Little Virgil didn't even try to hide his shock and instead, laughed as loudly as his mother, and then pushed the car's gas pedal to the floor, sending even more gravel shooting out behind them as Nellie laughed again. This time, much to Little Virgil's joy, she didn't even try to stifle it.

The gravel road quickly led them through the woods and into a large clearing, ringed by a board fence. Most of the boards were painted white, except for a short section off to the left where winter had slowed Little Virgil's progress and then finally stopped his painting some time in early November. Virgil Morrissey -Little Virgil's father - had finished building the fence in September. Along the right side of the clearing were three newly built sheds. One was painted white and the other two were still awaiting their paint. Chickens, too numerous and erratic to count, moved around between the sheds during the daylight hours. They were locked into their coop behind the sheds at night. Along the left side of the property was a tall red barn. The older Virgil had painted that with the help of his oldest son, Joe, almost five years earlier. Inside and behind the barn lived a dozen cows. Some were for milking, some for breeding, and some for butchering.

Inside a small shed behind the barn and in a fenced lot around the shed, lived three turkeys. Virgil painted that building himself and no one went inside the lot or the building but Virgil. Virgil's protectiveness of his turkeys was the stuff of local legend.

Along both sides of the barn and running parallel to the pine forest were stone fences built to reroute water and dissipate any flash floods. Although only one flood had occurred on the property as far back as anyone knew, Virgil built the walls to make Nellie feel secure in the fact that the property would never flood again. The walls had mainly been built by Joe, Joe's younger brother Jeb, and two of Joe's friends who worked for daily pay and board in the Morrissey's barn. The wall was finished by the end of the summer of 1935 and one of the friends, Monte Montgomery, had continued to come around for three more summers in hope of winning the heart of the oldest Morrissey daughter, Virginia. His hopes were dashed in 1939 when Ginny married a boy who lived across the creek on the Kaiser's estate. Ginny moved across the creek that year with her new husband, Josh, which caused Monte to join the Sheriff's Department as a jail guard. Eventually, Monte was promoted to Deputy.

The house was in the center of the property, built on the foundation of the original house which had been destroyed in a flood. The house was two stories with an attic. Virgil started building it in 1934 and finished it in 1936. The house was white and the roof and shutters were painted green. Nellie loved every square inch of the house. It was her dream home.

As they pulled up to the front of the house, Virgil Morrissey walked out on the porch and stood with one hand on a post and the other hand held up in a wave. A smile came across his face and he said, "How many times did he make you wanna jump out of the car?"

"Too many to count," Nellie said as she winked at her son and climbed out of the car and walked towards her husband.

"Did the Ladies League decide if they wanted fireworks tonight or not?" Virgil asked.

"Half of us want them. Half do not," she said. Her tone suggested she was annoyed, but not at Virgil.

"That's pretty much where the decision was sitting before the emergency meeting." He said "emergency" with a lilt to his voice. "The Kaiser has to know if they want them or not. We have to have time to set them up. It's not some quick process, Nell. Midnight is..." he looked at the pocket watch, "ten hours from now."

"We want them," Nellie answered quickly and confidently. "Start setting them up please." She stood still for a moment or two before opening her mouth as if to say something. She then closed it, and after a moment of thought, quickly said, "Do whatever you need to do to make it happen. Let's fill these skies with lights and colors."

Virgil almost pushed the issue to make sure she was certain but as she walked into the house, Nellie nodded her head and made a sound that told him she was certain enough for everyone.

"Charlene!" Little Virgil yelled towards the upstairs of the house. No answer. "Charrrrrleeeeen!" he yelled again.

"For land's sake," Nellie said as she walked back quickly onto the porch. "She's down in the basement bringing up jars."

"Tell her I'll pick her up at nine, please," he said quickly. He paused for a second and then corrected himself. "Tell her ten." He quickly added, "please."

"She won't need you to pick her up, son," Virgil said.

Nellie quickly added, "Your little sister will ride in with us and we'll all meet up around ten."

Little Virgil answered by sitting back down in the seat of his car and pulling on his hat. "I wasn't planning on going to the Kaiser's place. I was gonna take Charlene with me to the town dance."

"See you tonight," Virgil told his son as he walked towards his truck. "Check in with me when you get to the farm, okay?"

Little Virgil started to reply but then decided against it and gave his father a salute. After he started his car again, Little Virgil made a wide circle across the yard, and sped down the hill and out of sight. Virgil started his truck and was careful to stay on the gravel as he backed up and pulled forward a few times before following the same road his son had just driven down, except he made a right onto a road that led up through the pine trees and across a low point in the creek.

As Virgil drove onto the Kaiser's property, his eyes were busy surveying the land ahead and beside him, while his mind was busy mulling over thoughts of his youngest son. To hear Little Virgil tell it, life was smooth sailing and all was well. Lately, the older Virgil's heart and gut were telling him otherwise.

Chapter 2

Ralph Pourpin had still not gotten used to the thumping of the Mercy Creek bridge, even though he had been crossing it at least once a month for the better part of a year. He was coming back from a visit to the Kaiser's estate after yet again having his services rejected by the house manager. Though he had tried to convince the house manager, the property manager, and even the head of security, that the Kaiser needed an attorney on retainer, Pourpin had never even gotten a sit down with the owner of the estate which now covered close to 250 acres, plus an additional 500 acres worth of timber cutting rights. The man owned horses, cattle and several other types of smaller livestock. His employee total was over fifty. Ralph Pourpin was convinced the Kaiser needed an attorney. The hard part was convincing the Kaiser. Actually, that was the impossible part since no one would let him even meet with the man.

Another thing Pourpin knew was that he needed clients. He had just finalized a land sale one county over so that case was closed. And he had lost his one case in court at the county seat. He didn't get a fee and his client got thirty days. The way he had it figured, if he didn't get a client or two in the next few days, he wouldn't be able to pay rent past the second week of January. He had no more savings. Even his car wasn't his car. He had to borrow it from his landlord, Mrs. Beaumont. Bea Beaumont was the owner of the boarding house he had called home for the past several months. "Borrowing" her car meant he paid double rent on days he borrowed it. He once called it "renting" her car and she had given him a sour look and smaller portions at dinner that night. Since then he had called it borrowing and gladly paid double rent.

It was while crossing Mercy Creek bridge that he first got the idea. And this was an idea that just might have the Kaiser driving to meet with him, begging to pay his retainer fee. After thumping through the old covered bridge, he pulled off to the side of the road, shut the engine off, and jumped out of the car. The cold air caused him to make a strange sound and shake a little bit, so he reached back into the car and grabbed his coat. Putting the coat on helped, so he walked confidently back to the bridge and under the roof.

He walked straight across the bridge, the opposite way he had just crossed it in his car. Then he spun on his heel and crossed it again. This time he stopped when he heard a board thump. He bounced up and down and heard it thump again. It didn't sound quite the same as it did when he was in his car, but it was the same board. He thumped it again and then walked the length of the bridge and back out onto the end where he had first driven through when coming from the Kaiser's house. The road narrowed before the bridge, he noticed. The river was close on his left, which often caused the road to flood, but the bridge was raised up, which caused a dropoff down to where the creek and river met. Pourpin walked over to the right side of the road, opposite the river side and noticed outcroppings of rock, hidden behind brush. That rock was why the road narrowed before the bridge. Water on one side and rock on the other gave the road builder very little room, which gave the driver only one narrow lane before crossing the bridge. Pourpin looked up the hill towards the Kaiser's house and then down at the rock, which was on the Kaiser's property.

Pourpin stood still for a moment and then walked back onto the bridge and started pacing in small circles until he heard a creaking sound diagonally across from the thumping board. Pourpin jumped on the creaking spot and heard a louder creak and then walked slowly over to the thumping board and made it thump again. His weight, which usually slowed him down and worked against him, helped him as he moved in larger circles, finding sounds and identifying their origins. When he found a cracking spot he let out a howl and began to stomp around, trying to hear it again.

It was while he was stomping that the truck came up on him, so quickly he could barely get out of the way before it flew past him on the bridge. The thumping was so loud and the dust was so thick that Pourpin ran as fast as he could to get off of the bridge and onto the road. When he emerged from the darkness of the bridge, he saw two things at once.

The first thing he saw was the truck swerving to the left and off of the road towards the river. The second thing he saw, at almost the same time, was a large animal with skin like a deer but a giant head, run from the road and into the trees and up the mountain. Pourpin's eyes switched back to the truck, which was heading towards the river. He then quickly looked back to the woods. At this point, Pourpin's ears took over because he could no longer see the animal, but he could hear it crashing through the trees. And then it made a long bellowing sound. That sound was quickly swallowed up by the truck's horn which erupted from underneath the truck's hood, which had just been crumpled upon impact with a strong looking sycamore tree. In this instance, hitting the tree was a stroke of good fortune for the driver, because fifty feet away awaited the Shenandoah river, which was running high with freezing cold mountain water.

"That thing was bigger than our truck!" the woman shouted as she rolled out of the passenger's side door of the truck.

A girl that looked to be in her late teens climbed out of the truck and started pointing up the hill as well. "Is that smell comin' from that thing?"

"What was it?" the woman said. "And what's that smell? It's awful."

"Your truck is overheating," Pourpin said, trying to be helpful. They ignored him.

A boy in overalls shouted from the truck, "It was a bear!"

The driver emerged from the truck and immediately went around to check the damage the tree had caused.

When Pourpin walked up to them, the woman screamed and the teenager jumped into the back of the truck while the driver came around from the front of the truck, looking like he was ready to commit a killing.

"Where did you come from?" the woman yelled from inside the truck. The man was the only one not back in the truck.

"I was on the bridge when you drove past me," Pourpin said. "I'm fine. Don't worry." He brushed off his jacket and checked his shoes, which were dusty but not muddy. He did not mind dust, but he despised mud. He quickly looked up at the man who was now between Pourpin and what appeared to be the man's family. "Did you all see that...thing?"

"I seen it," he said.

The woman quickly jumped out of the truck. "What did you see? We saw what looked like a bear."

The World Comes To Mercy Creek

"It won't no bear," the man said. "It was red. Probably somebody's bull got out."

"And bears hibernate," Pourpin said.

"That's a lie," the man said.

Pourpin decided not to debate, especially since the man suddenly seemed to be holding a stick and brandishing it in what Pourpin immediately sensed was a threatening manner.

"Well then what was it?" the woman asked. "If it was a bull, it's the biggest bull I've ever seen. I don't think it was no bull."

"It's arms was long," the teenager said. She had suddenly emerged from the safety of the truck and was looking tentatively at the woods across the road. "Real long," she added for emphasis.

"It had arms?" the woman asked. "I thought those were front legs."

"No, No, No. They was arms," the teenager said.

The man looked back at his family and nodded his head towards the truck. They climbed back in and slammed the door.

Pourpin looked around for a minute and asked, "Did that loose board on the bridge cause you to wreck?"

The man looked at him for a second or two and then just turned around and got in his truck and started it up. The engine started but then made a loud screeching sound like metal on metal. The engine stopped and the man got out of the truck and disappeared under the hood again. Banging sounds were followed by a grunting sound followed by more banging sounds, and then the man came around again and got in the truck and started the engine a second time. This time, the screeching sound didn't happen.

Pourpin started to walk toward the truck but it began to move back towards him so he began to move backwards as well. When the truck stopped, the woman got out and put the hood down. It made a different screeching sound as it was lowered. The truck started backing up again before the driver changed gears and revved the engine while he pulled the truck back up onto the road and then drove away. Something was dragging from the front bumper and causing sparks on the road as the truck disappeared.

By the time he had gotten back to town, Attorney at law Ralph Pourpin had not forgotten about the animal he had seen, but he had switched his focus back to what could make him money. His first task was to draft a letter to Virginia's State Senator, then the Governor.

"Dear Sir," he wrote. "I hereby type out this letter to serve as due notice to you as a representative of this state of a dangerous hazard which lurks within our county. On state Route 606, there is a bridge..." The clacking of his typewriter keys went late into the evening.

Chapter 3

Virgil Morrissey despised the smell of gunpowder. It caused his stomach to churn and it often turned his mind back to battle. There had been times when the smell had nearly caused him to stop hunting, but the necessity of hunting caused him to always press on, despite the feelings it caused within his mind.

For that reason, and a few others, he had turned the fireworks duty over to Helmut, one of the young men who lived on the Kaiser's estate. He was eighteen, just a year younger than Jeb, and eager to do anything that would please the Kaiser. This made the fireworks job all the more perfect for him. The Kaiser loved fireworks as much as Virgil hated the smell of gunpowder.

Nellie Morrissey loved fireworks as well and she had fought hard to have them included in the New Year's Eve festivities on the mountain. She had no idea Virgil disliked them. If she knew, she would have hated them.

The town, Lyttle's Mill, had decided not to have fireworks that year. Instead, they planned to only do the annual dance marathon, which was held in the high school gym. It was set to start at 8pm on December 31st, and end when the second to last couple stopped dancing. Usually that was in the early morning hours of January 1st. At first, everyone in the area, including in Mercy Creek, was disappointed that the fireworks were canceled. Some were angry. But Nellie quickly came up with a plan to get the Kaiser to set off his own set of fireworks from a supply he kept for the Fourth of July - his favorite holiday. It was in this way that the folks on the mountain had become the ones who would set off the New Year's Eve fireworks display.

When Virgil had given Helmut the final okay after Nellie's meeting, Helmut had gone into full action mode, recruiting several other guards and estate workers to help him implement plans he had finalized in his mind since before Christmas. By the time the sun was setting, Helmut was searching for Virgil to report his readiness. Virgil was occupied by a crowd of housekeepers just outside the kitchen when Helmut found him.

"One at a time, please. One at a time," Virgil was saying with his voice raised, but not loud enough to imply anger. "I can't understand y'all unless everyone slows down."

"Show some respect and stop shouting down Mr. Morrissey," Leeza May, the Kaiser's cook, shouted. Her voice did reveal some anger. "All this hollering? All this hollering? It's unnecessary. It's unnecessary. IT IS UNNECESSARY!" she shouted so loud that one of the younger housekeepers named Eisel started crying. "And quit with the tears," Leeza May said to her quickly as she pointed to an older girl named Veronica and said, "Tell the man what you saw. And NOBODY else talk."

"Ronica thought it was a bear," Easil said. "But it looked at me." She started crying again but choked back her tears when she looked towards Leeza May. "It looked right at me like a human. And...." She looked around the small crowd that had gathered, before finishing. "...and it smiled at me." With this, she burst into frantic tears while half of the girls laughed at her and the other girls began to console her.

Veronica took over and said, "It was taller than the biggest bear I have ever seen, though I have only seen two in my life. But it didn't move like a bear. It moved like a...a man-bear."

"Which way was it heading?" Virgil asked.

"Towards the back end of the farm," Veronica said, pointing across the yard and through the maple trees.

Virgil walked across the yard to the side drive and reached in his truck. When he came back, he was carrying a rifle, which he slung quickly across his back.

"You plan on shooting it?" Leeza May asked.

"Only if you'll clean it and cook it," Virgil said as he unclasped the yard gate and walked down a lane through the maple trees.

"Helmut," Virgil said, "Make sure everything is ready to go for midnight. No need for me to check behind you. I trust you."

As he walked, Virgil switched his thinking away from party preparation and instead, he began to make a list in his mind of the things he needed to do as a result of the bear sighting. And that's what it was. Bears lived all over the mountain and they rarely hibernated like other types of bears in other states. The color the girls said the bear was didn't make sense, though. Reddish brown was the color of a grizzly. He had never heard of a grizzly ever in Virginia, but he couldn't be too careful when it came to bears.

    He found the tracks at the back of the property and he stood over them and walked alongside them for several minutes before kneeling next to the clearest set. By the time he stood up, he knew it wasn't a bear. These tracks belonged to something Virgil had never seen before.

Chapter 4

"He wasn't wearing a mask, but he had his hat pulled way down over his forehead. And he was wearing glasses with dark lenses," the bank teller said. "So I don't know his hair color or his eye color. I'm sorry. I told the police officer the same thing. I was afraid to look at him when he showed me the gun."

"Oh, I understand," the reporter said. "I bet it was scary. Because there wasn't anyone else out there working with you, correct? The others were in the back offices?"

"Right," she said slowly. "And in the vault. The other teller was back in the vault, counting our surplus change."

"I would be scared, too, if I was alone and that happened. And when you're scared, it's almost impossible to focus. And then everyone expects you to know all these details."

"Yeah," she said softly.

"What about when he was leaving? When he wasn't pointing the gun at you? Did you see him then?"

"No," she said. "He pulled the door shut behind him." She sniffed and rubbed her nose. "I'm sorry."

"Can I teach you a trick, I learned?" the reporter asked.

The teller looked up slowly. Her eyes moved around faster than the rest of her body. "Sure," she said, with a hint of caution.

"Take a walk," the reporter said. "And try not to think about all of this stuff."

She made a scoffing noise.

"I know it sounds ridiculous," he said. "But try not to think about it." The reporter looked around the room and then leaned in and lowered his voice. "You might be surprised what you remember when you're not trying to remember."

The teller showed just a hint of a smile, and said, "It's a great suggestion, but I think I'm fine staying in here." Her eyes went to the police officers that were standing around.

He took a step back but kept his voice low. "Is there somewhere around here where I can take a smoke?"

She whispered, "Out back and down the steps."

The reporter tapped his jacket pocket and said, "Care for one?"

She stood up quickly, adjusted her skirt and said, "Follow me."

Once out back, the reporter lit one and offered it to the teller. "Is a Lucky okay?"

"That's my favorite," she said as she took the cigarette and inhaled slowly.

The reporter watched her shoulders relax after exhaling slowly.

"Thank you," she said. "I needed this."

"Me too," he said. "I'm nervous, too."

"Why are you nervous?"

"This is my first big story," he said. "I usually cover the farm report and some sports."

"Those are big stories, aren't they?" she asked.

"They can be," he said. "And I love writing about those things, but when we got the call about the robbery, I was the only reporter not out for the holiday, so they sent me."

"You're gonna do great," she said.

"Thank you. I'm gonna try my best." The reporter took a long drag on his cigarette and asked, "Why are you all open today, by the way? It's New Year's Eve."

"We're always open," she said. "On New Year's Eve I mean. It's not a bank holiday or anything."

"That's funny," he said. "I always thought it was." The reporter watched her take another slow drag on the cigarette.

They both smoked in silence until she asked, "What's that type of ear boxers have?"

"I beg your pardon?" the reporter asked. A wrinkle ran across his brow as he looked at her through their mingled smoke. "What about boxers?"

"Their ears...They are called something when they get all...strange looking. What's that called?"

"Cauliflower ears?"

"That's it!" the teller said, before catching herself and lowering her voice. They shared a quick laugh because of her outburst. "The guy who showed me the gun had cauliflower ears."

The reporter nodded and finished his cigarette. "Be sure to tell one of the officers that, okay?" The teller nodded. "And ask one of them to keep an eye on your house. They'll do it."

"I live in a boarding house," she said.

"Here, in Lyttle's Mill?" the reporter asked.

"No. Right now I live in Winchester. I used to work at the Winchester branch, but they transferred me here when Mrs. Irene retired." She took another smoke and exhaled slowly. "I'm moving here soon. I just need to find a place."

"My brother is opening a boarding house over on Church Street," the reporter said. "He should be taking boarders next week. I can mention you to him." He pulled out his reporter's pad. "I'm sorry. I never asked your name."

"Esther," she said. "Esther Hausen."

"I'm Jeb Morrissey," the reporter said, as he shook her hand.

When he walked back out onto the sidewalk in front of the bank, he waited until he was a few blocks away before he stopped and pulled out his reporter's pad again. Writing quickly, he listed out several questions and noted some names he needed to investigate. When he was satisfied he had written down everything he needed, he headed back to the newspaper office.

The walk from the bank to the newspaper office took just over four minutes. The Lyttle's Mill Herald spread across two buildings near the center of town. The reporters, photographers and editors were all in one building together. It was three stories tall and brick. The third story made it the tallest building in the town, though the top floor was unfinished and used only for storage. Jeb's office was in the printing and distribution building across the street. It was a small block building, drab among the Victorian houses on either side of it.

Jeb's walk from the sidewalk to his desk took him up two separate flights of stairs, across a big warehouse space, and down a long hallway. From his window, Jeb could see the other office building. He was the only reporter with an office in the distribution building. In fact, he was the only person at all with an office in the distribution building. Artie Fox, who ran the department, ran it from the floor. His desk was in a corner near the conveyor belts. The typesetters and machine operators worked from the floor as well. Jeb was also the only reporter who had never had an article published on the front page before, or the second page, so that might explain his office situation.

Jeb rolled a blank sheet of paper into his typewriter and began to punch out the beginning of his story. Most of the reporters were off for the holiday. That's why he caught this story. And he planned on making the most of the chance to write a real one. Something more than a student athlete profile, or a piece about hay prices.

By nightfall, he had written as much as he could. For the rest of the story, he needed more information. He reached across his desk and slid his small notebook closer to himself. His intention was to write out a few questions and list some possible options for how to proceed with the story, but thirty minutes later he had filled several pages with his thoughts and questions and ideas.

When he looked up at the clock it said 8:25. He was supposed to pick Millicent up at 7. As he grabbed his hat and jacket from the hanger on the back of his office door, he prepared himself to end the year with another argument.

Chapter 5

Desperation will make good men do bad things. That proved itself to be true many times throughout the decade leading up to 1940. Hunger led to theft. Fear led to violence. So many crimes had been committed by desperate men during the Great Depression, that the number one building project throughout the country was new jails.

More people were hired for law enforcement jobs than any other field. One of those hired during this time was Deputy Monte Montgomery. He was Mac MacBatten's least favorite brother-in-law. He was Mac MacBatten's only brother-in-law.

"Good Evening Sheriff Tyson," Deputy Montgomery said.

"You don't have to call me Sheriff while we're in the office, Monte." Bo Tyson had been the county Sheriff for twenty years and he no longer tried to hide his irritation. No matter the subject and no matter the audience, if he was irritated, he showed it. He tried to keep reading the reports stacked in front of him, but the young Deputy kept making sounds that seemed designed to catch the Sheriff's attention. When he finally looked up, Monte was standing directly over him, at the edge of the big steel desk.

"Sheriff Tyson, I've been thinking. Well actually, I was reading. Which got me to thinking. Have you ever heard of the Trojan horse story? It's mythology."

"I have," the Sheriff said. "All the soldiers hide in a big wooden horse, and then the enemy brings the horse into its gates, and the soldiers slip out at night and take the city?"

Monte shook his head quickly and said, "No. Nope. It was this battle, see? I've been reading about it. In a big book I have. It's mythology."

"You said that already," Sheriff Tyson said.

Monte just kept talking. "This battle was a big one and I mean huge. One side was winning. But then the other side got this idea to hide out in a big horse made out of wood. And when the winning side rolled that big wooden horse into their city, they was bringing the enemy in without knowing it."

The Sheriff stared at his Deputy for a moment and then sighed and said, "Oh okay. I must have been thinking about a different story."

"Yeah there's all kinds of stories in mythology. Easy to get confused," he said. "It's okay. But what I was thinking after reading that story in my big mythology book, was about that car thief over in Jefferson County."

"Not our jurisdiction, Monte," the Sheriff said, as he looked back down at his reports.

"Yes sir, but Sheriff Tyson, whoever stole those cars over in West Virginia might come across the state line and cross into our county. Or they might even *be* from our county, and they're crossing the state line to steal cars from West Virginia. Either way, it's a matter of time before they strike here."

"And when they do," the Sheriff said, without looking up, "we will investigate the crime. We cannot investigate a crime which has never happened. We cannot and we will not. Am I understood?"

"Right," Monte said. He turned and walked back to the door. "Have a good night, Sheriff Tyson."

"You heading over to the fireworks?" the Sheriff asked. "It's your night off. Enjoy it."

"I will," he said as he opened the door.

"Hey Monte?" the Sheriff called out.

Monte turned and looked towards the Sheriff.

"What was it you were gonna tell me about the Trojan horse?"

"Oh, I don't remember," Monte said. He ran his hand along the edge of the door and then raised it in a wave. "I'm sure it was something foolish. Happy New Year, Sheriff Tyson," he said. And then he was out of the door and gone.

The phone rang as the door shut and Tyson answered with "Sheriff's Department."

From the desk on the far side of the big room, a woman's voice called out, "Dagnabbit, that's my job!"

The Sheriff raised his hand and waved towards the woman's desk. "Sheriff's Department," he repeated into the phone. While he listened, the Sheriff looked down and scribbled notes on a piece of paper he kept on his desk for calls. He knew Mernie, who also acted as their dispatcher, was standing over him. He kept listening and then said, "Your husband saw it?"

Mernie walked over and looked down at the paper on his desk and saw question marks and the word "bear". The Sheriff said, "No I believe you. I'm just asking who saw it besides your children. If Artie was near by and saw it, I just wanted to know." He wrote "daughters" and then "bear" again.

At Mernie's desk, the phone started ringing again, but she didn't move to answer it. She kept moving her eyes from the Sheriff to the piece of paper in front of him. As he was writing on the paper, he looked up and pointed towards the ringing phone but Mernie stayed long enough to read the word, "Bigfoot" surrounded by a circle of question marks.

Chapter 6

"Where's Uncle Yates?" Charlene asked, as she looked around at the crowd of people all over the Kaiser's Estate.

"He's away on a trip," Nellie said.

"Does he go away as much as Daddy does?" she asked.

"No, but working for the Kaiser causes people to have to travel more than we thought." Nellie put her arm around her youngest daughter and squeezed her close. "But thankfully they always get to come back home to us."

Virgil walked up and said, "Happy New Year" while he leaned down to hug Charlene. "Ready to see some fireworks?"

"Yes!" Charlene said. "But can I see the Kaiser's birds first?" The Kaiser had a bird sanctuary inside one of the buildings behind the house. During the warm days, the birds flew outside in a netted area, but during the cold months they stayed inside. At last count, there were over twenty-five different types of birds in there.

"Sure!" Virgil said. He looked at Nellie. "Wanna come with us?"

"I'm gonna try to find some of the ladies from the committee and warn them about the fireworks," she said. "You two go have fun."

A guard walked up as Nellie was talking and said to Virgil, "The Kaiser is asking for you in the trophy room. He's going hunting."

"Hunting?" Virgil asked. "What in the world?" He looked down at Charlene and said, "I'm sorry, honey. I've gotta work for a bit. I'll be right back and we'll go look at all the birds you wanna see."

Charlene didn't say anything. She just moved back to her momma's side.

"It's okay, Virgil. Go do what you need to do."

Virgil hesitated. Looked at the guard. And then back to Charlene and Nellie. "I'll be right back."

"I should've gone to the dance with Little Virgil," Charlene said.

"Little Virgil's not going to a dance either," Nellie said. "He's meeting us here."

"We'll see," Charlene said. "I'm gonna go find Abigail."

Before Nellie could say anything, Charlene had moved along the side of the crowd and was out of sight.

"Ma'am, is your husband nearby?" a man she didn't recognize, asked Nellie. "I just need a minute of his time."

"I hate to tell you. You're gonna have to find him and get in line," Nellie said. She pointed towards the Kaiser's house and then turned to find her friends.

"I can see fireworks on the Fourth of July," the Kaiser was saying in his trophy room, as he pulled his Mosin Nagant down off of the rack on the wall. "But one cannot hunt a Virginia grizzly just any day of the week."

"I don't know that it was a Grizzly," Virgil said. "I can't even be certain it's a bear, yet."

"What did the tracks tell you?"

"Not as much as I wished they would. To tell you the truth, I've never seen tracks like that before."

"Well, Veronica described a bear and Easil said it was reddish brown. I've never even heard of a reddish brown black bear. So it has to be a grizzly. And I intend to hunt it. I have killed on three continents, Virgil. Please cease your worrying about me. I need you worrying about a host of other things. But I should never be on that list."

"You're near the top of the list, if I'm being honest," Virgil said.

"Well move me to the bottom or off of it, please."

"I've tried," Virgil said. "And I've come to the conclusion, it's impossible."

"Have Yates and Uma returned from Richmond yet?"

"No, their train doesn't arrive until ten. I have Josh and Ginny picking them up."

"Did I know that?"

"That Josh and Ginny were picking them up? I doubt it. You shouldn't have to worry about stuff like that. "

"Good. I have enough to worry about," the Kaiser said. "There are grizzlies in my woods."

The World Comes To Mercy Creek

"I don't know that it's a grizzly if it's in Virginia," Virgil said.

"But you don't know that it is not. Do you?" the Kaiser asked.

Virgil changed the subject. "Ralph Pourpin came by here this morning and left a message with Otto. He wants to meet with you at some point tonight."

"Now I'm sorry I have to kill that grizzly."

"Why"

"Because I owe him one for giving me a reason not to have to meet with that tree stump."

"He's not that bad," Virgil said.

"Isn't he though? He's a blood sucker. I would call him a vampire, Virgil, but vampires have a mysticism about them that make them epic in nature. There is nothing epic about this man. He is more like a tick."

"You need to let me know what you want Leonid doing on the Estate." Virgil said. "Am I saying his name right?"

"How the hell should I know?" the Kaiser said. "I can only assume that my sister named him after two names and pushed them together. I will most likely call him Leonard."

"Regardless, I will need to know what you want him to do here, once he arrives," Virgil said.

"What do you mean? He will of course be doing whatever it is you need him to be doing," the Kaiser said, as he selected a hunting knife from a drawer and slipped his belt through the sheath loop and then buckled his belt and adjusted his jacket.

"He's your nephew. I know nothing about what he can or can't do," Virgil said.

"He's a nephew I've never met. His mother wants him out of Germany, so she is sending him here. I'm sure he will be happy to do whatever it is you choose for him to do. But whatever it is, I would like him doing it within twenty-four hours of his arrival."

"You're not much help," Virgil said.

"As I'm sure he will not be either." A knock on the door caused the Kaiser to call out, "Come in."

Josh, who was one of the lead guards and Ginny's husband, walked only one step into the room and said," The dogs are ready, sir."

"You're taking the dogs?" Virgil asked the Kaiser.

"Oh, yes. They would never forgive me if I hunted a grizzly without them."

"Will you be back in time to watch the fireworks, Sir?" Josh asked.

"I'm not sure if I will be back to the house, but I plan to enjoy them no matter where upon the mountain I find myself."

"Will you at least take a few of the guards with you?" Virgil asked.

The Kaiser looked like he was going to argue, but instead he smiled and said, "Anyone is welcome to tag along, of course."

"Thank you," Virgil said, as he turned and directed Josh to find a few men to go along on the hunt.

"Do not send anyone who might try to steal my shot, Virgil. I make this clear to you, so you can make it clear to everyone else. Yes?"

"Nobody steals your shot," Virgil said.

"Right oh!" the Kaiser said as he stomped down his right boot and spun to pick up his rifle.

As they exited the house together by the side door, the Kaiser began walking towards the forest along the back of his property. He was quickly joined by an older guard named Otto and a younger man named Werner. Virgil went in the opposite direction and circled back along the edge of the crowd. He wanted to take Charlene to see the birds before the fireworks started. He had less than an hour, but that was plenty of time for her to see them and they could spend some time together.

"Mr. Morrissey!" a voice called out for him. He recognized it immediately. It belonged to Ralph Pourpin.

Virgil turned around and greeted him. "What can I do for you, Ralph?"

"I know he's here," Ralph said. "This is his party. This is his home. I left a message for him."

"He's actually not here, right now," Virgil said.

"Virgil..." Ralph said slowly. "I'm not from around here."

"I know that, Ralph. You're from Vermont, right?"

"Pittsburgh," Ralph said.

"Okay. What's that mean to me?"

"It means I'm not like the people you're used to dealing with."

"Oh I see," Virgil said quickly. "You're smarter than the people I'm used to dealing with. Right?"

"Now you've got it. You catch on quickly. One of your grammaws must be from the North."

The World Comes To Mercy Creek

Virgil laughed. "No. Both of my grandmothers were from Virginia. And they both taught me how to behave. That's why I'm not punching you in the nose right now."

"I don't mean to upset you, Virgil. But come on. How many times do I have to come by here, before you all get the picture?"

"Well," Virgil said, as he looked around the crowd. "I have to admit, that's the question I'd like to ask you right now, Ralph."

"I was hoping I could sit down with the Kaiser and discuss something of pressing importance to everyone in this community. How many times a day would you say he and all of the people who work here cross that bridge on the road down there?" He pointed towards the river.

Virgil sighed. "Too many to count, Ralph."

"That's what I thought," Ralph said. "I need to sit down with him. Tonight."

"He's not here." Virgil was starting to get frustrated. "I don't know what else to say, Ralph. I really don't. But there's fireworks in just a little bit, and I hope you stay for them."

Ralph looked around and said, "Maybe next time you see me, I won't be asking to be his lawyer. Maybe he'll be asking me."

"I hope not, Ralph," Virgil said. "And I mean that in the nicest way possible, but I hope not."

Before Ralph Pourpin could say anything else, a large woman and an older man with dark skin and silver hair came up to Virgil. The woman grabbed his arm.

Virgil turned as Leeza May led him away and behind them, Ralph Pourpin started the long walk down the hill to where he had parked.

"What's wrong?" Virgil asked.

"I can't get into the root cellar," Leeza May said. "It's locked."

"It's always locked," Virgil said. "Don't you have a key?"

"No. I mean the inside door is locked. And I don't have a key to it, because that door is never locked. The outside door is, but I don't ever need to go through that door. That's why I have access to it from the kitchen."

"I'll take care of it, Leeza May," Virgil said.

"I'm sorry to bother you, Virgil," she said. "I know Yates is out of town and so is Miss Uma, so--"

"I will take care of it," Virgil said quickly. As he reached the house, Leeza May went towards the kitchen area, and Virgil went to the back of the house and put his key into the padlock, and turned it. As he made his way down the stairs, he looked around the room and then moved over to a spot on the floor. He kicked dirt over the spot and looked past it and saw another shoe print. A small one. He scuffed that one as well and then looked around the entire floor before he called out, "I'm down here, Leeza May. I'm gonna open up your door from this side. On my way now."

From the other side of the door at the top of a small set of stairs, he heard Leeza May's muffled voice.

Once he opened the door leading to the kitchen, Leeza May thanked him repeatedly while gathering up all the jars and bags of food she needed.

As Virgil emerged from the root cellar into the back yard, he could hear cheering and clapping. A whistling sound cut through the night air, followed by an explosion of white light. Then more whistling and more explosions of different colors. Red. Green. More white and then blue and red. As the fireworks continued, Virgil searched the crowd during the bursts of light, hoping to catch the familiar silhouette of Nellie or Charlene, but he could not find them. At the end of the fireworks, someone shouted out a countdown and everyone cheered and shouted Happy New Year! It was a beautiful fireworks display and everyone around Virgil seemed happy and enthusiastic.

On the other side of the yard, Virgil's wife and daughter made their way to the front porch steps to wait for him to be done for the night.

Chapter 7

At the train station in Richmond there was a long bench which ran along the wall next to the ticket office. At the corner of the room, a smaller bench continued down the side wall and stopped. A gap of five feet remained between that bench and a new bench which was much longer and ran the remaining length of the wall. Leonid, the Kaiser's nephew, had been instructed by letter, many months earlier, to stand near that gap, under the big Virginia flag on the wall.

"That's him over there," Uma said, pointing at a young man sitting on the edge of the bench nearest the flag. He was leaning back against the wall with his eyes closed.

"He looks older than I thought he'd be," Yates said, as he led them across the station. As they neared the sleeping man, Yates asked, "Does he speak any English at all?"

"We are not sure. I think no. I will talk to him." When they neared the man, Uma spoke a few words of German and then stepped back, anticipating his reaction.

The man opened one eye, and then both eyes after the one eye focused on Uma.

"Leonid?" she asked.

"No," the man said. He had an accent but it was a Boston one.

When they turned away from him, he said loudly, "Hey I can be anybody you need me to be, Miss."

"I don't see anyone else even close to his description," Yates said.

"What should we do?"

"We wait. Nothing else we can do. His train got here on time. We're on time. So we wait."

Yates lifted his pack and Uma's suitcase and carried them both to an empty stretch of bench where he sat them down. Uma set her travel case down and sat next to it. Yates dug through his pack and pulled out a small silver flask. He pointed the bottle at Uma and she shook her head no. After lighting a cigarette from a leather case, she offered one to Yates and he took it. He started to offer a light to Uma, but she had already lit hers. She was quietly watching travelers pass by.

From a far corner, the sounds of a small brass band made their way across the station. Yates thought he recognized the tune. Something he had heard Glenn Miller play, most likely. He loved Glenn Miller.

Uma made a sound as she exhaled and lowered her chin to her upturned palms, while her elbows rested near her knees.

"You tired?" Yates asked.

"Ready to be home," she said.

Yates nodded. "How was New York?"

"It was fine. I got to see a show before I met with the bankers. It wasn't all business. How was Chicago?"

"Cold," Yates said.

"I don't know that I've ever known Chicago to not be cold," Uma said.

Yates chuckled. "The Kaiser must like you more. He sent you to the better city."

"You, however, got the better task," Uma said, and laughed.

"That could be debated," he said. "Those guys were ruthless. The rate they wanted for converting gold was ridiculous.

"Well, they know our choices for assistance are limited," Uma said.

Yates didn't reply. The brass band reached his ears again and he let himself enjoy it before abruptly saying, "Oh and I got them."

"The cigars?" she asked quickly.

"Yep. I picked out the type you said to choose and I even got the red box."

"Oh! He will be pleased," she said. "So pleased. He was saying just last week how much he missed European cigars."

"I found them in a shop downtown. The taxi driver helped me find them."

"Thank you so much, Yates. He will love them."

"Not as much as you love him," he teased.

Immediately her face tightened and the smile left. "What made you say that?" she snapped.

"I don't know, Uma. I was just trying to be funny. No disrespect intended. To either of you."

"That's not something we joke about. I'm his employee. That's how he sees me, and that's convenient, because that is what I am."

"Well, I bought a gift for my sweetheart," Yates said to continue the humor but break the tension.

"Who is the lucky lady?" she asked.

"Why, me of course," he said and laughed.

"You purchased yourself a gift?" Uma said as she shook her head while smiling.

"Yep. It'll be delivered this coming week."

"Well, what is it?"

"You'll have to find out like everyone else. Wait and see." With that, Yates leaned back against the wall and closed his eyes.

His closed eyes led him to sleep and he woke up several minutes later to Uma asking, "Are you hungry?"

Yates looked around quickly, disoriented for a moment. "I think so. Yes. What time is it?" He looked around for a clock, but then quickly remembered his watch.

Uma beat him to it. A quarter past eleven. He was supposed to be here two hours ago.

"Uncle Yates!" a voice yelled from near the front set of doors.

He looked up and smiled. "Ginny girl!" It was his niece and her new husband, Josh. "What are you two doing here?"

"We are your ride," Josh said.

"Well, Happy New Year," Yates said. "We're hungry and Leon isn't here yet. Wanna go across the street for a meal?"

"Leonid," Uma corrected.

"Close enough," Yates said.

The young couple agreed quickly to the offer of dinner and followed Yates as he exited the train station and led them along the narrow street that ran alongside the depot. At the corner, he looked back and Uma, who was walking at the rear, pointed to the restaurant on the other side of the road. "Let's try that one," she called out.

The restaurant side was almost empty because of the late hour, but the side with the bar was packed. A nice waitress with blonde hair and bright red cheeks led them to a table. Ginny ordered a club sandwich. Josh said he didn't want to be full while trying to drive so late at night, so he just had coffee. Uma ordered a bowl of potato soup. Yates said to the waitress, "I guess I'm the only hungry guy in the bunch. I'd like your fried catfish basket, please."

The atmosphere in the room was happy. From the bar, laughter would rise up and then another group would compete with it for superiority. At some point, near the end of their meal, a man stood up on the bar and began a countdown. By the time he yelled "Happy New Year!" Everyone at the table was in agreement that the young man standing on the bar had spoken with a German accent.

As the crowd all cheered and couples all around the room kissed in the new year, Yates walked up to the young man who had fallen off of the bar and was now laughing hysterically from the floor. "Happy New Year, Leon," Yates said.

The man slowly pulled himself up to a standing position and with a confused look and a thick German accent, he responded, "Happy New Year for you! And God Bless America!" before passing out into Yates' arms.

Chapter 8

"Apple trees maybe?" He said this out loud, but might as well have been talking to himself. Claire was counting money like she did every night, no matter where they were. "Or maybe cherries?" Bill reached out and touched one of the limbs, causing snow to fall down onto him. "Hard to tell without the leaves," he said, as he shook his hand quickly toward the darkness. The snow flung off of his fingers and dispersed in the night air.

The orchard was quiet except for the sound of Bill brushing the snow off of his shirt and Claire rustling paper from one pile to another. He wanted to ask about Georgie, but he was afraid of making Claire angry and one sure way to do that was to interrupt her while she was counting. Instead of asking about Georgie, he started thinking about him. No matter how hard he tried to distract himself by analyzing the trees in the orchard all around them, his thoughts kept going back to what had happened.

From the get go, Georgie was the worst choice of the three of them to be the one to actually go into the banks. His temper was bad and he got frustrated easily. Plus, he was a terrible shot. Georgie Lutz could fire a revolver six times at a big tree from ten paces away and be lucky to scar bark. Bill had the calmer demeanor and the steadier hand. The problem was, Bill was so tall, he had to duck down to talk to the tellers. And there was one bank in Yuma, one of the first ones they hit, where he walked straight into a hanging chandelier and nearly decapitated himself. His height wasn't just a negative because of the awkwardness it caused. It was also because of his recognizability. Once people in Arizona had started telling the stories of the giant bank robber, Bill couldn't even go out in public anymore. When you're almost seven feet tall, a mask doesn't change your appearance all that much.

Jason L. Queen

Before they headed East, Claire had insisted on being the one to go into the next bank. The bank manager had laughed at her from his desk and went right on back to his paperwork. It was a full day and a half of driving towards the Mississippi River before she finally explained why she had come out with an empty money sack as well as an empty revolver.

By the time they crossed the big river, Claire had come up with a new way they would do their robberies. There was never any discussion about it. She just thought it up and announced it.

The first place they had robbed using their new system was a post office in Arkansas. It was actually a combination General Store and Post Office. Bill and Georgie waited in the car while Claire walked to a corner where she could be a lookout and direct Georgie into the store when it was least crowded. While Georgie was inside the Post Office, Claire would wave Bill forward at just the right moment so that she and Georgie could jump in the vehicle while Bill drove.

The Post Office was a test run - a successful one. They walked away with $157.00 and a tray of pork chops Georgie stole from the meat counter on his way out. That night, over a late autumn campfire, while they roasted the chops and counted the money, Claire presented a plan to rob their way East. By then, Bill and Georgie had learned not to ask questions. If Claire wanted to head East, East was where the car was gonna point.

Bill secretly hoped they would go to Florida. He had worked with a man who once worked on a fishing boat in the Florida Keys and he told many stories about boating off of the coast of Florida. Bill could imagine them in Florida. Bright sun. Tanned skin. Claire's laughter rising above the sound of the ocean's waves. He had seen the ocean once, as a boy. It had not impressed him much then. Not like it had his brothers and sisters. But in Florida, he felt like the ocean sounds and smells would take his breath away. Not to mention the sight of Claire in the sun. In Bill's dreams of Florida, he had a hard time picturing Georgie.

Georgie managed to control his temper all the way to West Virginia and most of the way through December. On the morning of the Monday after Christmas, he walked out of a bank, carrying a bag of cash and a bullet in his leg. The bag was open and spilling money all over the sidewalk at just about the same pace his bullet wound was spilling blood. Claire had gotten so focused on the scene in front of the bank that she forgot to wave Bill forward from where he was parked out of view around the corner. By the time he had finished his second cigarette, he realized something was wrong because Claire looked like a statue and normally she tried her best to blend in.

At first he thought about honking the horn, but he didn't want to draw any attention to himself so he stared at Claire who was staring at something he couldn't see. His hand went to the pistol he always carried in a holster on his hip underneath his jacket. But then he saw Georgie stumble out into the street. Sirens sounded from somewhere behind Bill as he floored the gas pedal and steered the big car up to Claire who suddenly moved as if waking from a dream. She looked at Bill and then at Georgie who was rising up from his knees and holding out his hands towards the car. One of the hands briefly held up the money bag before Claire grabbed it and ran the few steps to the car. She threw open the door and as her body hit the floor, she yelled, "Go! Go! Go!"

Bill went. They drove for at least three hours before Bill finally asked if they could stop for gas. She nodded but didn't say anything else. After they got gas, Claire went into the store and bought them two cokes. She handed one to Bill and he couldn't help but smile. She had not bought him anything until that Coke, and he knew it was her way of making sure he wasn't upset with her. After that, they still drove in silence, but the tension had decreased greatly. At some point, Claire told him to start heading North, and he did, though he was a bit disappointed they were now heading away from Florida. She assured him they would head East again at the top of the state and by the time they crossed into Virginia the sun was low in the afternoon sky.

Claire had told him to pull down into the middle of one of the orchards on either side of the main road. She said it would be a great place to hide because it felt like snow was in the air and the snow would cover their tracks.

Once in the orchard, she told him she needed to go into town to get some supplies. He thought that was risky, but he didn't want to upset her by saying so. So he didn't. She returned an hour later with a box full of canned vegetables and a pie.

By then, it had started to snow. She had been right about that too. She always was. The snow started falling faster and heavier so they both moved back into the car to wait it out. The smell of Claire's perfume filled the quiet car and intoxicated Bill. After it had been dark for several hours, Claire said it was safe to start a small fire and cook some beans. As soon as the fire was started, the snow had stopped falling and Bill was able to think through what had happened that morning. At least now he didn't feel like a third wheel. He could still hear her voice telling him to calm down. Telling him everything would be alright. Telling him they were in this together now. Together. Bill pushed the feelings of guilt back into a dark part of his mind and leaned towards the fire.

She finished counting the money and looked across the fire towards Bill. "Seven thousand dollars." She looked down at the money and then back to Bill. Directly at Bill. "Seven thousand, three hundred and ninety six dollars," she said slowly. And then she moved around the fire and draped her jacket across a rock, sitting slowly down on it.

Bill couldn't hide his excitement. "That's a fortune," he said. He had been stirring the fire with a stick and a shower of sparks shot towards the area where Claire had been sitting before she moved.

Claire rested a hand on his shoulder and said, "Our fortune."

And with that, he pushed the memory of Georgie back there in that West Virginia street, right out of his mind.

"We are gonna make a lot more while we're at it," she said, moving her hand down to his hip.

Her use of the word "we" took his words away and he admitted to himself that he was glad Georgie was gone.

He snuck a look at her as she leaned towards the warmth of the fire, letting his eyes move along the side of her cheek and to her mouth. She looked around quickly and her face hardened. He started to apologize but then a smile spread across her face and she pointed past Bill toward the night sky. At first he thought they were shooting stars, but they were fireworks. The orchard was too far away from where they were being set off for them to hear anything, but the clear winter sky provided the perfect backdrop for the lights and colors.

A burst of blue faded and was replaced by fiery trails of red and then a burst of green. A cluster of yellow and another burst of blue. Bill had been too young for the first War, but he remembered the fireworks shows in the years after the return of the soldiers. His whole town in California had come together to celebrate. Those were good times. Warm times. He hadn't felt the warmth of good times like that for many years, but sitting next to that fire, he felt it again. "Would you look at that?" Bill said.

The World Comes To Mercy Creek

"It's wonderful," she said, as she made a rustling sound.

Bill wondered if she was counting money again. "We've almost got half of what we need to get to Florida, don't we?"

He heard the burst of fireworks close by and tried to figure out why he felt like his hair was on fire. Was someone else setting them off? He felt the cold of the snow on his cheek and heard another burst of fireworks, this time very close, before everything went dark around him.

Claire's voice reached through the darkness and said, "They're apple trees, Bill. Such a shame you'll never see them in the spring."

Chapter 9

After a few hours of laying wait inside the trunk of the Oldsmobile F, Deputy Monte Montgomery began to wish he had thought to remove the spare tire before climbing in. Leaving it in the trunk had caused him to have to lay on his side with his leg bent. It wasn't long before his left leg began to cramp up. By leaning back as far as he could and twisting his shoulders towards the front of the car, he was able to move his leg and straighten it enough to relieve the pain in his cramped muscle. His face was pressed against a piece of rubber and the smell of it was thick and filled his nose.

He had no idea what time it was, so he moved his body again and lifted his left arm up in front of him. Next he had to shift his right shoulder towards the top of the trunk so he could grab hold of his flashlight. Freeing it from his gun belt was a more difficult task than he thought, but once he had the flashlight on, he read the time. Half past two in the morning. Operation Trojan Oldsmobile had been a failure. Deputy Montgomery had been planning the mission for over a week. After reading about another car theft in neighboring Jefferson County, Monte had canvassed the other crime scenes and mapped out what he saw as a pattern. All seven of the other cars had been no older than five years. They had been parked along the highway near some nature trail or landmark. In three of the cases, the driver was hiking. One was hunting. One was a surveyor plotting out property. The other two were what the Sheriff of Jefferson County had designated as "dalliances". In the newspaper articles, the reporter had used the word "picnic".

Despite the fact that Sheriff Tyson rejected his plan, Monte pressed on and four miles from the Jefferson County line, off of Highway 340, he had pulled into an orchard entrance and parked. The car was far enough from the highway to make a thief think they were safe to case it, but close enough to be seen by anyone looking hard enough. It had started snowing just as he had climbed into the trunk. He considered calling off the whole thing and coming back on a day with clear weather, but he would never be more ready and prepared than he was then. And he didn't know if Jimmy Dye would let him borrow the Oldsmobile off of his lot again, so instead of leaving, he climbed into the trunk. Five hours later, he was done. The plan had not worked. Perhaps it was the holiday. Or just a poor choice of location. But he would have to try it again some other time. He had the trunk rigged so he could pop himself out easily and make an arrest once the stolen car was stopped, but he also had unscrewed the cushions and the rear lining of the back seat so he could climb through and apprehend the thief while he was driving, if necessary.

Monte shined his light towards the rear of the trunk and as he reached for the latch to free himself, he heard a sound. The door handle had been turned. One of the doors, presumably the driver's side, was being opened! Monte cut off his light and froze. He strained to listen for any other sounds. His ears buzzed with the electricity of the moment. And then the door clicked, and the front seat squeaked. A metal clicking sound was followed by the engine cranking and coming to life.

As the car started moving, Monte moved himself around to prepare for a quick attack if necessary. Operation Trojan Oldsmobile was about to be even more successful than he had realistically hoped. The car began to move forward slowly and Monte tensed his muscles, but then relaxed them in anticipation for the length of the ride as the thief drove him back to their lair.

The car lurched suddenly over a bump and threw Monte's body to the left and as he fell, he made a thumping sound and then his foot hit something and he made a louder sound. Did he? Was it in his mind? Did he yell? Or just breathe? The car stopped and slid gravel at the same time. The sound of a door opening was so loud it filled every inch inside Monte's skull. Monte had been flipped around in the car and as he tried to rise up onto his knees, he bumped against the trunk lid. This time he was certain he had made a loud sound so he readied himself and drew his sidearm. All around him, there was only silence, except for the low idling of the car engine. Monte reminded himself to breathe and he did. Slowly and quietly.

The silence continued and he relaxed his grip on the pistol for a second to let his muscles rest. The trunk flew open and the cold air pushed him back and took his breath away. He fired into the darkness twice and jumped up, but his left leg wasn't working and then fire exploded in the night. Burning in his chest was followed by more fire from his left and he felt burning all over his side. When he hit the ground, he felt two more bullets hit him and he wished to himself that he was back in his room on Elm Street, reading that big Greek mythology book.

Chapter 10

Everyone in the town of Lyttle's Mill knew about The Beaumont Boarding House and Dining Room. It wasn't only the finest looking house in the neighborhood, it was the finest looking house in the whole town. The blue painted siding stood out among the other white houses and its plush green lawn was twice the size of the next biggest lawn on the street. The original owners of the home had bought the lot behind it and turned it into their backyard. A white wooden fence ran around the yard of the house and inside the perimeter of the fence, every twenty feet, stood a white pine tree. For more than twenty years, the Beaumont's boarding house never had a vacancy. Once one person moved out, there was always a line of people waiting to move in. While most boarding houses rented rooms by the night or the week, the rooms in the Beaumont house were rented by the month, and some were leased for a year at a time. There wasn't a more successful boarding house in the Shenandoah Valley.

In the same neighborhood, halfway down Church Street, was what had to be one of the least successful boarding houses, not only in the Shenandoah Valley, but most probably in the entire country. It was only two stories tall, and the white siding had faded in the Virginia sun. The lawn was filled with shrubbery and less than half of the yard had green grass. The front porch was huge, but one whole side of it was unusable because the boards were warped and cracked. When the boarding house was owned by the Reynolds family, the porch was full of people each evening, rocking in rocking chairs or singing along with someone playing guitar or banjo.

At some point early on during the Depression, the type of boarder changed. They never had enough money to stay more than a night or two, and eventually only trouble makers knocked on their door. By 1934, the boarding house was empty. No one knew exactly what happened to the family. One day they were there, and then the next they were gone.

For the next few years a string of owners were in and out of the house, none of them staying long and none of them re-opening the boarding house business. Eventually, a man from Front Royal had moved to town and re-opened the boarding house in 1939, but he closed it at the end of the year. No one saw him leave. One day, Frank Mackey, one of his regular boarders, woke up after a three day bender and was hungry. He went downstairs to see which meal was next to be served and no one ever came to the table. The furniture and most of the household items were still in place. But the owner was gone. Frank rummaged through the pantry, found a jar of pickles, ate it at the table, and left.

On the first day of 1941, Bea Beaumont's husband, Ben, brought his wife some news. "New owners at the Reynolds place." No matter who had owned it over the last few years, it was still referred to by the Reynolds name.

Bea looked up from her seat at the kitchen table where she was tasting the gravy Mabel Greene had just sat in front of her. "More pepper, Mabel," she said. And then to Ben, "Are they opening the business back up, or just living there?"

"Hard to say," Ben said. "I've seen people in and out all week. A few I recognize from the mountain. Carrying wood from the mill. And toolboxes."

"They're opening the business back up." She said "business" with a tone that implied negativity, which was curious, since she owned and operated the same type of business.

"I suspect so," Ben said. "They carried all of the mattresses out on Monday and new ones got delivered yesterday morning."

Bea looked up. "Any other furniture going or coming?"

"Just some carpet. And curtains. And a few sitting chairs."

"Just how long has this all been happening?" she asked.

"A week or so," Ben said.

"And you're just now telling me?"

"Yep."

"Why?"

"Why what?"

"Why are you just now telling me about this?"

"I didn't want to upset you."

The World Comes To Mercy Creek

"What kind of hambone redneck thinking is that?" she said. "I wouldn't have gotten upset except for you making me find out a week late. Probably even two weeks, if I pushed the issue and made you recall real hard."

Mabel set down a plate of biscuits and gravy in front of Ben. Before he could even lift his fork, Bea slid it away from him and said, "Get your biscuits and gravy down the street since you're so interested in keeping their secrets."

"Nobody is keeping secrets from or for anybody. Anyways, I think they're locals," Ben said. "Not outsiders. I recognize the couple from the Post Office and around the way. And some of the men who are working are definitely from the mountain."

"You think it's better to have my business attacked by someone we know? That makes it better than if a stranger does it?"

"Nobody's attacking our business, Bea," Ben said. By now her back was turned and she was telling Mabel it was time to serve breakfast. Abigail Greene came into the kitchen where she had been waiting for her momma in a small side room designed for the help. Abigail knew to never look directly at Mrs. Beaumont, so she took all of her direction from her mother.

Ben turned around and walked back out on the porch. Behind him, he could hear his wife's voice growing louder and sharper as she directed and corrected Mabel in preparation for the boarders coming down for breakfast.

Ben opened the front door again and slipped quickly over to the coat closet. He grabbed his heavy coat and put it on as he walked down off of the porch and onto the sidewalk. As he neared the old Reynolds place, he was just in time to see Frank Mackey, a few men from the mountain, and the young couple he recognized but did not officially know. They were hanging a sign. Ben moved a bit further along the sidewalk until he could read the green lettering on the white sign. At the top it said: "Lyttle's Mill Room and Board" and at the bottom: "Est. 1941". Across the street, just out of earshot, the two men were talking.

"Can I have my old room back, Joe?" Frank Mackey said, as he adjusted the length of the short chain attached to the sign.

"It's gotta come down just a little bit on the right," Joe Morrissey said as he held both arms out in front of him and framed the sign with his fingers. "No, no. YOU'RE right. That's it. That is perfect."

Joe's voice strained out the last few words as he ran forward and went up on his toes to help Frank slip the chain over the hook.

The chain made a clinking sound and then from the porch, Joe's wife called out, "That looks magnificent." Her mother and twin sister called her Hope, which was her middle name. Joe started calling her by her first name, Emily, when she told him one evening that she thought she would give her first name a try.

Joe smiled and called out towards the porch. "It was supposed to be a surprise. I thought you were still asleep."

"I'm still young enough to ring in the new year and wake up on time to make breakfast," Emily said as she walked down the steps and weaved her way between the shrubs and stumps that had overtaken the sidewalk. "I've got a big old plate of eggs and grits ready for you." She looked at Frank and smiled. "And a plate for you too, Mr. Mackey."

Frank blushed and looked towards Joe who said, "Come on in. Seeing as how you're our first boarder and all."

"Well now, Joe, I need to get my money together first. I can't board just yet."

"How about you trade us work for your room and board?" Joe asked. "That way, we get what we need and you get what you need." Joe looked at Frank for a moment and added quickly, "That is, if you want to stay with us. I know it's in rough shape."

"Ain't we all?" Frank asked, as they all laughed together.

Down the street, Ben stood out front of the big blue boarding house and watched as the young couple and the town drunk walked back into the old Reynolds place. Ben Beaumont wasn't worried about the competition the way his wife was. Their boarding house was successful in every way. They always ended the month with a profit and they always turned people away from their full rooms and full table. Besides, better people than that bunch had tried and failed to make a boarding house out of that old shack down the street. No, Ben Beaumont wasn't worried a bit. As he heard his wife yelling at Mabel for baking too many biscuits, Ben almost felt sorry for the young couple. She would make them wish they had stayed up on the mountain.

Chapter 11

Jeb knew this new year was going to be a great one because it had already begun with him being assigned a story on the crime beat. A story that would make the front page. Technically it was assigned to him on the last day of last year, but Jeb would write it and the newspaper would publish it in the new year. To make his day even brighter, he had arrived at work to find a note from the Chief Editor's secretary, telling him to report to the Chief's office at 9am. He spent the forty-five minutes he had before the meeting finishing the article. His main hook for the story was the fact that the bank was robbed on a quiet afternoon when no one was out in the main bank lobby but one teller. And that while the police did not have a full description of the bank robber, he had disfigured ears, possibly from boxing. This was going to be his bombshell.

While writing the story, he couldn't help but let his mind keep going back to Esther. Not because she had been the main witness but because... Well, because he liked the way he felt when he thought about her. Thinking of Millicent, his first and current girlfriend, brought him the opposite feeling. Whether it was angst, or worry, or jealousy, or confusion, the emotions he now associated with Millicent had nothing to do with love. Not that he was in love with Esther, either. That would be insane. He had only met her a day ago, and only for a few minutes, at that. But whatever he was feeling, he liked it, and he wouldn't mind feeling that way some more.

At five minutes to nine, he crossed the busy street with accelerated steps, not just because of his meeting but because the day was cold and the wind blowing between the concrete and brick buildings made everything colder. The first thing he noticed as he opened the door to the offices, was how warm it was in there. He had to wear a coat and sometimes gloves in his office. Immediately he felt the warmth wrap around him as he walked to the steps and made the ascent to the second floor, where the administrative offices were.

The Chief Editor was named Jim Marbling. Jeb had been at the paper for two years, mostly in production and distribution, so he had never before had a meeting with the Editor. When he walked into the Chief's office, he was met by his local news editor, Andy Diers and Jim Marbling, who was on the telephone.

"Have a seat," Andy said as he waved at someone over Jeb's shoulder.

The door opened behind him and Jeb turned, after sitting down, to see the lead reporter, Charles Hathaway, enter the room.

"Tell him to take her for a walk," the Chief said into the phone. "It doesn't have to be a long walk, no. But she loves getting out." He looked up but didn't acknowledge they were there. "Oh I know. Yes. Okay." He turned in his chair to look out the window. His chair was one of the newer models that let the seated person turn around without having to get up. Jeb's desk chair was wooden. It didn't swivel, but it did squeak when he moved in it. And sometimes the crack along the back would pinch his shirt and he would have to swivel his shoulders quickly to free himself. "I have to go now, Connie." He hung up the phone and turned around, this time looking at each of them before calling out over their heads, "Hey Jerry? Jerry was a photographer. "Jerry?"

Behind Jeb and Andy, a voice answered back, "Yes Chief?"

"I need you to run to Mac's and order a cord of wood for me. His boys are selling it. Tell them I want it stacked on the back porch."

"Yessir," Jerry said from behind them.

For a moment, the Chief stared past them and then looked at Andy, "Pull the boy from the bank robbery. I want Chip on it."

Jeb looked quickly from the Chief to Andy.

"Okey dokey," Andy said as he stood up and moved his head in a motion to Jeb to stand up. Jeb started to say something, but Andy was already out the door before he could even start to get his thoughts straight. Instead of talking, he stood up and followed Andy.

"Hey Morrissey," Chip said as he followed them out.

Jeb looked over at him but didn't answer.

"Bring me your notes, pal. You did take notes yesterday?"

"Of course I did," Jeb said, defensively.

"Of course you did. Drop 'em off at my desk this morning. I'm gonna be hard pressed to finish this up, now that I have to pick it up where you dropped it." Chip slapped Jeb on the arm as he went past him and down the hall. "Oh and I've moved my office up here, by the way," he called out over his shoulder. And then, the sound of a door closing.

Jeb took a few steps down the stairs and looked at his editor and asked, "What the hell just happened, Andy?"

Andy, continuing down the stairs, replied, "office politics." And with a shrug of his shoulders, Andy turned and headed away from the front door and towards his tiny office on the first floor. Jeb went back outside and crossed the street at a considerably slower pace than when he had crossed less than an hour earlier.

Chapter 12

Seven calls had come in before Sheriff Tyson even finished his first cup of coffee at Max's Cafe. He always started his day at Max's and then reported to the office to go through any phone messages, take any new arrests to the Magistrate, and give the day Deputies their assignments. By the time the call total had reached ten, Mernie decided that she had to send someone over to the cafe to get the Sheriff. For the three years she had worked for the Sheriff, she had been told to never interrupt his breakfast unless it was an emergency of Old Testament proportions. They had now reached what she was prepared to call "emergency status". Whether it was biblical or not, she didn't know. She was not a church going woman.

When Deputy Newcomb came back through the door, he tried to make what looked like a hand gesture of warning to Mernie, but the Sheriff had already come around him, heading straight for Mernie's desk. Before he got within ten feet of her he was shouting, "Give 'em to me one at a time. In the order they came in."

"The first one was Monte's mother, asking if he had worked an extra shift last night. She said he always comes right home after work, but no one in his family had seen him since he left to start his shift yesterday."

"Newcomb?" The Sheriff shouted while still looking at Mernie, "Run by Deputy Montgomery's house. On the way, stop by the Horseshoe and see if he was there last night. Call me from their house if he hasn't shown up by then. Next?"

"Bull Maddow." Bull was the perfect name for a man, but Bull Maddow was a woman. Anyone who knew her for long came to the conclusion that it was the perfect name for her.

"Next," the Sheriff said. Bull was always calling in strange occurrences in her orchards.

The World Comes To Mercy Creek

Mernie ignored the Sheriff and continued. "She says there's two cars in her orchards. One is deep in it back past her saplings. No one is in it. The other one is in her State line orchard. No one is in that one either."

The Sheriff started to say something and then stopped himself. "Next."

Mernie stammered for a bit and then shuffled the messages in her hand. "This one was *for* Monte. Jim Dye, asking if Monte was done with his Oldsmobile. He said it was supposed to be back on the lot this morning."

"Who borrowed his Oldsmobile? Monte?" Sheriff Tyson asked, looking around the room and back to Mernie. "What does that have to do with us?"

"According to Jimmy, Deputy Montgomery told him he needed it for police business."

The Sheriff turned and looked around. "Where's Dale?" Dale Benedict was the Sheriff's right hand man. They had fought in the War together and it had been Dale, who was a jail guard first, who had brought Tyson into law enforcement.

"Right here, boss" Dale said from the other side of Mernie's desk. He had come in from the jail door.

"Call over to the Maddow place and ask Bull to describe the cars to you. If she tells you one of them is an Oldsmobile, come tell me. If neither one is an Olds, just head over there, check the cars, and have them towed. Or do whatever. You know what to do."

The Sheriff turned back to Mernie, quickly. "Next," he said. "Give me the damn next one."

"Why are you so upset with me?" Mernie asked. "I just answer the phone."

"Not now, Mernie. What's the next one?"

"One was about fireworks in the orchards. Possibly connected to the cars? Maybe a bunch of teenagers had a party and set off fireworks and a few of them left their cars."

"Next," the Sheriff said, his look of irritation had changed to concern. "Trojan horse," he said softly.

"Right. Vance Robertson called to let us know about a bear that had scared his horses. I guess he called you too?"

"No. Huh?" Dale walked up quickly from behind him so the Sheriff held up a finger towards Mernie and said, "It was an Oldsmobile?"

"Yes sir," Dale said. "A green one."

"Did any of the other messages have anything to do with Monte or the cars?" he asked quickly.

"No. Bear sightings."

"Grab two of the boys," Tyson said to Dale. "Bring shotguns. Meet me out front." The Sheriff walked in a small circle and then turned back to Mernie. "Call Yates Morrissey about the bear. I was gonna call him today. Tell him the County will put a ten dollar bounty on it. He can keep the meat and the fur. Tell him to present himself as the County Game Warden. I can deputize him from here. Tell him I'm asking personally."

"I think he might still be in Richmond," Deputy Newcomb said.

"No, he got back this morning," Mernie said.

"How do you know that?" Newcomb asked.

"I'm a single woman and I live on the mountain. It's my business to know where Yates Morrissey is. I'll call him now," Mernie said quickly. She had seen every mood imaginable working with the Sheriff over the years, but this was the first time he had ever seemed worried. She just wasn't sure which one of the calls bothered him the most.

Chapter 13

It wasn't unusual for reporters to stay late at the newspaper office, especially on days they went to press, so Jeb knew it wouldn't catch much attention if he waited around long enough to catch a copy as it came off the presses. He had already finished his story about a record number of car wrecks on Centenary Road, but if anyone asked him what he was up to, he could simply say he was finishing up his article.

By the time the first issues were being stacked and tied on the loading dock, Jeb was poised to grab the first one available. All of the distribution guys knew him and liked him. After all, he was the only reporter who shared their building with them. They saw him everyday and considered him part of their work family.

Artie Fox had already offered him a cup of coffee from his personal percolator. Jeb had happily accepted.

After taking the new issues off to the side, it didn't take Jeb long to find the article with the headline: Bank Robbed On New Year's Eve

> While the rest of the area was saying goodbye to 1940, The Old Dominion Bank said goodbye to over $14,000.00 on New Year's Eve. An armed gunman entered the bank in the late afternoon, just an hour prior to closing.
>
> According to Bank Manager, Clive Fedlo, at the end of each quarter, the bank counts all currency and reports the bills and coins it has to the Banking Commission. Every fourth quarter, at the end of the calendar year, any old bills are bagged up and sent back to the Banking Commission to be exchanged for new bills.

During this yearly inventory, the old bills were bagged up and sitting behind the teller counter. The bandit exited the building less than five minutes later with the money from the teller's drawer and the bags of old currency.

There is no description of the bank robber at this time and no indication that there was more than one person involved in this crime. The Sheriff's Department had no comment at this time.

Jeb read the article twice. And then a third time. It was his article word for word, except Chip, or someone, had intentionally removed the description of the bank robber.

"Why?" he said to himself as he laid the newspaper back on the stack and crossed the street towards the offices for the third time that day. When he got to the front doors they were locked. Jeb didn't have a key to that building, so he had to knock on the glass door. He couldn't see through the frosted glass, but he could tell lights were on and he could hear people talking in the distance.

When he got back to his office, the phone was ringing. When he picked it up, it was Andy's voice. "City desk has a story for you to cover," he said.

"Why not Chip?" Jeb asked.

"I don't know. I guess he's not available. Who cares? You want the big story don't you? This is a big story. The Sheriff and every one of his Deputies is over at the Maddow Orchards. Been there for hours."

As Jeb hung up the phone and put his coat and hat on, he searched around his desk for his gloves and when he could only find one, he grabbed it and ran out the door to his car.

It took ten minutes to get to Bull Maddow's apple orchard. The whole way over, Jeb practiced what questions he wanted to ask, but they all went right out of his mind when he saw the bodies. Right there on the edge of the road, lined up with the first row of apple trees, were two bodies. The headlights of several cars lit up the area. One body was covered with a white sheet. The other was wrapped in burlap. Three Deputies stood nearby. The Sheriff was nowhere to be seen.

Down the hill was a Deputy Jeb knew from school. John Morton. He knew the other two from around town. "Is Deputy

Montgomery nearby?" Jeb asked one of the Deputies. Monte would tell him what was going on. The two Deputies stared at him and one of them looked like they wanted to murder him. He started to apologize but realized he didn't know what he would be apologizing for.

"He's right there, Jeb," Deputy Morton said as he walked up from the bottom of the hill. Jeb followed his pointing finger and realized he was showing him one of the dead.

"What in the world happened?" Jeb asked. "What in the world?"

"You asking as his friend, or as a reporter?" Deputy Morton asked.

"Both," Jeb replied.

"You're gonna need to ask the Sheriff that question," Morton said, pointing up the hill to a newer looking Oldsmobile. Sheriff Tyson had the trunk open and another man, wearing a suit and holding a camera, was taking pictures while another man held two flashlights. Both were pointed into the trunk.

"Sheriff Tyson?" Jeb called out.

"Jeb Morrissey," the Sheriff said. "This is a crime scene."

"Yes sir," Jeb said. Sheriff Tyson had been Sheriff of the county for Jeb's whole life, and he had always been kind and fair to the Morrissey family. Jeb intended on keeping things that way. "The paper sent me here, Sheriff. To ask a few questions. Find out what's going on."

"We've got two dead, Jeb. One was my Deputy. That's what's going on."

"How were they killed?" Jeb asked. He was in shock, but trying to remind himself he was a reporter and reporters asked the hard questions when necessary.

"We're not ready to make a statement about this, Jeb," the Sheriff said while lowering his voice. "I can tell you, we're looking at two murders. And the perpetrator is not in custody."

"Any suspects, Sheriff?" Jeb asked.

"Can't say, Jeb."

"Can I ask what the murder weapon was?"

"A pistol," the Sheriff said. "And a shotgun."

"You're looking for two killers?" Jeb asked.

"I didn't say that," the Sheriff said. "I said there were two weapons."

"Can I ask the property owner a few questions."

"The owner was Bull Maddow. She went on home," the Sheriff said. "It's probably time for you to do the same, Jeb."

Jeb walked back over to the road and leaned against his old Ford while he wrote a few notes down on paper.

Within an hour, the bodies were loaded into an ambulance, and the Deputies all got back into their cars. The Sheriff walked past Jeb on the way to his car. Jeb started to ask him a question, but he stopped. He reminded himself that one of the victims was a Deputy. He knew the Sheriff wasn't in the mood to talk.

Chapter 14

At nineteen, Millicent Robertson was the oldest of the Robertson sisters. Andrea had just turned eighteen. And Fern was about to turn sixteen. Most folks agreed that Andrea would probably be the first to be married, since she had been dating Albert Landover for three years. The Landovers owned one of the biggest horse farms in Fauquier County and Andrea's father Vance, who planned on having the largest horse farm on the mountain, had already given his blessing to the wedding, though Albert had not yet asked for it. He would, though. Everyone knew that.

Millicent had no plans of being the second to be married. She was the oldest and she would not walk her sister down the aisle as a spinster. She knew her boyfriend, Jeb, would propose soon, but she would of course turn him down at least twice. She had read in a Jane Austen novel that this was the most expeditious way to guarantee a long marriage. She would make him work for it and earn her "I do".

As the Robertson sisters rode their horses the short distance from their barn to the lower pasture of what had once been the Baker farm, Fern asked, "How can we go skating without skates?" Her sisters laughed and Andrea said, "You'll see Sissy. We're almost there."

The kids and teenagers of Mercy Creek had been proving for years that you didn't need skates in order to go ice skating. Baker's pond had been the place everyone gathered whenever the ice froze solid enough to walk on. Sometimes it happened several times a winter. That year, the first time it had frozen solid enough to skate on was the first day of the year. A few teenagers from town had walked out on it and deemed it ready.

By dusk, there were over thirty people spread out skating, or standing on the shore or sitting around small campfires. On the far end of the pond, some boys from town had brought a load of wood from the lumber yard and started a bonfire. The full moon reflected off of the silver surface of the lake and competed with the nearby bonfire for brightness.

On the side of the pond closest to the bonfire, boys were running out and skating as far as they could on the soles of their boots. Jerry McCall had gone the farthest so far. Over at one of the small fires, Pete and Pat MacBatten had brought some of their father's whiskey and they were telling stories about their adventures on Baker's Pond over the years. A few girls from town were hanging onto their every word. Whenever Pete would pause in his story, Pat would spit a blast of shine into the fire, causing it to flame up and hiss loudly, which in turn caused the girls to jump and edge closer to the closest MacBatten brother.

Across the pond, at the darkest corner, a girl screamed and a wolf howled. Or was it a coyote? Another scream was followed by a man yelling and pointing at a dark figure running along the edge of the pond, just outside the edge of light. And as it disappeared over the hillside, nearest the trail where the Robertson girls had stopped, the animal let out another howl that sounded like a combination of groaning and roaring.

At the same time, a horse whinnied loudly and two girls screamed.

"She's hurt!" a boy's voice yelled.

And then another voice shouted, "Help! She's hurt bad!"

Several of the boys ran over and helped Andrea and Millicent lift their youngest sister up out of the snow and carry her over to the fire. Millicent quickly looked around and then grabbed Andrea by both shoulders and said, "Ride home and get Dad!" Without saying a word, Andrea ran back to her horse, mounted it and started out across the dark field. The full moon lit her silhouette and then she was gone. The sound of the galloping horse faded with her.

Pete MacBatten quickly moved to the fallen girl's horse and undid her saddle, letting it drop to the ground as he pulled the horse blanket out from under it and spread it out on the ground right next to the fire. Millicent quickly moved Fern over onto the blanket so she wasn't down in the cold snow.

"Did anyone drive here?" Pat MacBatten called out. 'Does anyone have their car close by?"

"I do!" Virgy Morrissey yelled as he came around the large bonfire, looking worried. "My car is just down the hill." He pointed into the darkness. "On the old logging road. If y'all help me get her to the car, I can drive her to a doctor."

The MacBatten brothers and a few other boys from the mountain picked the blanket up with the young girl still on it and worked together to carry her down to Virgy's car.

"I'm going with you to the hospital," Millicent said. "Will someone stay here and tell my Daddy where we went?"

"I will," Pat MacBatten said.

Virgy backed the car down the logging road until he found a wide place in the road to turn around. He sped away with Millicent in his only other seat, cradling Fern across their laps.

Chapter 15

By the time Jeb finished writing his article about the bodies in the orchard, he knew it was the best thing he had ever written. Better than the short story he wrote in high school. Better than the poem he wrote for Millicent when he first met her. And far better than any of the farm and livestock articles he had written for the newspaper. He set the scene perfectly. Followed it up with questions. And then presented possible explanations. After editing it three times, he knew it was his ticket to the front page. He might even get as many bylines per issue as Chip. Maybe more.

He knew he should wash up and change clothes before he took his article down to Jim Marbling, but he didn't have time. The offices were opening in a few minutes and he could see people arriving for work all along the street. Jeb realized at about that same time that he had not been home since the morning of New Year's Eve, and he had to check the calendar to see that it was January 2nd.

When he walked through the front door of the office building, the first person he saw was Chip. "500 words on sheep shearing?" Chip asked.

"Nope. This is a headliner," Jeb said.

"I just handed him a headliner," Chip said.

"Is it another article about the bank robbery that doesn't even mention the robber?"

Chip stared at him and then smiled. "Maybe it is, rookie. Maybe it is."

This time when he walked into Jim Marbling's office, the Chief Editor wasn't on the phone. "Is that for me?" he asked and pointed at the two sheets of paper in Jeb's hand.

"Yes sir," Jeb said. "It's an article about the killings last night."

"In the orchards?" he asked.

"Yes," Jeb said. "I think once you read it, you'll want to put it on the front page.

"Is that so?" the Chief asked.

"Yes sir," Jeb said. "It's the best thing I've ever written."

"Isn't it the only thing you've ever written?" the Chief said. "Leave it. I'll decide where it goes."

Jeb set the pages down on the Chief Editor's desk and turned around and walked out.

Before he was through the door, the Chief called out, "And next time you come to my office, take a bath first. You smell like you've been shearing sheep. Or something unmentionable."

When he got to the street, he started to cross back over to his office, but instead, he took a left and followed the sidewalk until he got to the front door of the bank.

Through the glass and across the lobby he could see her, behind the counter, smiling and greeting a customer. Jeb started to pull the door open but then he remembered Millicent. Despite their many arguments lately, she was still his girlfriend. He had woken up many days thinking he needed to end things with her. And today seemed to be the day to do it. But he wanted to know in his own heart at least, he had always stayed honorable and done the right thing. So he let the door shut, turned back down the sidewalk, got into his car, and drove back towards Mercy Creek. He would finally have the hard conversation he had been putting off for weeks. But first, he would sleep. And there is no kind of sleep comparable to the kind you get when you're home.

Chapter 16

Virgil heard the roaring before he saw what was making it. The sound had gotten louder right before it stopped on the other side of the big white gate which separated the road leading up to the Kaiser's Estate from his driveway, which led straight up to the house. From Virgil's office, which sat up on the second floor of a renovated barn, Virgil could look down and see the other side of the gate if he stood at the window instead of sitting at his desk. Curiosity got the better of him and he turned his chair around, stood up and walked over to the window.

Two guards were talking to a man wearing a leather hat and a leather jacket - the style of clothing pilots wore in Europe. They were all standing by the source of the roaring sound Virgil had heard. It was a red motorcycle. One of the guards walked through a smaller gate next to the guardhouse and made his way to a small block building. He knocked on the door and Yates opened it and walked out. They stood still talking for only a moment before Yates started jogging towards the gate, leaving the other guard behind.

Yates yelled over the gate and it slowly swung open. As Yates walked through the gate, Virgil contemplated going back to the work on his desk, but there was a motorcycle out there. That was something he couldn't help but want a closer look at.

By the time he made it down to the driveway, Yates was roaring up, astride the motorcycle. He stopped right in front of Virgil who asked in a loud voice, "An Indian?"

"Sure is!" Yates shouted back as he revved the motor before cutting it off. "I found it in Chicago!"

"Found it?" Virgil asked. "Most of my finds are free. Was this...?

The World Comes To Mercy Creek

"No," Yates laughed. "Not hardly. I guess I'll be working for the Kaiser for the rest of my life to save that money back up, but..." He put his arms out wide as if to showcase the motorcycle. "She's worth it."

Virgil couldn't help but agree. "I saw a few of these in the War. By god, Yates, is this a Scout?"

"Good eye, old man. Scout 101."

"Original paint?"

"Oh hell, I don't know," Yates said. "I'm guessing so."

"This bike is wasted on you," Virgil said. "I bet you don't even know its history."

"Maybe so, big brother," Yates said. "But with you it would just be a piece of history. The way I see it, this thing still has some history left to make."

Virgil smiled and took a step back from the bike so he could look it over better. "Somebody customized the back rack. And the seat looks different from what I remember."

"Virgil, this thing was made after the War. You had two babies by the time it made its way into the world."

"I've seen 'em since the War," Virgil said. "The last one I saw was in 1930. At the World's Fair. Probably this same model. I wonder how it rides?"

"Like a thirsty horse smelling water in the wind." Yates and Virgil turned around and it was the man in the leather jacket. He smiled and said, "I was tempted to turn South at the Virginia line and run away with this sweetheart."

"I would've chased you to the ocean," Yates said, as he shook the man's hand. "Virgil this is...?"

"Wallace," the man said.

"Virgil this is Wallace. All the way from Chicago, Illinois. And Wallace, this is my brother, Virgil. All the way from across the creek over there." Yates pointed over the man's shoulder and he turned to look.

"I've never been to the mountains before," Wallace said.

"Do you have time to eat lunch with us before you head on back?" Yates asked. "What time does your train leave? If you have time, you can have lunch before one of the boys drives you over to the station."

Wallace looked confused for a second and then his face looked sick. "I don't have a ticket," he said. "They told me I'd get my pay and train fare from you."

"Oh they did?" Yates asked, not giving time for an answer. "I gave your boss an extra twenty and also bought a train ticket for you."

"They told me you would pay me twenty and give me a train ticket when I got here," he said.

Yates stood for a moment, staring at the boy. He clinched his fists and started to say something, but instead looked at Virgil.

"He didn't do wrong by you," Virgil said. "It looks like you both got taken."

Yates switched his stare back to Wallace and after a few long moments said, "I'm gonna ask once. And I'm gonna ask you to look me in the eye when you answer."

"Okay," Wallace said, his voice getting shaky.

"Are you trying to con me out of more money?"

"No sir," the boy said quickly and clearly. And then he slowed his breathing down and said again, "I wouldn't do that."

Yates was quiet for almost a minute. Then he shrugged his shoulders and said, "Let's get you some lunch. And then we'll get you a ticket back home and get you the pay they promised you."

The boy followed them around to the back of the house and into the Kaiser's house.

Virgil's original plan was to get a lunch for the boy and let him eat it back in the barn or in Yates' office, but before they even opened the pantry, they could hear the familiar voice of the Kaiser. "And why is my property manager and head of security making their own bologna sandwiches?" And as he entered the pantry area, "There you all are. I'm not sure what is happening, but I am not aware of any mass layoffs or mutinies of my staff. I'm also not sure where Uma is, so perhaps I have missed some very important event on my own estate." He stopped and looked at Wallace. "And you are?"

"This is Wallace," Yates said. "He delivered a motorcycle to me."

"And now my curiosity is at maximum. We will address the motorcycle after introductions are complete."

Virgil quickly spoke up, "And Wallace, this is Kaiser Wilhelm the 27th."

The World Comes To Mercy Creek

Wallace looked confused at first, but without hesitation said, "It's nice to meet you sir. Kaiser, sir."

"Leeza May! Leeza May!" the Kaiser shouted.

From the dish room on the other side of the kitchen, a woman's voice said, "We're washing up from breakfast still!"

"That's so nice of you. Please send someone over to make some sandwiches please."

After an exchange of voices down the hall and the sound of clattering pans, an older man named Johan came around the corner. "Yes sir. What type of sandwiches would you all like?"

"Mine will be cheese, please," the Kaiser said. As he walked out of the pantry and over to the small dining table he called back. "Tell Johan what you would like and then come in here, please. Yates, do I have to ask this young man about your motorcycle, or do you plan on telling me yourself?"

"It's an Indian," Yates said as he followed the Kaiser. "And it's red."

"Why on earth did you choose red?" the Kaiser asked. "I think silver or black would look better."

"You need to see it first to say that, don't you?" Yates asked.

"I don't agree with that at all," the Kaiser said. "I didn't need to see my Mercedes to know it would look best in black. And the Rolls Royce was best in Silver. Everyone knows that. Even people who do not own one."

Yates laughed. "As always, you make a logical argument, Kaiser."

"And what brings you to our table this afternoon?" the Kaiser asked Wallace.

Wallace looked like a possum in a lantern light, so Virgil spoke up and told the whole story.

"And you're heading back to these...these charlatans?" the Kaiser asked. "Why would you do that?"

"'Cause I got nowhere else to go," Wallace said.

Virgil and Yates both looked at the Kaiser, who asked, "What if you had a job here?"

Chapter 17

Vance Robertson found himself in the oddly conflicting situation of being angry at one Morrissey boy and grateful to the other. He was angry with Jeb Morrissey because he had broken Millie's heart and Millie's heart was something he would always try to protect. But ask any father of older children, and they will all tell you the same thing. You can protect your children from many things, but heartache is not one of them.

He had originally thought Jeb was a good young man, but he had been late to pick Millie up on New Year's Eve and then he had canceled their date the next night. Of course he said he had a good reason. Don't they all? The boy had a good reputation around town as a hard worker and a smart young man. He wasn't the first choice for his oldest daughter, but he wasn't a terrible one. The Morrissey family would have given Vance the credibility he needed with the mountain people, since he came from one of the most respected families in the county. One of the original mountain families, actually.

If the boy was too dumb to know how lucky he was to have Millie, then he didn't deserve Millie. He deserved one of these backwoods women who only made dinner and kids. The more he thought about it, the more he loathed that stupid boy.

However, his younger brother had suddenly proven to be different from Jeb. At just the right time, when Fern was in danger, he had stepped up to help her. The Doctor had told Vance that if Fern had gotten to the hospital any later, she would not have made it through that first night. Vance would never forget what the younger Virgil Morrissey had done for his little girl, but for now, he wanted to stay angry.

Vance Robertson was not normally an angry man. He was often sullen. He was sometimes mean. But he was rarely angry. It was in one of these rare angry moods that Robertson sent for and met with two men he used from time to time to hunt any animal that hunted his horses. These men were predators of predators.

Ian Akewater and Zeke Duggan made a good team, but they couldn't have been more different. Akewater was from Hampshire, England. He had moved to America with his father after the Great War and was orphaned within a month after reaching America. He had been taught to shoot by a man who paid him to feed his kennel of hunting hounds. Eventually, Ian became a hunter for the man and, together, they would sell the furs on the weekend in Washington, D.C.

Zeke Duggan was a local. He had grown up in the valley near Lyttle's Mill but spent more time on the mountain and the river than he did in school. There was no better local shot than Ian Akewater. But there was no better local hunter than Zeke Duggan. They teamed up during the Great Depression when Duggan's little house on the lake burned to the ground. Akewater offered him a room in his cabin on the mountain in exchange for Duggan showing him how to track animals on the mountain. Akewater had always been able to hunt from a tree stand or blind, but on foot, he rarely bagged anything. Within a few weeks of Duggan moving in, Akewater's smokehouse was full and his fur wall was covered. In fact, Akewater's hide business started making so much money, some of the locals started to wonder if someone burned Duggan's house down on purpose. Maybe it was somebody who needed a hunting partner.

Duggan never put value to any such suspicion. He liked Akewater and considered his house burning down to be one of the best things to ever happen to him.

"We spoke to most everyone who saw the beast at the pond. They didn't tell us much more than some of your neighbors told us," Ian Akewater said. He twisted the heel of his black leather boot into the plush white carpet and then moved his foot so he could watch the carpet slowly take shape again. It was as if the carpet were rejuvenating and healing itself. Just as the carpet re-formed, he would jam his heel back down onto it and twist again. "It would be helpful if you allowed us to talk to your daughters."

"I agree," Zeke Duggan said. "Nobody has gotten closer to...that thing than them."

"I don't give a damn what you think," he said to Akewater. "Or what you agree with," he said to Duggan. "I'm paying you to do what I tell you to do."

"You're paying us to hunt an animal," Akewater said. "Let's not get Shakespearian about it."

Under normal circumstances, Robertson would have appreciated the European hunter's brashness. But the circumstances were not normal. His daughter had almost been killed and his sense of humor was nowhere to be found. "Mr. Duggan, can you hunt this animal on your own?"

Duggan was the younger of the three men there, but his weathered and scarred face made him look older. "I don't work alone," he said. "Ian and I are partners. If you don't use him, you don't get me." He looked around for a place to spit his tobacco. When he couldn't spot one, he spit into his hand and rubbed it down an already filthy part of his jeans.

"We're what you would call, an all or nothing, package," Akewater said with a flash of a smile.

Robertson stood so abruptly; the back of his legs pushed his chair against the wall with a solid thump. "Then I choose the nothing," he said. "You two may leave now."

"Come on now, Robertson, we were negotiating terms. Why end them so abruptly? We've always been able to reach an agreement," Akewater said.

"Yeah, you know I didn't grow up on no horse farm," Zeke Duggan said. "My family raised smaller livestock. And sometimes you gotta smack a pig on the ass to get him where he needs to be."

"Am I the pig in this analogy?" Robertson asked.

"Oh no. Of course not. The deal is, Sir. The deal is the pig. Let's kick this deal in the ass and make it happen. "

"No, I don't think you two are the right men for the job after all," Vance said as he pointed to the butler who had suddenly appeared in the doorway. "Alex please show these men out." He stood up and buttoned the bottom button of his jacket. "Through the servant's entrance, please."

"You understand this means we won't ever hunt for you again, Robertson. Do you understand the ramifications of that?"

The World Comes To Mercy Creek

"Oh I understand, Mr. Akewater. I don't think you do, but that is neither here nor there." He stopped at the door leading out of the parlor and pointed towards the hallway. "Alex?"

As the big shouldered butler led the men out the door, Duggan said, "Do you know what kind of man you work for?"

"I sure do," Alex said, and closed the door behind them.

Vance continued down the hallway, went up the stairs slowly and entered his library. He needed to clear his mind. Although he did his best thinking and planning while walking outside, he had discovered that the best way to clear his mind was to get lost in a good book. On a small table next to his reading chair was a small pile of books he had been planning to read during any snow storms they might experience. He sorted through them and decided to read a Western. For several minutes he read the words and turned the pages and found himself drawn into the story. After an hour passed, he sat back in his chair and stared into the distance. Laying the book back on the table, he walked out of his house and down to the stables. The book, titled "Day Of The Posse," had not only allowed him to relax; it had given him a plan on how to kill the animal that had almost killed his baby girl.

At the barn he quickly found two of the boys he paid to muck the stalls and stack hay, straw, and feed. He called them boys but they were out of high school - too young for him to call them men, but too old to call boys any longer. "I need you two men to round up as many men as you can and meet me back here tomorrow at noon. I will announce then that I am putting a bounty on the head of that bear or beast or whatever it is."

"Some people are saying it's Bigfoot," Henry Hanks said.

"I don't care what anyone is calling it. I want it dead," he said.

"We'll round up plenty of help, Mr. Robertson," the other man said.

"Thank you. If you get forty men here with guns, I will give you each an extra week's pay."

Both men thanked him. They shook his hand excitedly and left to find anyone who might say yes.

Less than twenty hours later, the front porch, front steps, and front yard of the Robertson house was full of men ready to go hunting.

"Men, the first thing I want to say is thank you. There isn't another county in Virginia that could round up so many fine hunters in such a short amount of time. Time is of the essence, gentlemen, so I won't make some long speech." The men laughed. This annoyed Vance, but he knew he needed them. "I am putting a bounty on the head of this animal which is rampaging through our woods. This bounty is for his death. Bring me the body of bigfoot and I will pay you fifty dollars."

Within an hour, hunters were spread out up and down Mercy Creek and all over the mountain.

Chapter 18

Yates secretly wished he could have chosen Josh and Helmut to take with him, but he figured if anyone had to get stuck with the two new guys, it should be him. It didn't matter that they were both barely more than teenagers or that Leonid spoke only broken English. It was because they were basically strangers. When you're hunting, it's best to have people you know and trust with you. Yates couldn't say that about either of these boys.

Their job was to go to the back of the property at the corner above Mercy Creek and post up along the ridgeline. This would give them a clear view of the woods coming up from the creek, and of the Kaiser's largest pasture, which ran the length of the back of his property.

The boys thought they were there to hunt the mountain monster, but their job was actually to make sure no one, in their quest to get the bounty Vance Robertson had offered, came onto the Kaiser's land. They had done a good job of making sure this didn't happen for several months now. However, the sudden appearance of this animal, whatever it was, and the bounty put on it by Robertson, had the mountain boiling over with people walking all throughout the woods. It was worse than back in the Depression, when the deer were almost nonexistent, and the hunters used to scour the hills looking for one to kill for meat.

As far as Yates was concerned, if one of them killed what everyone was calling the mountain monster, the kid would make fifty dollars and he would make ten from the sheriff, plus the meat and fur. Yates was convinced it was a bear of some sort - maybe a grizzly a long way from home. While the others were hunting, he was on the lookout to make sure no one came along and saw something they shouldn't see. Virgil was worried to death about it, and if Virgil was worried about it, Yates was too. That had been true since they were little. The Kaiser wasn't exactly worried about someone seeing what he was doing. He was more of a pragmatic thinker. His concern was that what he was doing would be slowed down or stopped. He made clear to Yates that could not happen.

"How far are we walkin'?" Wallace asked, as they crested the hill above the creek. He was clearly still annoyed that he hadn't been given a firearm.

Back at the barn, when Yates had asked both Wallace and Leonid if they had used a rifle or a shotgun before, both claimed they had used both. When Yates handed Wallace a double barrel shotgun, he had stared at it and didn't even know how to break it open to load it. Leonid, on the other hand, had quickly opened and loaded the shotgun and showed accuracy when firing it. Accuracy with a shotgun is not particularly impressive. However, the way he handled the .308 bolt action was truly impressive, especially since he put three of five shots in the center of the target. The other two were his first shots as he got used to the weapon.

"Did you hunt a lot back in Germany?" Yates had asked. Leonid had shaken his head no and put the rifle over his shoulder.

"No," Leonid said, with a thick German accent.

Yates took the shotgun and strapped on his gun belt. If they came across a bear, they might need more firepower, so Yates selected another rifle and put the sling across his chest.

It occurred to Yates, as they finally stopped above the creek, that the fact that he was carrying three guns while Wallace carried none was most likely adding to his negative attitude.

"Finally," Wallace said, as he dropped their ammunition packs on the ground. He opened their canteen and took a long drink before sinking down against a white pine and leaning his head back against the soft trunk.

Yates scanned his eyes along the creek and tapped Leonid on the shoulder and pointed to his eyes and then dragged his finger along the field behind them. Leonid nodded and walked back to the edge of the woods and began to watch the fields.

Since arriving at the Estate, Leonid had been quiet. Uma told Yates and the Kaiser that she suspected he spoke more English than he was letting on. The Kaiser admitted little knowledge of him other than the fact that his half-sister had written and asked him to please allow the boy to come to America. Something had happened in Germany to cause her to ask, but the Kaiser had simply replied with an envelope containing a ship ticket from London to Norfolk, Virginia, and a bus ticket from Norfolk to Richmond.

Yates had immediately disliked the young man, but he was beginning to change his opinion. Interestingly, he had started out liking Wallace, but that opinion was beginning to change as well. Yates found he judged people by how they worked. How they acted in the woods. Sitting beside someone at the Kaiser's dinner table a few times a week didn't tell him much about their character. Walking with them on a two mile hike often did.

"Tell us about Adolf," Wallace said. Yates cut a look over to him, but decided to let it play out.

Leonid, who was standing rigid and unmoving twenty feet away, said nothing.

"Nothin'?" Wallace asked, speaking louder.

Leonid stood still. Occasionally his head would move as he scanned the horizon.

"I heard they're killing Jews over there," Wallace said. "That's what they're saying back home."

"Who's saying that?" Yates asked.

"Hebs," Wallace said.

"I don't know who that is," Yates said. This kid was annoying him to the point where he was about to send him down to the logging road by himself.

"Hebs are Jews. The Jews are saying it. They're filling up Rogers Park like the rats filled up the warehouses down by the river. I'm not saying I believe 'em." Wallace took another long drink from his canteen. "That's why I'm asking him." He pointed at Leonid and leaned his head back against the tree again.

"How are the Jews being treated in Chicago?" Yates asked.

Wallace answered quickly. "Not great. No one wants them there. Why the hell would we? They're eating up everything. 'Cause I'm talking thousands of them pouring in. Trying to take work, but they can't get a Union card, so..."

"So they get food from bread lines? Or what? How do they eat? It's gotta cost a lot to feed that many people."

"People. Other Jews. I mean the ones already here. They're helping. Trying to. But it's a mess, I'm not gonna lie to you."

A rustle of leaves echoed up from the creek below and Wallace jumped up. Yates walked quickly but softly on the carpet of pine needles and tried to spot the source of the noise. "Squirrel," he said, pointing to a tree halfway down where a squirrel was making his way up the tree from the ground below.

Wallace walked in a small circle and asked, "Can you show me how to use that shotgun?"

"Yes, but not out here," Yates said.

"I didn't mean out here," he said. "I meant some other time." He widened his circle and while he walked he asked again, "So are you gonna tell us?" He was directing his question at Leonid, who turned and looked past him and pointed.

A deer was making its way down to the creek from the other side. Yates watched the deer with Leonid, both of them taking quick glances behind them to make sure no one was coming across the field.

"Who lives over there?" Wallace asked, pointing at a trail of smoke coming from an unseen chimney.

"My family," Yates said in a tone that told Wallace to stop asking questions.

"Truck."

At first, Yates was startled because he wasn't sure who was talking. He jerked his head around and it was Leonid. He chambered a shell in the rifle and looked to Yates, as if awaiting a command.

"It's ours," Yates said quickly. "They weren't supposed to come today, but we never know."

"What the hell is that?" Wallace asked. A large truck pulling a long flat trailer, covered in a canvas tarp moved slowly along the horizon on the gravel road that cut from one end of the farm to the other.

"It's a lumber delivery," Yates said.

"I thought we shipped lumber out," Wallace said.

"Leonid, I need you to head on up to that corner." Yates pointed across the field and towards the back of the property. "Wallace, I need you to go on down to the creek."

"Can I take the shotgun?" Wallace asked.

"No," Yates said, as he handed the double barrel to Leonid.

"What do I do if that monster comes along," Wallace shouted as Yates walked swiftly away from them.

"Don't let it eat you," Yates said over his shoulder

Chapter 19

Little Virgil wasn't sure how close the first shot had come to hitting him, but the second blast blew bark into his eyes. His first reaction was to run away, but the stilt on his right leg had come unstrapped when the shots startled him. He took two hops on the left stilt, but the right stilt had slipped down and sideways, which pulled the bearskin down over his eyes and he went down in a heap, slamming into one big tree and several small ones as he fell off of a small dropoff and into a patch of briars. The briars were brittle from the cold and as he freed himself from the thorns, he managed to rip the bearskin free, but he had to shake off both stilts. He tried to cover the stilts with leaves, but he couldn't spend enough time to hide them properly, so they were barely out of sight as he spun around and thrashed his way through the briars and into a pine forest.

Little Virgil cut his eyes to the left as he ran but he only saw more pine trees as he felt cones crack and explode under the soles of his boots. To the right were thickets in the distance so he cut diagonally in that direction. Branches lashed his face as he weaved between saplings. The pines offered very little camouflage or coverage so he ran faster towards the thickets. The anticipation of another shot caused his muscles to tense and his heart to pound.

At the edge of the pine forest, he slipped on pine needles and fell again. The sound of his breathing filled his ears and he felt his heart beating all the way down into his numb fingers. This time, as he fell, he managed to turn so that his right shoulder took the brunt of the fall and he fell into the edge of the thicket and crashed down through the dense shrubbery and undergrowth. For a moment, he panicked. The roots and branches of the undergrowth were so tangled that he felt caught in a net. Once he broke out of the snares, he looked around, still on his hands and knees, and felt like he was in a cage, with the sapling trunks rising up all around him like iron bars. His bad leg was starting to hurt. It rarely did, but it was a weakness he always hated to be reminded of.

Somewhere behind him, he thought he heard a shout, which pushed him to get moving again, this time he used his elbows and forearms to propel himself forward and he rolled onto his side and squeezed through two of the trees. He found a rhythm of raising up on his palms and toes when the underbrush wasn't low, and then dropping to his elbows when it dropped lower, and then flipping onto his side and throwing himself through the narrow bushes and shrubbery. He moved like this for several minutes before stopping. He checked his watch.

It has been almost an hour since he left the trail, wearing the stilts and the old bear rug. Ellis Jensen had left just ahead of him and was positioned by the river. The plan was for the mountain monster to run around until he was spotted by someone hiking or driving by. After that, Ellis and Little Virgil would meet up near the river, fire a few shots into the air, throw the bearskin and stilts into the river, and go back to town to report the kill. This would allow them to end the story of the Bigfoot, which had started out as a way to get laughs, but had gone way beyond their intentions. On top of that, Ellis would collect the bounty. He had offered to split it with Little Virgil, since they had created the monster together, a week or so before Christmas, but Little Virgil just wanted the bigfoot to die. He felt so guilty about what had happened to Fern that he could barely sleep at night. And if Ellis took the money, it would make him just as guilty, and seal his mouth from ever telling the truth.

What the boys had not expected was to cross paths with the hunters. Little Virgil had to admit to himself that he hadn't even considered that possibility until the first shot was fired. At first he thought it was Ellis firing prematurely, as he had once done when they were hunting hogs out in Hickory Hollow, but it had not been Ellis' shot.

He had quickly found himself crawling through the underbrush and rooting through the dirt like a feral hog on the run. He felt panic come upon him and for almost a full minute he was consumed by the knowledge that he was about to die. But death had come his way once before and after a time, moved along. His mind brought back a memory he didn't have - couldn't have - of his father carrying him up a hill, his nearly lifeless finger tips bobbing up and down in the air and occasionally dragging through the snow.

The thought, at first, brought him sadness. But then a resolve. He did not want to die. And he would do whatever he needed to do to make sure he didn't. Little Virgil had grown up in these mountains and walked this land from one end to another with his brothers and his daddy and by himself. He closed his eyes and lowered his forehead down until it rested on his muddy knuckles. He tried to see where he was as if he were a cardinal flying above. The thicket would stop at the base of the mountain and at the creek. He listened for the water and heard it to his left. Slowly he made his way towards the water and when it was loud in his ears, he stopped, made himself as small as he possibly could, and waited, in the thicket, for darkness.

Darkness comes early to Virginia in the wintertime, and it only took a few hours for him to feel safe to finally crawl out of his hiding spot. When he stood up, his legs were numb and stiff and he moved slowly to the edge of the creek. The plan he had hatched all afternoon was to walk in the creek, but it was partly iced over, so he backed away from it and walked in the woods, keeping the sound of the creek to his left. He realized too late that he had left the bearskin back in the thicket. It was too dark to go back, so he followed the creek for at least an hour until he reached what he was trying to find: a four-board fence that ran from Mercy Creek and along the back of the Baker farm. From there, he would make his way to the logging road where his car was parked. It was the same place he parked it on the night Fern was thrown by her horse.

Making his way down the creekline was harder than he thought. Rocks tripped him. Wet leaves and ice made him slip and sometimes fall. His bad leg was numb and dragging. Tree limbs slapped him in the face. Briars wrapped around his legs and scratched out at his hands and clothes. Mud grabbed hold of his shoes and threatened not to let go. The darkness was thicker than normal and the woods were more quiet than ever in his memory. As the clouds parted and the moon lit his path, he spotted the four-board fence ahead. He let out a small shout of glee when he got close enough to confirm it was the fence he was looking for. He turned right and walked along the fenceline with his left hand occasionally reaching out to touch the fence posts and feel the roughness of the oak boards.

Little Virgil knew the road he was looking for would curve alongside the fence and turn at the corner, so as long as he kept the fence next to him, he couldn't miss the road. Then it was there, barely able to be seen in the moonlight, but it was there. His car was only a few minutes away now and he was relieved. His whole body was cold and aching and he was so scared and worried -he couldn't make his mind concentrate and think past getting to the car. One thing he knew for sure - the mountain monster was dead.

To his right he heard the metallic click of a bolt action loading a bullet into the chamber of a rifle. His mind didn't even tell his body to run before a lantern lit up the night and a voice said, "I don't know about you Zeke, but I thought we were hunting something a whole lot bigger."

Chapter 20

On the way to the hunting cabin, Yates had to pull over twice to let Ellis throw up. The first time he didn't get to the edge of the road fast enough. The second time they sat for almost ten minutes before he was finished. Halfway through the second time, Yates was tempted to leave him behind. He needed to get to the cabin quickly, and the boy wasn't going to be any help once they got there.

He waited for him, though, because that was part of the message Zeke Duggan had sent the boy to tell Yates. He was to come up to the hunting cabin, without calling the Sheriff or bringing anyone except Ellis Jensen. And if he didn't follow those rules, both Ellis and Little Virgil would be in jail before sunup.

As he pulled up to the cabin, Yates decided to leave his rifle in the truck - his pistol too. He stood a better chance of leaving with everyone unharmed if he didn't go in with a gun. No matter how much he wished he lived in the Old West, they were in the modern world now. Since the depression, laws were being strictly enforced throughout the country like never before. With that in mind, he still needed to remember that these men he was meeting were seasoned hunters. He knew them and more importantly, they knew him. So if they were emboldened enough to hold his nephew against his will in order to lure Yates there, they must think the risk was worth the reward.

Rather than wonder any longer, Yates made his way up to the door of the cabin, which looked more like a shed or a shack, and knocked on the door.

Little Virgil opened the door. He looked young, and small. Yates locked eyes with him and put his hand on his forearm and gripped it for a moment. And then moved past him to the center of the small room. Only Ian Akewater was there. Yates looked past him. One closed door off to the right. One open door at the end of the room.

Yates knew from looking at the outside of the cabin that at least one of the rooms was a closet. The only other room had to be at the rear - the one with the open door. He moved to the right, next to the closet door and said to Little Virgil, "Come on over here with me, son."

Little Virgil moved quickly and made a sound that made Yates feel a mixture of pity for his nephew and anger towards the men who were doing this.

"Thank you for coming so quickly," Akewater said.

It struck Yates as an awkward thing to say, and it made him realize these men had not thought this through well. They were making it up as they went along, or at the most, only a move or two ahead. His original plan was to give them whatever they wanted, leave with the boys, and then make things straight later. But Akewater was nervous and showed it. "Five minutes from now, I'm leaving here with these two boys," Yates said, as he took a step away from Little Virgil and towards Akewater.

The hunter took a step sideways, causing the open door to be directly lined up with Yates, so Yates moved over to a table, and sat down. This put him at an odd angle from the open door and Akewater. "Well...I'm here," Yates said, trying to keep his voice steady. His anger was giving him more trouble than he had anticipated.

Akewater stammered for a moment - just a moment - but it revealed even more of his hand. "Your nephew pretended to be that monster everyone is hunting," he said slowly. He swallowed and raised his voice and picked up a bit of speed with his words. "My partner took a shot at the beast and I flanked it to go in for the kill shot. But instead of this...creature everyone's been scared about, imagine my surprise when I saw one of Virgil Morrissey's boys stripping off an old bear fur and running for his life." Akewater paused a moment to steady his voice. "Think of the damage this boy has done. He scared the Robertson girl's horse and put her in the hospital. Ran off some of Doc Thompson's cows on his farm. They broke a fence and one of them has not been located yet. Benji Mathers smashed up his truck. And a whole bunch of men from this community are running around the hills, right now, hunting something that is not real."

The shock Yates felt from Akewater's words caught him in the jaw like a bar room right hook. He tried to shake it off, but his mind was distracted by it. And this revelation had caused a mix of other emotions to come forth. Yates felt his anger turning towards Little

Virgil - some of it at least - but when he turned and looked at the boy, he could tell the fear and regret from all of this had crushed him down to where he looked eight years old again.

"So you kidnapped the boy to punish him because he led you all on a wild goose chase?"

"No. We're in a county that has a constable law," Akewater said, gaining more confidence. "That means we can make a citizen's arrest, which we have done. And we have twelve hours to take him and his accomplice to the Magistrate or to the Sheriff. We're five hours along. Plenty of time left."

"If you and your partner have your mind made up," Yates shifted his eyes to the open door and then back to Akewater, "then why am I here?"

"Because we respect your family, Yates. Your brother is a good man. And that Nellie? Boy, Zeke says she was a peach in her day."

Yates sensed Little Virgil moving forward at the mention of his mother, and he looked over at him long enough to see that the fear was still there, but anger was fighting its way to the forefront. "I appreciate the respect and the courtesy," Yates said. "I'm guessing you aren't just surrendering these boys into my custody?"

"I just wouldn't feel like a good citizen," Akewater said. "I just wouldn't, so no, I cannot do that. However, I could bond them out to you. I'd be willing to do that. You could pay their bail, and if you never mention this to anyone, I will never call that bond in."

Yates considered their odds of fighting their way out of the cabin. Yates knew he could handle Akewater in seconds, but by the time he did, Duggan would come out firing whatever weapon he had at the ready in that other room. Little Virgil was a fighter, but this situation had him rattled, and he probably wouldn't be any help. To underestimate these two hunters would be a mistake. "I think that's more than fair and just," Yates said. "I would like to post his bond."

"I knew you were a gentleman and now you have proved yourself to be a scholar, sir." Akewater moved over to the table where Yates was sitting and leaned his rifle on the wall to his left.

Yates knew he must have strong confidence in his partner to sit down like that and to let go of his weapon. Or was it arrogance?

"We want hunting rights to the Kaiser's Estate, in perpetuity," Akewater said.

"I can't give that to you," Yates said. "There's only two men who can, and I'm not one of them."

"You can get it though," Akewater said.

"Not this time of night," Yates replied. He began to ask himself if he could smash this man in the face and grab his rifle quick enough to defend himself from Duggan. He was sure the answer was yes, but if the gun wasn't loaded or the ammunition wasn't chambered, it would end badly.

"Oh I plan on letting you take the boys on home tonight, in your custody. But to do that, I need you to write us permission to hunt on the Kaiser's estate. Make it look pretty and official and sign it. The German will honor it."

Yates knew he was right. And after he told Virgil why he had done it, Virgil would honor it as well. "I can do that," Yates said.

Akewater slid a piece of paper and a fountain pen over to him. "Just write it as a "To Whom It May Concern". Yates did that and wrote a few quick sentences before turning the paper so Akewater could read it. "That's fine," he said. "Now sign it and date it."

Yates signed it and laid the pen down on the paper.

"Now I need him to sign a confession," Akewater said, nodding towards Little Virgil.

"He's not doing that," Yates said. "You got your bail."

"I need some insurance you won't renege," Akewater said.

"You've got my word and my signature. That's all you need, and that's all you're getting," Yates said.

"No," Akwater said calmly. "I need the confession, or he ends this night and every night for many years to come, behind bars." Akewater looked over at Little Virgil. "Do you know what state prisons are like these days, boy?"

"I'll write it for him and he will sign it," Yates said. He needed to get the boy out of there, and agreeing to their terms was all he could do for now. "That's the best you're gonna get."

Akewater leaned forward. "You don't tell me what I will and won't accept."

"I'm asking you to," Yates said.

"Be polite," Akewater said. "Mind your manners. Say please."

Yates tensed his jaw and readied himself to fight back. His eyes went to the rifle. The bolt was in position. The safety was off.

The World Comes To Mercy Creek

"I'll write it and sign it," Little Virgil said. His voice was low, but steady. "I caused all this. I'll write it and sign it."

"Now that's a lad," Akewater said as he waved the boy over. After a couple of long minutes, the paper had several sentences on it, and Little Virgil's signature at the bottom of the page.

"Our business is done here," Yates said, as he stood up.

"I want his motorcycle," a voice said from the back room.

Akewater lost control of his eyes for a moment and they cut towards the open door, where the voice came from. And when his eyes moved, his smug smile turned into a grimace. "Zeke wants your motorcycle," he said.

"I heard him," Yates replied. He was quiet for a time. Somewhere in the room something was making a gnawing noise. A dog or some other kind of animal was in the closet or under the old floorboards. Yates listened to the rhythm of it for a minute or two and finally spoke. "If I can take the boys with me now, I'll bring the motorcycle to you in three days," Yates said.

"By tomorrow," Duggan said as he stepped into the doorway of the adjoining room. He had a coach gun cradled in his arm. "Let's not play this game about trusting each other. We all know what this is. It's a business deal. And business deals need to be done within twenty-four hours."

"It's a judicial deal," Akewater corrected. "This is about justice."

"If I bring you that motorcycle that quickly, Virgil is gonna suspect something. He loves that thing more than me and he asked me to sell it to him first if I ever sold it."

"No one can claim the right to buy something," Akewater said. "This is America. The land of capitalism."

"This is the South. The land of unspoken understandings," Yates replied.

"He's talking about the right of first refusal," Duggan said. "It's real."

"I need a few days to complain about it. Say it's junk," Yates said. "And then tell Virgil I'm selling it."

"But you're agreeing to these terms?" Akewater asked.

"I agree," Yates said.

"I need to hear him say it," Duggan said, stepping out into the room and turning to Yates. "I need to hear you say it."

Yates measured the distance between himself and the two men who were now less than a foot apart. His muscles tensed and his fists tightened. He stood there for a moment and then leaned forward and said, "I agree to the terms, Zeke. I give you my word I'm gonna follow this thing through all the way to the end."

Zeke laughed and looked at Akewater. "Told you so," he said as he looked back at Yates and spit tobacco down on the floor between them.

Yates turned to Little Virgil and nodded his head towards the door. Little Virgil moved quickly and was gone. Yates walked to the door and turned after he stepped out onto the little front porch. "I'll be seeing you boys," he said.

"Within three days," Duggan said. Akewater folded the papers in his hand and walked to the door and shut it as Yates climbed into the driver's seat of his truck and drove back down the narrow road.

"I'm so sorry I caused you to lose your motorcycle, Uncle Yates," Little Virgil eventually said from the darkness.

"You can be sorry, nephew. And you need to be. And I appreciate that you are. But I'm not planning on losing a damn thing."

Chapter 21

"That's the kind of guy I am," Jeb said to himself as he knelt down and started picking up the pieces of the picture he had shattered against his desk a few minutes earlier. "The kind of guy who loses his temper about someone stealing his article, and then cleans up everything he broke during his temper tantrum." He said it out loud, but no one was anywhere near Jeb's office since everyone in the distribution arm of the paper would come in after lunch. Jeb was currently picking up tiny pieces of glass and listening to them clink against the sides and bottom of his metal trash can.

"And apparently I'm the kind of guy that makes everyone else think they can walk all over him."

After he had seen the lead article was written by Chip, he read it quickly and realized it was his article. Word for word. The one he had handed Marbling himself. So that meant it had been the Chief's idea to give the article to Chip. He tried to calm down, but the more he thought about it, the angrier he felt himself getting. When he looked at the framed picture on his wall, the one of Jim Marbling and Andy Reid shaking hands with his father, he felt his anger at two of the men in the picture boil over and he smashed it and busted the frame. After that he grabbed pieces of the frame and snapped them in half.

And then he saw his dad in the picture. That was the day the Mill had reopened back in 1934. The whole town had been so happy and people had lined up, thanking his father and wanting to shake his hand. Thinking back to that day, Jeb remembered all the years his father had quietly taken care of his family and worked with no one seeing him or clapping for him or wanting to shake his hand. Jeb knew his dad didn't need to be thanked by hundreds of people. He just did what he was supposed to do, and often what he wanted to do, without worrying who was going to honor him for it.

With his daddy in his mind, Jeb sat back down at his desk and started writing questions for his next article. Why were these two men killed? Who was the unidentified man? Who killed them? Why did the first man still have a gold pocket watch in his pocket? Why did the Deputy still have his badge and wallet and gun?

And all the questions he felt like he couldn't ask publicly yet, he was asking himself. What was his connection to the Deputy? Was Monte investigating a crime? If so, why didn't he tell the Sheriff? Would he investigate something on his own without telling the Sheriff?

The best answer for the town was the worst answer for the article. Two people were passing through and one killed the other. Deputy Montgomery had interrupted it and was killed. And the person passing through kept on going down the highway.

While there was some satisfaction in the article being able to propose what happened and suggest the killer was gone, Jeb asked himself if the article was thrilling. Because that's what everyone seemed to want. They didn't just want straight news reporting. They wanted to be thrilled. And this wasn't thrilling. A man was dead - maybe a drifter. But maybe he had a family somewhere. At least at some point in time he did and probably still did. And a Deputy had been killed. A Deputy who was part of something bigger. A group of other Deputies who worked for a Sheriff who had taken an oath to protect his people. And someone had come in and killed one of the protectors. A Deputy who had a momma and a daddy and a little sister. Monte was an only son and his father was an only son. His family line died out in that orchard.

Jeb slowly began to type. He didn't have answers. But he did have a story to tell.

While writing the story, he heard a knocking at his door. When he opened it, Sheriff Tyson was standing there.

"Good Morning Jeb," the Sheriff said.

"Good Morning Sheriff," Jeb said. He found himself wondering what he had done wrong. He looked nervously at the shattered picture frame on his desk and then back to the Sheriff.

"Walk with me down to the diner, Jeb," he said. "I'll buy you lunch."

While they walked, they made small talk. The Sheriff asked about Jeb's mom and dad. And they talked about Joe's boarding house and his chances of making any money from it.

The World Comes To Mercy Creek

By the time they walked into the diner, the Sheriff seemed ready to talk about more serious things. "Let's grab that table over there, Jeb," he said, pointing to a small table in a corner.

When they sat down, the waitress came along and sat down a tomato juice for the Sheriff. "Can I get you anything, Jeb?" she asked.

Jeb looked up, surprised she knew his name. "I guess I..." He looked quickly at the Sheriff's tomato juice and said, "Can I get what he has?" he asked, awkwardly.

The waitress smiled and said, "You sure can."

Before she could walk away, the Sheriff quickly added, "His needs to be just tomato juice Shirley, honey."

"Sure thing, Sheriff," Shirley said as she disappeared through a swinging door behind the counter.

"Jeb, I need your help," the Sheriff said.

"I'll help in any way I can," Jeb said.

"Around the newsroom, have you heard anything? Anything at all? About some crimes that might fit what happened to Monte and that drifter?"

"Well. There's that car theft thing over in West Virginia," Jeb said.

"Yeah, I think that's what Monte was investigating," the Sheriff said. "His murder doesn't fit those crimes. We actually know a lot more about the car thefts than we are letting on to the public." He leaned in and lowered his voice. "We think it's two teenagers from Bunker Hill. The Sheriff over there is talking to their parents as we speak."

Shirley brought Jeb his tomato juice. While the Sheriff ordered a chili dog with fries, Jeb sipped from his glass and grimaced before adding salt and trying it again.

"What can I get you Jeb?" she asked.

"Can I get a grilled cheese sandwich?" he asked.

"You sure can," she said.

While they waited on their lunch to be served, an older man Jeb recognized but couldn't remember his name walked by and said, "When are you gonna take care of that mountain monster, Sheriff?"

"Working on it Floyd," the Sheriff said.

When Shirley walked back up with their food, she said, "That's all everyone wants to talk about these days. The mountain monster. Some people are calling it Bigfoot. And Monte getting shot, of course," she added quickly. "Sorry, Sheriff."

"It's okay, honey," he said. "Can I get another one of my...tomato juices please?" he asked.

"Sure thing," she said, and retreated quickly to the kitchen.

The Sheriff didn't start talking again until she returned with his drink. As she walked away, he leaned forward and said, "The bank got robbed. That bigfoot thing started showing up. And two people get shot to death. All in the same day. That don't make sense." He ate a few fries and then said, "You're a reporter. Does your gut tell you something is strange about all that?"

"Yes. But my gut also tells me they aren't related."

"Mine says they are. Wanna hear how?"

"Definitely," Jeb said.

"This is off the record."

"I understand. Ethically, I can't report it if you say it's off the record."

"I don't care about ethics. If you report it or leak it or even mention it, I'll kick your butt from here to Inwood. You're an adult now, so I wouldn't even have to get your daddy's permission. I would. But I wouldn't have to."

"Understood," Jeb said. While Jeb ate his sandwich, he listened to the Sheriff go into great detail as to why he thought the monster on the mountain wasn't real. The main point of his argument was that he had lived on that mountain his whole life and never seen it.

As the Sheriff finished his chili dog, he wrapped up that part of his theory with, "And I bet you could talk to every old timer in the county and they would tell you they haven't ever seen it, either."

"So what does the fake monster on the mountain have to do with the bank robbery?" Jeb asked.

"Distraction," the Sheriff said as he held up his empty glass. After Shirley came over to fill it, He sipped from it and breathed out a long, satisfied exhale. "Man that is good. Distraction, Jeb. They thought more people would call my office and we'd all be up on the mountain, while they robbed the bank."

"Did they?" Jeb asked.

"Rob the bank? Of course. You know that."

"No, I mean, did people call to report the monster?"

"Oh. Yes. They did. Later. Not at the time."

"So, did anyone see it during the bank robbery or before?"

"No. At least none that called. I think there were some that didn't report it."

"Okay," Jeb said. He reminded himself to be careful not to show too much skepticism. The last thing he wanted to do was upset the Sheriff. "That makes sense," he said. "So how does that connect with the murders in the orchard?"

"Monte somehow came up on the gang where they were camped, and they killed him."

"What about the other man?"

"His partners got greedy and killed him."

"Why are you sharing this with me, Sheriff?"

"Well, once I solve this thing, you could have an article all ready to go. Look like you're ahead of the curve."

"And what do you want from me in return."

"Fair treatment from somebody at your paper. Everyone around here reads the Herald. And that reporter, Chuck?"

"Chip," Jeb corrected.

"Yeah, that's the one. He always tries to make everybody in this county look dumb compared to Loudoun and Fairfax where he's originally from. Hell, he even makes Warren County look better."

"Why would he do that?" Jeb asked, being careful not to share his own feelings about Chip.

"It all goes back to a football grudge. One of my Deputies, Jimmy McCall, before he was a deputy, rang that Chip's bell during a Homecoming game. The boy fumbled, and one of my jail guards, Phil Petris, before he was a jail guard, picked the ball up and ran it in for a touchdown. Won the game for us. That's the only thing that could explain it."

"But Chip lives here now. Right here in town. And he works here."

"Right. What better way to get back at us then to attack from the inside."

"Like some kind of Trojan horse?" Jeb asked.

"Yeah," the Sheriff said. "Just like one of those."

For a moment, Jeb thought the Sheriff had gotten emotional. He was wiping his eyes with his shirt sleeve. "Are you asking for a friend at the paper?" Jeb asked quickly. " Because that gets into ethical problems."

"Jeb, I'm just asking for someone who isn't an enemy. That's all. It's not abnormal for the police to report facts to the local paper. I just don't feel safe doing that lately, so I haven't. You could open that line of communication back up."

Two men from the mill came over at that point. Jeb had known them both since he was little. After exchanging hellos, they began to ask the Sheriff about the murders in the orchard.

As the Sheriff was telling them that was classified information, Jeb stood up and said, "I'm sorry Sheriff, but I've gotta get back to work."

"You do that, Jeb," the Sheriff said. "And tell your family I said hello. They've always been good friends."

As Jeb walked out of the diner, he heard the youngest of the mill workers say, "And what about that monster up on the mountain? I heard Vance Robertson put a bounty on it."

On the way to his car, Jeb walked past the bank, and tried to see if he could spot Esther through the window, but the glare from the sun prevented him from seeing much of anything.

Chapter 22

When the sun comes up over the Blue Ridge Mountains, the reason for their name is obvious. They become a shade of blue that surely makes the sky jealous and causes the clouds to reach down to try to touch them. The only comparable shade of blue is the ocean from the sky. But from the ground, nothing rivals the Blue Ridge. Not for color, or beauty, or calming effect.

Virgil Morrissey was looking to his beloved Blue Ridge for any amount of calm it could give him. He used to walk the mountains, or ride his horse along the ridge. But the world seemed to be spinning a bit faster lately and the time between sunrise and sunset was as narrow as the space between hope and despair.

Though the busy times had been stressful, Virgil was thankful for them because they not only promised hope - they delivered. But despair can come along in an instant, and Virgil was feeling that right there on his front porch with his wife and youngest daughter inside, and his youngest son just a few feet away, at the bottom of the porch steps. He was facing his father, but Little Virgil was angled in such a way as to suggest he might run at any time. And perhaps that is what he was preparing to do. Little Virgil had seen his father angry before. And he had seen him lost and desperate and panicked. At that moment, he was every one of those. It scared Little Virgil, and though his father had never given him any reason to ever be fearful, he seemed poised for escape.

"There's a girl in the hospital because of you, son," Virgil said.

Silence.

"If anyone knows that feeling – that damned desperate feeling of helplessness. Lying in a bed while doctors and nurses... If anyone knows that feeling, it's you. And instead of spending your life making sure other people don't have to feel that way - Because you know, your momma said that's how a bad thing becomes good – if we use what we learned to help other people. But instead, you put a girl in the hospital."

Silence.

"I'm gonna need you to say something. I try not to ask a lot of you. I'm sure you think I do, but I try not to ask a lot. I'm gonna need you to say something."

Little Virgil was standing with his back to his father. He looked so small down there in the yard, and as he turned and moved slowly up the steps to the porch, Virgil could see the way exhaustion and fear and guilt had twisted his face into a mask of shame. When Little Virgil sat down on the top step, he stared out across the field for several minutes. Virgil wanted to say something, but instead he walked across the porch and sat next to his son and waited.

"I don't know what you want me to say," Little Virgil said. "I just don't know."

"Are you even sorry?" his father asked.

"I don't know," he said. He was more sorry than anyone could possibly know. He felt sorry down into the pit of his stomach. The sound of Fern crying on the way to the hospital was a ringing in his ears he couldn't make stop. And the truth is, he didn't want to make it stop. He wanted to suffer. But he didn't want to go to jail. He didn't want to face her father or anyone else and say what he had done. He didn't want to see the hurt on his father's face. Or the disappointment. So he looked away and repeated himself. "I don't know."

From behind him, Yates walked out of the front door and passed him, down the steps where he turned around. He was holding a biscuit in one hand while he lit a cigarette.

Little Virgil looked at his father and tried to think of the right thing to say. When he couldn't, he walked back into the house.

Virgil sat for a moment, thinking.

Yates took a long drag on the cigarette, exhaled, started to say something, and then took a bite from the biscuit instead. He knew his brother. He would eventually say something.

"What was the one thing I repeated to you so much you got sick of hearing it?"

"Take better care of your stuff?" Yates said, with a laugh. "Take better care of your toys, Yatesy. Take better care of your tools, Yatesy. Take better care of your horse. Take better care of that girl. Take better care of yourself."

Virgil smiled. It was a small one, but it was a smile. "What was the other thing I used to say?"

"I know what you're getting at and it ain't just something you used to say. You still say it all the time."

"When you come to a crossroads..." Virgil said as Yates joined in on the last part, "follow whatever path the right thing to do went down."

Yates took another bite of the biscuit, and let the smoke from the cigarette run up his fingers, along his tanned forearm and into the air. "The right thing to do here is to let him suffer the consequences of a stupid, stupid thing to do."

"He isn't even sorry," Virgil said.

"Oh he's sorry," Yates said. I listened to him cry like a baby the whole way home. "He's sorry, alright."

"Sorry he got caught?" Virgil asked.

"No, I don't think it's just that. He told me he was sorry about it. Sounded sincere."

"Then why wouldn't he tell me at least. That he's sorry."

"Virgil," Yates said, pointing the cigarette at him. "You're damn near perfect. You don't know how hard it is to tell Perfect that you messed up. God forbid, you gotta admit you did something wrong on purpose." Yates paused again and scuffed at the hardened clay with his boot. "Perfect ain't easy to make a confession to."

Virgil stood up and walked in a small circle in the front yard. Nellie came out and handed him a cup of coffee. She spoke low enough so Yates couldn't hear. "You fix problems all day long, Virgil. That's what you do. Do that now."

"He has a lesson he has to learn here, Nell. A big one. I--"

"We will teach him what he needs to learn. Us. Our family. We don't need outsiders doing it."

Virgil looked at her. The weight of the situation pushed even harder down on his neck and shoulders. "I don't think you understand how deep he's gotten himself in here."

"Then pull him out. He's always been the one we needed to rescue. Rescue our little boy, Virgil. I don't ask for much. I swear anyone would agree that I do not. But I'm asking this now."

With that, she turned and walked slowly towards the house. "There's more biscuits left, Yates. No one else seems to have an appetite. I won't see them go to waste." She closed the front door behind her.

Yates finished his cigarette and remained on the top step. After a while he went into the house, leaving Virgil in the yard, walking slowly in circles. Inside the house, everyone was quiet. Charlene was sitting by the woodstove, reading a magazine. Nellie was leaning against the kitchen counter, drinking a cup of hot tea. She had both hands cupped around it, watching the steam rise above the rim of the mug. Yates sat down at the table and took another biscuit. This one he cut in half and buttered. He slowly ate one half as he tried to think of what to do next.

Everyone looked up at the sound of the door opening. Virgil walked in only a few steps and then looked at Nellie. "Would you mind packing a few lunches for us, Nell? Yates and I are gonna take a little road trip to Waynesboro."

"I don't mind at all," Nellie said. "What's in Waynesboro?"

"Yates sold some horses to a wild west show that used to be a big deal back before hard times hit. He thinks they might have something we can borrow to help out with this whole situation."

"Do you want Little Virgil to come with you?" she asked, nodding towards the boy who had come downstairs and was standing on the landing.

"No," Virgil said slowly. "He needs to stay here and not go anywhere."

Little Virgil turned and walked back up the stairs. He was tired and felt sick, so he laid down in his bed and listened for the sound of his father's truck leaving.

Chapter 23

The motorcycle really did run like a dream. It climbed the old road up the mountain like it was made for it. Weaving through the ruts. Jumping the bumps. Wallace couldn't even tell it was the same motorcycle he had ridden through the cities and highways on his way to Virginia. It had performed then like it was designed for that type of travel. Traveling the roads like a thoroughbred. But leaving the foothills and heading for the highlands of the Blue Ridge, it seemed to almost reinvent itself first into a work horse, and then a mountain goat.

Yates had told him he would come to the cabin before he even knew he was in a clearing. The road would end at the steps of the old shack. His directions were accurate and true. Wallace braked to a stop beside the porch and then swung the motorcycle around so it was sitting parallel to the cabin.

"Whooo-eee," Duggan called from the steps as he came out of the cabin and down to the yard. He was carrying a rifle and hesitated only a moment when Wallace took the helmet and goggles off. "Didn't even want to come face us again," Duggan called back over his shoulder as he walked up to the bike. "Sent some spring rabbit to do his business. Hop off," he said as he pushed Wallace's arm. His eyes were bloodshot and he spoke just as loud before the motor was off as after. "This is mine. Hop off it rabbit!"

"Come on out and see it Ian," Duggan called out to the cabin, but there was no movement from within.

Wallace turned to go and Duggan was so busy pretending to ride the motorcycle that he didn't notice until the young man was several yards down the road and almost out of the clearing. "Where're you going so fast, rabbit?" Duggan called out. "You still got something that belongs to me," he said as he climbed off of the motorcycle and charged across the clearing. I want the helmet and those driving glasses too. And the jacket."

Wallace started to walk fast before breaking into a run. This caused Duggan to bellow like a bull and charge after him. Zeke Duggan was a big man and as he rounded the corner of the clearing to follow Wallace down the hill, he realized three things too late to do anything about any of them. First, there was a man standing in the middle of the road with a shotgun pointed right at him. Second, his own gun was leaning against the motorcycle. And third, his weight and his speed didn't allow him to stop on the gravel the way his mind told him to. So before he knew it, Zeke Duggan was swimming through the air like the river turtles swam in the water right before he and Akewater shot them during the Spring. When he hit the ground he made a grunting sound and then something like a whimper. He felt handcuffs close in around his wrists before he could put up any fight at all.

Back at the cabin, Ian Akewater was realizing he should have hidden the written confession better, because it was laying right on the table within arms reach of Yates Morrissey. Instead of picking the papers up, though, Yates came across the room like a mountain lion and before Akewater could pull his own pistol, he felt the steel of Morrissey's revolver strike him above the left ear. And then, darkness.

It wasn't the throbbing in Akewater's head that finally woke him back up. Or the car he was riding in hitting bumps in the road and tossing his body around in the back seat. And even though the handcuffs were digging into his wrists every time his arms twisted, that pain didn't wake him up either. It was Zeke Duggan screaming, "False arrest! False arrest!" over and over and over again.

"Shut up," he said. But when he heard himself talk, his words were jumbled and muffled. He felt like he had something stuffed into his mouth. He tried talking around it before realizing it was his tongue. He shouted this time and the words almost made sense. He was loud enough to catch the attention of Duggan, who abruptly stopped yelling.

"They arrested us Ian! They arrested us! Can you believe it?"

"For what?" Akewater said. His words were coming out better. "Why did they arrest us?"

"Ask him," Duggan said, pointing his finger towards the front seat.

The World Comes To Mercy Creek

Akewater's eyes followed Duggan's finger and saw a man in a khaki shirt and a green hat driving the car.

"How did you arrest us?" Akewater asked.

"That's a badly worded question, Mr. Akewater," the man said as he took his right hand off the wheel and tugged at the end of his mustache, almost as if he were checking to see it was still attached. "I think you're asking 'How could I?'" The answer to this is because I am a Game Warden. And under the laws of the state of Virginia, as enforced by the Virginia Department of Game and Inland Fisheries, I am duly allowed to arrest anyone who has committed crimes against those laws, that department, or that state. You sirs have committed many crimes."

"You're gonna regret arrestin' us," Duggan said.

"I doubt that. Because right now, I wish I could arrest you more than once. Which, of course I can't. But I can charge you more than once, and once we reach Richmond, my boss, and his boss will decide just how many charges we can drop on you two *fine* citizens."

"Sir, you are an officer of the law, and it seems a fine one, but I must, and I do this with the greatest level of sorrow, inform you that you have been duped. You see, Sir, the Morrissey family is trying to cover up a very serious crime by pinning a very small one on us."

"Oh now, this sounds very intriguing, sirs. Please do tell me more. We're about an hour away from the capitol, so you can take your time. Don't feel like you need to rush."

"Oh it won't take us long," Akewater said. "This is a sordid tale, but a short one, I assure you." Akewater swallowed a few times and tried to make his jaw stop hurting. He moved his tongue and the pain shot up along his jaw and into his ear. "Forgive me. I find myself in a bit more pain. May I have some water? Perhaps we could pull over at a service station or auto park?"

"No, but I've got a sack of potatoes back there on the floorboards. Should be right around your partner's boots. You can bite on one of those. They shouldn't be dried out."

Akewater sat for a moment, trying to figure out how a potato was supposed to quench his thirst, before deciding to press on with his story. "It all started with the Morrissey boy. Virgil, Jr. He and his friend pretended to be a bigfoot. And they caused a very serious accident. We were hunting up on the mountain and spotted him, and subsequently placed him under citizen's arrest. You seem to have been brought into this based on a set of false facts given to you by the Morrisseys in an attempt to free the boy and his friend from any charges they might face in connection with the injury of Vance Robertson's youngest daughter. And I understand why they would want to do that, and I don't blame them. And I don't blame you for falling for their lies. But, Sir, we are not the guilty ones."

"Where did you make this arrest, Mr. Akewater?" the game warden asked. "You certainly have my interest piqued now, as your story has entered into the topical area of law enforcement. If you don't mind me asking, please give me some more details about this citizen's arrest."

"Oh certainly, sir," Akewater said. "Most certainly. I can see you appreciate the skill of conversational exchange. You see we were up on the top of the mountain on the back end of the old Baker farm and we--"

"So you were on the old Baker property when this happened?"

"No, the property past it."

"Oh, I see. The property on the other side of the old four board fence."

"That's the one," Akewater said.

"My goodness boys. This is unfortunate, but that is now Federal land. There must have been some flags on the ground showing that. In fact, I know there are, because I walked with the Federal surveyor when he put them out up there. Golly. You were right. This is bigger than I thought. You boys are now guilty of trespassing on federal property."

"Now hold on a minute," Akewater shouted.

"You need to shut up, Ian," Duggan said.

"No, no, Zeke. We need to make him understand. The Morrissey boy was on that property as well. If they charge us, they will have to charge him with the same crime."

"Well, the Morrissey boy claims you all shot at him up there and he was running across the property to save his life and get back to his farm."

"That is correct. We did shoot at him. When we thought he was the mountain monster. Which he was dressed up as," Akwater said.

"So you admit you shot at him?"

"No, I'm saying we thought he was an animal."

The World Comes To Mercy Creek

"Oh." The game warden lifted his head as if he was thinking through a very difficult puzzle. "Well, damn, boys. This just keeps getting worse."

"Oh we know," Akewater said. "I told you it was a sordid tale."

"Well now it seems you two will be charged with hunting on Federal property. Or attempted murder. My goodness gracious, this has certainly become a very sordid tale. You are correct, Sir."

"He went to war with Virgil Morrissey," Duggan said. He sounded like he was tired and wanted to sleep. There was no fight in his voice.

"Went to war with him?" Akewater asked, still trying to carry the air of someone who wasn't going to jail.

"Well that's not fully accurate, Mr. Duggan," the game warden said. "It was more like Virgil Morrissey saved my life and carried me about two miles to a medic station. If we're wanting to be accurate, and I can tell, accuracy is of the utmost importance to you."

Akewater made a sound from the back seat. It was a combination of a sigh and a groan.

After a few miles had passed, Zeke Duggan spoke up. Akewater found a moment of peace when he heard Zeke's voice, because Zeke was a trapper, and if there is anyone who knows how to get out of traps, it's a trapper. "If we end up in jail, we are gonna have plenty of letter writing time," Zeke said. "My partner writes very well. And I bet he will write every newspaper in Virginia, every citizen of Lyttle's Mill, and any police officer who didn't go to war with Virgil Morrissey. And he will tell our story. And we'll see if that Morrissey boy has any kind of future after people hear what he did. Running around pretending to be some monster. Nearly killed a girl. Embarrassed the Sheriff's department. Yeah, we'll see how this plays. Now the flip side of this dirty coin is you let us go, and we keep our mouth's shut, and Ian keeps his writing hand away from pen and paper."

"Oh, didn't you hear?" the game warden said as he stuffed a fingerful of tobacco into the right side of his mouth. "Virgil's little brother Yates corralled the monster up on the Robertson property. It turned out to be a bull buffalo. Can you believe that?"

Chapter 24

"Park it right here, Virgil!" Sheriff Tyson called out from the sidewalk in front of Mac's Trading Post.

"Sheriff, shouldn't you be up on the mountain chasing that bigfoot instead of down here directing traffic?" Lyle McDonald asked from the crowd. Lyle's brother had run against Sheriff Tyson ten years earlier and although Lyle's brother had long since settled his grudge with the Sheriff, Lyle had not. Horns began to sound up and down the street. Two trucks pulled off to the side and the drivers and passengers all got out and started across the street to see what was going on.

It had been the Sheriff's idea to load the buffalo onto a cattle trailer and take it down to Main street of Lyttle's Mill. Nobody wanted the Mountain Monster disproved as a myth more than the Sheriff. Between the bank robbery and the murders in the orchard, he had no time to deal with a bunch of bigfoot sightings and a mountain full of angry farmers. When Virgil Morrissey told him they had caught a buffalo on the mountain, he knew immediately, this was the so-called mountain monster everyone was going so crazy about.

"That big scary Bigfoot, or Mountain Monster, or whatever it is you want to call it, is right here in this here trailer," the Sheriff said towards Lyle.

It didn't take long for a crowd to form as people stopped, first on the sidewalk, and then in the street. When traffic started backing up and more horns began to honk, Sheriff Tyson directed his Deputies to block off both ends of that portion of the street. Within a few minutes the trailer was surrounded.

"Who caught this thing?" a man asked from the street side of the trailer.

"I did," Yates said, as he leaned against the rear door of the trailer. "We spotted it up on the mountain in one of the Kaiser's fields.

It was ruttin' up against a tree so rough, we thought he was gonna uproot it. When we tried to go up to it, it ran off from us."

"Did y'all chase it?" a boy asked.

"No," Yates said. "We didn't do that. It was too fast. Faster than any buffalo I've ever seen, I'll say that much."

"What did y'all do?" Little Virgil's friend, Davey Gray asked. "Did somebody lasso it?"

"Who the hell would lasso a buffalo?" Little Virgil asked his friend.

"I don't know. I figured if anybody could, it would be your uncle."

Little Virgil nodded and tried to move back into the crowd.

"Tell us how ya'll caught it, Virgy," a girl said from the sidewalk.

Little Virgil looked to Yates and then walked back up to the truck to sit. He didn't realize his dad was still sitting in the driver's seat. He stopped for a moment with the door open, but got in and sat. He tried to think of something to say, but he couldn't. After a few seconds, Sheriff Tyson's voice could be heard calling, "Virgil? Virgil!?" from the back of the trailer.

Virgil looked over at his son and then just nodded before opening his door and stepping out. He closed the door with a metallic click and even over the crowd, Little Virgil could hear his father's boots walking away from the truck.

By noon, when Virgil told the Sheriff it was time to take the buffalo back to the Kaiser's estate, hundreds of people had seen the buffalo and agreed it must have been what everyone was calling the Mountain Monster.

"I wish they'd found the man that killed your brother-in-law as fast as they found that mountain monster," Lyle McDonald said to Mac MacBatten, who had come out of his trading post to ask Virgil what his plans were for the buffalo. Mac already had plans for bison burgers and steaks for his new butcher counter. Much to Mac's dismay, the Kaiser had decided to keep it on his estate.

"They're doing everything they can, Lyle," Mac said. "I bet they make an arrest any day now."

"That's a bet I would make any day," Lyle said. "The killer is probably long gone. Tyson was so busy chasing that dumb buffalo, he let the man who murdered Monte get away."

"The Sheriff knows what he's doing," Mac said, as he walked back into his store. It was a statement he had made already that week to his wife and to his sons, Pete and Pat. The boys were convinced there was more to the story, while Penelope was grieving and looking for someone to blame. She had quickly chosen the Sheriff.

Once back in the store, Pete immediately launched into his theory of how the Sheriff had killed Monte because he didn't want competition for his job. Pat chimed in immediately and added, "Why *wouldn't* he be worried about losing his job to Uncle Monte?"

"Because that lazy old man knew less in his pinky than Uncle Monte knew in his whole hand," Pat said.

"Yes!" Pete agreed enthusiastically.

Mac shook his head and said, "Well, at least you have a valid argument. Come on out back and help me lift these grain sacks." For Mac MacBatten, the best way to process grief was to work. He had faced his share of grief in his time, but had not yet met a sorrow that couldn't be outworked.

Chapter 25

Of all the Morrissey children, Ginny was the oldest. With each additional son or daughter, Ginny's responsibilities in the family increased. By the time Charlene was walking, Ginny had assumed much of her care, and even some of the care of Little Virgil, the youngest son. This was not at all due to her mother's negligence or laziness of any sort. Lazy was something none of the Morrisseys could ever be accused of. And Nellie loved each and everyone of her children and tried to care for all of them equally. But when a mother has an oldest daughter, she often begins to rely on her to help with and to do many of the things that need to be done for a family of seven on a farm in rural Virginia.

When Ginny married and moved away, she was less than two miles from her home, but she immediately began to try to find things to be responsible for. She soon discovered that many of the things she knew how to do and had gotten good at doing back home, were things that other people took care of on the Kaiser's estate.

She knew how to cook and bake, but the Kaiser's kitchen was full of people who were paid to cook and bake. She knew how to clean, but the Kaiser's house had several people living there who were paid to clean. She knew how to care for children, but the kids of the workers and guards were all over the age of fifteen and well able to take care of themselves.

She was happy with Josh and had everything she could ever want at the Estate, where the Kaiser treated her like family. In contrast, there were many nights she went to sleep feeling homesick and many mornings she woke up feeling lost. With the new year, Ginny promised herself she would take control of her own life and use all of her experience of taking care of others and apply it to taking care of herself. After several days of going out and taking long walks around the estate, she decided to start writing about her family history again. Her family's ancestry had always intrigued her and she had done some research by using three family bibles her parent's had. While walking down by Mercy Creek she decided to start writing about her grandparents. She would start with the many stories she had her Momma and Daddy tell. Once she wrote those down, she would spend time researching both sets of grandparents and then put all of those stories and facts into some form of narrative.

It was after this walk that she went into her father's office, which was in the renovated barn, across the property from the main house. She would begin by cleaning his office. It was a big office, but because her dad was in charge of so many things, his office was a big catch-all. She started by taking all of the tools and moving them out into the hallway. She would have someone carry them back down to the toolshed as soon as she was done. She wondered how many shovels the Kaiser owned, since there were at least four in her father's office. Also two rakes, an axe, two hatchets, and something that looked like a big knife. These were all piled up next to a big grindstone where apparently he had been sharpening blades. A pair of pruners and several smaller gardening tools were sitting in a wooden bucket. Ginny moved all of those to the hallway, but she couldn't lift the grindstone. She left it. She would ask someone to move that as well.

Next, she turned her attention to the piles of books. They were everywhere. She started with a table in a corner. It looked like Virgil originally had it set up for meetings. There were three chairs, but now each one was loaded with books, just like the tabletop. It took her almost an hour to move the books to a bookshelf along the far wall. Most of the books were on gardening or animal husbandry. Two were atlases too big to fit on the shelf so she left them on the table.

In another corner was a pile of map tubes and empty boxes. Ginny looked around to see where she could put them and spotted a door across from Virgil's desk. It was a smaller framed door, so she assumed it was a closet. Opening the door, she confirmed her first thought. It was a closet and very little was in it except for a pair of pants and an old suit, which were on hangers, and a pile of clothes on the floor, pushed to the rear of the small closet. Ginny leaned in and dragged the pile out into the room. A raincoat, a pair of boots and a pair of shoes. All were crusted with dried mud. Probably from the rain the other day. Or from all the melting snow.

The World Comes To Mercy Creek

Ginny leaned down and onto her knees where she could see the back of the closet better. What she thought was the wall was a stack of something. She touched the stack and it felt like paper. Ginny crawled forward and stood up enough to find the top of the stack. With her fingers, she tried to grip the top of the stack and she lifted up something the size of a small brick. It was wrapped. Like a big deck of cards. Money. Her heart drowned out the sound of her own voice as she whispered a question to herself. She stood suspended between wanting to look closer at what she had found and wanting more intensely to run away.

Outside, a man's voice called out to another and she moved towards the open door, standing at the top of the stairs, listening. Not sure what she would do if someone did come in, Ginny's eyes moved to the bottom of the staircase, ready to react at any shaft of light let in by the opening door. No more sounds came from outside, so after several minutes, Ginny went back to the closet and leaned in enough to count at least three rows of stacked money. Each row was waist high except for the front, which was several inches shy of the height of the others. The rows were at last three feet long, taking up the entire width of the closet. She pulled a bundle and moved out into the light. The top bills were hundreds. She assumed the rest were as well. She grabbed another bundle. The top bills were twenties. Another bundle. Fifties. Her mind tried to calculate the amount of money in the closet and she lost track at tens of thousands. At least.

Ginny quickly put the boots along with the raincoat. She wanted to leave quickly but instead she knew it would be obvious she had seen it. Instead, she continued to clean, sweeping the floor and calling down for help moving all of the tools. As she was finishing up stacking the boxes and tubes in the corner, her father walked in. Ginny's back was to him so she couldn't see his initial reaction.

"Virginia, you never fail to surprise me," Virgil said with no trace of anything but happiness in his voice.

Ginny turned and said quickly, "One more hour, and I would have finished. I've got big plans for whatever is in that room." She pointed at the closet door, trying to hide the worry on her face. She wasn't scared of her father. He had never given her reason to be. As he thanked her again for cleaning his office and told her not to worry about the other room because it was just an old closet, Ginny Morrissey felt something towards her father that she had never thought she would. Suspicion.

Part 2

Chapter 1

A mountain is never quiet. There are always sounds. They might change a bit depending upon the time of year, but there are always sounds on a mountain. Crickets chirp a majority of the year. Dogs in the distance bark up and down the ridges and valleys. Gunshots sound off from hunters. A woodpecker on a tree stays busy for hours. Crows land on a limb and call to the sky. Geese fly over and make their presence known. Scattered whistlings and songs come from birds never seen. Breezes stir leaves, and winds move branches and trees, producing scuffling and scraping sounds.

Down on Mercy Creek, where the covered bridge carries the road across the flowing water, the creek itself provides the main sounds which fill the day. The water is muffled as it flows under the ice, but its voice is still heard. The occasional car roars along and thumps over the bridge, but traffic was sparse on this particular day. The wind blew louder than the water, and flakes of snow turned the road, and the roof of the bridge, white. This late April snow falls to the surprise of everyone. Spring in Virginia usually brings rain and planting. The snow is a sign of winter weather making one final show of its existence.

Prints of the paws of a fox cut the road in half long wise, and disappeared on the bridge, only to reappear diagonally across the road and up the mountain. The hooves of deer have scarred the snow near the rocks on the Kaiser's property. Next to the rock is a wooden stake with an orange ribbon tied to it. Five feet away, near the bridge, is another stake with an orange ribbon. Across the road are two more. On the other end of the bridge, a line of stakes run into the woods for close to fifty yards and another line, ten feet further into the woods is marked with stakes as well. This area has been cleared of trees. Scattered stumps spread across this small area seem to reach for the snow, gathering it to hide their disfigurement. A pile of underbrush from weeks of clearing and cutting, lays piled up the hill. The falling snow, once it covers it, will make the pile look like a grassy knoll, instead of the mesh of briars and branches it really is.

On the river side, one stake with a yellow ribbon marked where a surveyor's tri-pod sat a few days earlier. Ten feet away stands a giant oak tree, out of which a nail sticks. On the nail is a tiny scrap of paper torn from a larger sheet of paper which served as a rough map. That rough map has since been rolled up in the surveyor's bag. On that map, a larger bridge is drawn. This new, larger bridge is not covered, and it runs across the stream deeper into the woods and further up the stream. Snow continues to fall and a few flakes land on the nail, and a few more on the scrap of paper. An hour later, as time passes and the snow falls, the scrap of paper and the head of the nail are no longer visible to the human eye.

Chapter 2

From the little room off of the kitchen, Abigail could hear voices coming from the dining room. The sounds of voices mingled with the clinking of silverware and dishes, along with the occasional scraping of chairlegs on the hardwood floor. Mrs. Beaumont had rugs in every room in the boarding house except for the dining room, because any carpet near that big dining room table would be ruined in weeks. Bea Beaumont protected her floors with a passion and had them stripped and waxed every March. The only thing she protected more than her floors was her money, and once she saw how much it cost to replace dining room rugs, she pulled them out. Of course the kitchen and what Mabel called the waiting room, where Abigail was at the moment, were also exceptions to the rug rule.

Mrs. Beaumont had many rules, including the one that required Abigail to limit her presence in the boarding house to two rooms - those rooms being the waiting room and the kitchen. No one was speaking in the kitchen, so she knew it was safe to open the thick wooden door and walk in. When she did, she saw the remains of the morning laid out before her. Scraps of dough. Piles of pans and baking sheets. The dirty dishes would come in soon. The cleaning of all of this would consume Abigail's morning.

After cleanup would come preparation for lunch; after that, lunch clean up; and after that, preparation for dinner; and after that, more clean up.

The door to the dining room swung into the kitchen. Mabel bumped it with her hip and swung a tray of dishes onto the counter while throwing eyes toward Abigail, who quickly jumped up to grab the tray. At the table she could see Mr. Beaumont facing her direction. Mrs. Beaumont's back was towards the kitchen door. They sat at different ends of the table, with Mrs. Beaumont taking what she called the head chair. Mr. Beaumont called his chair the head as well, so when Mamie would say the spot she would call it "his head" and "her head".

Next to Mr. Beaumont was the lawyer. In her mind she called him Mr. Porky. Not because he looked like a pig, although he did, but because he made such a mess when he ate and slurped his tea as well as his soup. She didn't recognize the man sitting across from the lawyer. He was wearing a black suit with a black tie. Abigail made a mental note to ask her momma about him. She couldn't see Miss Coalson, but Abigail knew she sat near Mrs. Beaumont. They served on the board of the League of Methodist Minister's Wives. Neither of them were Methodists or wives of ministers, according to her momma, so Abigail could never figure out why they were members, much less board members.

Over at the stove, Mabel was rattling pans and running water. "Get me two boiled eggs real quick," she said over her shoulder to Abigail. "One of the boarders sent his eggs back. Too hardboiled for him," Mabel said. "I asked if he wanted soft boiled. He says no. He just wanted a softer hard boiled."

"Who?" Abigail said. She knew most of the boarders by name.

"Mr. Chip. Come peel these eggs."

"They gonna be the same amount of boiled as the other ones. They boiled in the same pan, didn't they?" Abigail asked.

"Don't sass me. Just peel them two eggs," Mabel said.

"I didn't sass. I just asked. That's all."

"They been sittin' in that hot water for an hour longer. They more hard boiled than those others. Use your head, girl."

Abigail quickly peeled the two eggs and placed them in a small bowl.

"Paprika please," Mabel said.

Abigail sighed loud enough so her momma could hear her and then she sprinkled paprika on the side of each egg. "Salad fork?"

"He ain't gonna eat it with his hands is he?" Mabel said this over her shoulder while reaching up into a cabinet. She turned, set down a small sack of corn flour, grabbed the bowl, and bumped through the swinging door again. Mabel came back carrying another tray full of dishes. "Make me some more tea, will ya?" she asked.

"Is it snowing yet?" Abigail asked.

"Yep. Why do you think I'm runnin' around like a chicken. This snow ain't gonna stop now that it's started. Not today. Not tomorrow. Almanac says this is the big one. Man on the radio says five straight days. Five straight days of snow and here we are smack dab in the last days of April."

"I don't wanna be stuck here," Abigail said. That house out back is cold. And it smells bad."

"Then you best hurry up so we can do lunch and prep dinner," Mabel said, as she added corn flour to whatever else she already had in a big mixing bowl. "We need to finish up quick like."

If they finished in time, Mabel's husband would be able to pick them up and get them back home to the mountain. He prided himself on where he could go in the snow when he loaded the truck bed with firewood and strapped the big chains around the tires of his truck, but he had warned Mabel earlier in the day when he stopped by, that the snow was falling faster than anyone expected and they only had a small window of time for him to get them home.

That window of opportunity closed with a thud when Mrs. Beaumont decided she needed Mabel to polish the silver. She liked it done before the holidays, but had suddenly decided it should be done again, though it was only April.

"And after they are all polished, I want them wrapped in the silk napkins the way we saw them done at a restaurant in New York. I will demonstrate how, once they are polished."

By the time the silverware was polished and wrapped in silk napkins, the rooftops and yards and roads in Lyttle's Mill and Mercy Creek and everything in between were all wrapped in white as well.

"Will Daddy come get us after the snow stops?" Abigail asked.

"He'll be on his way as the last flake falls," Mabel said.

"I sure hope so," Abigail said, as a dish shattered on the hardwood floor of the dining room and Mrs. Beaumont shrieked out Mabel's name.

Chapter 3

At first, Josh thought it was cabin fever - this thing that had his wife so down and out. She hadn't been herself for several weeks, but in the last few days it had gotten worse. Far worse. It would make sense that she was tired of being cooped up. Weeks of freezing cold temperatures had limited their trips outside and she hadn't been to town or to her parent's farm in over a week. Josh had offered to take her several times on cold days, but she had declined. On the few sunny days, he had encouraged her to take a walk across the creek, and she had said she might. But she hadn't.

She had been quiet lately, but after the meeting a few days earlier when Uma had announced that there would be cutbacks and some rationing, as finances were not as strong as they normally were, Ginny had become particularly withdrawn. For some reason, that meeting had caused Ginny to go silent, and behind her tired eyes, Josh could tell she was worried. Maybe it was about how hard her dad was working. Or maybe she was thinking hard times were on the way again.

Across the room from Josh, Ginny sat and stared out the window. Her husband was right. Ginny was very worried. But it was not how much her father was working that had her so upset. It was more than that. The worry and fear and sadness came from a tangible source. Something that could be seen and touched and counted. Something she hated. The money. The image of all of that money stood in stark contrast to Uma's speech about reducing spending and going into a "temporary depression era" mindset. What did that even mean? They were barely out of those years and now they were being asked to go back to it? With all that money hidden in a closet?

Why would Uma say finances were low if that much cash was sitting in a closet not one hundred yards away? The alternative was that the only person who knew about the money was her father. That wouldn't make sense, though. If he was hiding money from the Kaiser, he could just take it home and hide it. Maybe he was worried about Momma finding it.

All of this caused her to worry, but the look in her father's eyes lately - that's what broke her heart. He had the same voice. Same face. But his eyes. They were hollow and cold. She had seen much as the oldest child. Lost jobs. Hunger. The near loss of Little Virgil. The flooding of the house. The rest of him may have shown the weight he carried, but his eyes back then, had never lost their spark. Now, however, he looked worried all the time. And his eyes were the eyes of a man who was keeping a secret.

Abruptly, Ginny stood up and told Josh she was going to see her momma. She knew she needed to talk to her about all of this. Momma would know what to do.

While walking across the fields to cut down through the back drive, the first flakes started falling. When she got to the creek, the wind was blowing so severely that she wasn't sure if she should keep going or turn around. She didn't want to get snowed in away from Josh, but she also knew this was something she needed to get out of her system and into the open as soon as possible. Her mom would know what to do. She always did. Talking to her momma was worth the risk of not being able to get back to that Estate. In fact, getting snowed in at her home place would have been desirable if not for the fact she would be snowed in with her father. This concept, which once would have brought her total security and comfort, now made her feel pangs of insecurity and discomfort.

As Ginny continued walking, she heard the horn of a truck and turned to see her father on the side of a hill. He had climbed out onto the running board of his truck and was waving for her to come to him. Sheets of snow blew up quickly and for a moment she lost sight of him. The sun came back out and there he was. He ran around and opened the door for her. When she climbed in, the cold of the seats was still warmer than the harsh outside air. She shivered as her daddy jumped into the driver's seat. "What in the world has you all the way down here, honey?" he asked.

"I was just on a walk," she said. She couldn't recall ever lying to her father before. Such a small sounding one, but big at the same time. She couldn't say what she was really doing. "This storm came up on me so quickly. Thank goodness you came along."

The World Comes To Mercy Creek

"Let's get you back home." Virgil turned the truck around in a big circle in the field and drove back towards the Estate up on the hill. "I feel like I haven't seen you much over the past few weeks, Virginia."

She fought back tears. He had used her full name. Hardly anyone did that, but he did it when he was concerned. Did he suspect something? He knew her so well. Surely he could tell something was wrong. But he wouldn't know what. She didn't even know fully what was wrong, so surely he couldn't. "I've just been trying to stay busy. Find my place."

"What do you mean?" he asked.

"It's such a big estate, you know. And so many people are paid to do things. It makes it hard for me to know what's needed."

"Well, maybe it isn't about doing what's needed," he said. "Maybe it's about doing what you want to do."

She was silent for a moment and then said, "I like pitching in. I like working and helping."

"I know," he said. "You're good at that." He accelerated up a hill and the truck spun tires for a bit, trying to find traction. When it did, the truck surged over the hill and Virgil deftly steered it through a gate and onto a gravel lane. "But life isn't only about working and pitching in. I feel bad that we only showed you that part of life. But we were so busy surviving that maybe we didn't give you as good a life as I had hoped we could."

"Oh, Daddy, you gave us a great life. You and Momma took great care of us."

"We did the best we could," he said after a moment. "But we never had money. Never. And there was so much you all couldn't do. So much you never had."

"We didn't care about all that. That stuff is not all it's cracked up to be. Money isn't some fix all or cure all. Sometimes it causes more problems than it solves!" She realized she had an edge to her voice and when she looked over at him, she could tell by the look on his face that he had been shocked by her reaction. She lowered her volume. "I just mean we had a good childhood. Money didn't matter then and it doesn't now."

He was silent for a long time and then said softly, "Money makes a lot of things possible. Important things."

She started to reply but decided against it, as the truck pulled up to the side door of the house. "I can go in through the mudroom," she said.

"Be careful, honey," he said softly.

When she looked at him, the coldness was there in his eyes again. If it had ever left during their conversation, it had returned.

On her way through the mudroom, she passed the hall that led down to the kitchen and she heard Leeza May's voice. "I can't understand it. I'm just saying, I know how much I can cook and how many supplies I need to do it. This does not make sense. I haven't cooked all that."

"I will look into it. I promise you I will figure out what's going on." It was Uma.

"I know you will," Leeza May said. "And I'm not complaining. I'm just....worried I guess. Last time food came up missing, all hell broke loose. And none of us want to live through all that again. It just does not make sense," she said again.

"Everything will be fine," Uma said. "We're just living in strange times. As soon as all the timber is cut and sold, we'll be back to normal around here."

Leeza May said something else, lower, almost in a whisper, so Ginny quickly continued down the hallway and into the great room, which she cut across quickly. She sensed someone was in the corner, near the Victrola, but she didn't look over.

She exited the room and went down the hallway to the room where she and Josh called home.

Chapter 4

Over in Lyttle's Mill, lunch was just starting at what people in town were calling "that other boarding house". Emily had figured out that serving lunch at 1pm instead of Noon gave her a few free hours between cleaning up for breakfast and preparing lunch. They had decided against hiring help in order to keep their expenses low, so her assistant cook and lead dishwasher was Joe whenever he wasn't working at his family's farm. He also made buttermilk biscuits just like his mother taught him, so the boarders always asked at lunchtime if there were any leftover breakfast biscuits. Frank always ate so many at breakfast that Joe had to start making a double batch so there would still be leftovers for lunch, at which time, Frank ate just as many as he did earlier in the day.

"You're going to need to start making your biscuits twice a day now," Emily said.

"I'm already going through a week's worth of buttermilk every few days," Joe said. "If we keep this up, we'll have to buy another milk cow."

"Well until that happens, the biscuits are the cheapest things we make around here for food, so keep making them." While piling a plate high with pickled cucumbers and beets, she smiled at Joe. "And they are a lot more popular than my vegetables."

"How do we stand on our jar supply?" Joe asked.

"Running low," Emily said. "We're down to beets and okra after these pickles run out."

"Who would've thought Mrs. Newberry eats so much. She finished off a jar of dill pickles all by herself. And still ate a big lunch."

"Shhhh. She'll hear you Joe," Emily said quickly.

Joe lowered his voice. "And she's so grumpy all the time. Can she make it any more clear that she doesn't want to be here?"

"Joe be nice," Emily said. "If you got kicked out of a place you've been living for three years, you'd be upset too."

"Well, we aren't the ones who kicked her out," Joe said. "She should be mad at old lady Beaumont. That's who kicked her out. To make room for that government man."

"And how would that make you feel Joseph?"

"Happy to be at the boarding house that *didn't* kick me out," Joe said, as he laid slices of bologna on a serving plate.

"Be nice. That's all I'm saying," Emily said. She picked up the plate of biscuits and the plate of pickles. "Let's eat."

As they walked into the dining room, Mrs. Newberry and Frank were already waiting.

"No biscuits?" Frank asked as he took three of the nine slices of bologna.

"They're on a plate in the kitchen," Joe said. "Don't worry about getting up. I'll go get them."

Emily locked eyes with Joe and shook her head. Later, she would remind him that the boarders were their guests and guests were to be treated with respect and generosity. That's how she wanted to run the boarding house. Joe had heard her say that a hundred times already in the three months since they had first opened. For now, in front of the guests, she would communicate everything through that single look. Joe nodded and went quickly into the kitchen and returned with the plate of biscuits, which he sat down in front of Frank.

Joe sat down and passed the plate of pickles to Esther. Esther was a bank teller Jeb had sent to them on their first week open. She was their second boarder, after Frank. Within a few days, Beth came along. She was Esther's friend and they were willing to room together. This was a stroke of luck for Joe and Emily because it meant two guests were paying the same for sharing a room that they would for one by themselves. Both of the young ladies were so skinny, Joe joked to Emily that they would cost them less in food combined than Mrs. Newberry. Emily had shushed him but he noticed that she didn't disagree.

At the table, per the usual, Frank was doing most of the talking. Esther and Beth would occasionally nod their heads. This time, though, he had their full attention as he talked between bites of his bologna sandwich. "The Sheriff's days are numbered. That's what they say at least." He used that phrase often, but never seemed to

The World Comes To Mercy Creek

identify who "they" were. "The Sheriff is expected to solve crimes. And a murder? A murder that goes three months without being solved? When one of the victims is his own deputy?" He took another big bite and then continued talking through the sandwich. "No. Nope. Nah. He can't expect to keep his job."

"They don't have any clues at all yet?" Esther asked. "You would think they would at least have a suspect by now."

From the front of the house, a crashing sound and the roaring of wind caused Joe to jump up while others around the table reacted to the shock in several different ways. Mrs. Newberry let out a howl. Emily gasped but quickly stood up to follow her husband. Esther dropped her butter knife while Beth quickly reacted by picking it up. Frank looked around and swiftly gathered up two handfuls of biscuits and retreated to the kitchen.

"Were you born in a barn, boy?" Joe yelled as he realized it was Jeb.

Jeb wrestled to close the door and when he finally got it shut, he stomped the remaining snow off of his feet and said, louder than he had planned, "Same one you grew up in, brother."

As they hugged, Emily jumped from surprise for the second time in only a few minutes. By the piano, in a puddle of melting snow stood a young man. He had a knapsack over his shoulder and was not even dressed for cold weather, much less a blizzard.

"This is Wallace," Jeb said quickly. "I picked him up out on the highway, just outside of town."

The man looked down at his boots. Realizing he had created a puddle, he looked up nervously at Emily and started to apologize but she cut him off quickly. "Let's get y'all in here to the dining room. It's warmer near the stove," she said. "Joe, take your brother and Wallace in where they can warm up and eat." She was already walking to the mud room for the mop when Joe stopped her.

"I'll mop all of this up," Joe said quietly. And then raised his voice and said, "I've been cleaning this boy's messes up for most of my life. No need to stop now."

Emily smiled and walked past the boys and into the dining room. "Folks, some of you may know my brother, Jeb." Jeb smiled to himself. She never used the term "in-law". From the table, Frank answered back with his mouth full. He did not look happy about having to share food with these two new quests. Mrs. Newberry gave them what some would mistake for a smile. "Are you published yet, Jeb? I keep checking the paper, but I don't ever see your name."

"I've had a few articles," Jeb said.

"Well none that I've seen, and I read front to back," Mrs. Newberry said.

"This is Wallace," Emily said. "He will be joining us as well."

As Wallace and Jeb shook hands with everyone, Jeb froze while leaning towards the two young women when he realized it was Esther. "Well, don't look so shocked," Esther said. "You're the one who sent me here, Jeb."

"I did," Jeb said. "I sure did, I just--" Jeb looked around like he was trying to find his lost words in the air somewhere. "It's good to meet you again. I mean it's good that I saw you again." He caught himself and tried once again to correct it. "I'm glad we met," he said. His face flushed red and he looked to Emily like a deer caught in old fencing wire.

"Well we sure are glad you sent her our way, Jeb," Emily said. "She and Beth have been great boarders."

If Jeb had thought he was struggling for the right words with Esther, one look at Beth caused him to lose all speech. He nodded. And then tried to smile, but his smile felt like anything other than a smile and it probably looked even worse. He finally just shook her hand and sat down on the bench next to Frank, who neither scooted down or made any effort to give Jeb room to sit comfortably. Jeb didn't seem to notice. He focused instead on reaching for a slice of bologna and some Saltine crackers.

Emily, after filling Wallace's plate, went into the kitchen to the coffee pot. It was still warm but almost empty. When she came back out to the dining room, she had two tea cups filled with black coffee. Handing one to Jeb and the other to Wallace, she saw that Joe had returned and they both sat down quickly.

"We were just talking about the murder of that Deputy," Mrs. Newberry said. "Does our reporter friend have anything to add?" She said reporter the same way she said Presbyterian. Like she was trying to say a word quickly so as not to allow it in her mouth for very long.

"Well," Jeb said. "The killer was never caught. And it seems like the, uh, the Sheriff's investigation hasn't gone much further."

"We already knew all that," Mrs. Newberry said. "Some reporter. Emily dear my tea is cold."

The World Comes To Mercy Creek

"I'll get you some fresh," Emily said as she rushed into the kitchen. As she prepared the cup of tea, Emily reminded herself to slow down and breathe. In her mind, the more they pleased their guests, the more money they made, which would allow them to keep doing this job they thought they would love. But she didn't love it. Because she spent all of her time rushing and trying to please the guests.

Back at the table, as Emily was sitting down, Frank, between bites, called out, "I need more butter down here."

A quick look around the table by the few who listened to him revealed that the butter dish was empty in front of Frank. "I'll get some more," Joe said. He was happy to be able to help Emily with lunch. Normally he was at the farm with his father. He and Emily had chickens and pigs there, not only to supplement their food supply, but also their income. They sold pigs at the market whenever Virgil took a load in. Joe planned on adding a few dairy cows, but for now he traded labor to his dad for milk and cream and butter. This worked out well for his father, who found himself over at the Kaiser's Estate more and more these days so he appreciated all the help he could get, so it didn't all fall on Nellie.

Joe set the butter dish back down in front of Frank and asked, "Does anyone else need anything else before we sit down?"

"You don't have to shout," Mrs. Newberry said. "We hear just fine."

Jeb smiled and shook his head as he ate a slice of cheese and some pickles. He felt bad eating their food, so he left the last bologna slice on the plate and offered it to Esther, who declined with a smile. While this was happening, Frank plucked the slice from the plate and finished it quickly.

"Tell us a story, Jeb," Emily said. "I know you got one. Coming in here all covered with snow. We thought you'd be tucked in back at the Creek."

"I was on my way there in fact," Jeb said, "but my car tires and this snow didn't get along very well. And my car tires and the ditches seemed to be getting along a lot better by comparison, so I slowed down to a crawl, but couldn't see a thing. I damn near hit this hitcher here," while pointing out Wallace. Mrs. Newberry made a sound of disapproval. It was unclear if she was directing her huff at the obscenity Jeb used, or the fact that he picked up Wallace.

"I wasn't hitch hiking," Wallace said. "I just underestimated this storm. It got worse once I got off the mountain. I thought it would let up. I was planning on walking to the bus station."

"I didn't realize you were coming from the mountain," Jeb said.

"That's where we're all from," Joe said as he drank from his glass of ice water. He preferred iced tea, but he and Emily usually let the boarders drink their fill before they poured any for themselves. "You living up there? Or just passing through?"

"I was staying up there and working," Wallace said. "But that work isn't for me. I just... I prefer a different type of work I guess."

"It's cold up there in the winters," Jeb said.

"It's not that," Wallace said. "I'm from Chicago. So it's not that."

"I would love to see Chicago," Beth said.

"You like to travel?" Wallace asked.

"I want to, but I've always lived in Virginia," Beth said.

"So you decided to stop here before you ended up in a ditch somewhere?" Joe asked Jeb.

"Something along those lines," Jeb said. He ate a pickle and then stood up with Emily and Joe as they stood up to end lunch. The boarders quickly dispersed, though no one could go outside with the blizzard hitting so hard. Even the porch was covered with snow.

Frank disappeared so quickly, Jeb didn't even see him leave. Mrs. Newberry moved slowly past them and to the stairs. With each step up, she grunted and then exhaled loudly as she rested every few minutes. Jeb balanced a stack of plates and carried them into the kitchen. When he came out, Esther was gone. So was Beth.

"Can we help you with anything?" Jeb asked.

"No, we'll take care of cleaning up. Unless you can think of a way we don't lose this place by summer," Joe said, after Emily went through the kitchen door, her arms loaded up with dishes and pitchers and utensils.

Chapter 5

Bea Beaumont was whistling while Mabel worked. That's how her husband knew she was happy. He wasn't used to Bea being happy, but this was undeniable. She was usually stressed out while Mabel prepared dinner, and with the snow piling up outside, Ben had expected her to be especially on edge, since Mabel's daughter Abigail was snowed in with them. They wouldn't sleep in the boarding house of course. There was a little place out back where they would stay. But her presence always caused Bea's face to flush red and when her face was red, her voice was loud, and when her voice was loud, her blood pressure was up, and when her blood pressure was up, her temper was up. But not today. Today, she moved around like she didn't have a care in the world. And that whistling. That was a very strange thing for Bea to be doing, but Ben wasn't asking any questions. Anything that caused his wife to be happy was good by him. It didn't matter much what it was.

Bea knew what it was, but she wasn't telling anyone. If she told anybody, they might tell someone else, who might tell someone else and one of those someones might beat her to the thing that would finally make them rich. So she would keep her mouth shut, but her mind was moving at a pace it hadn't reached in years. She kept playing the conversation back over and over. That lawyer, Ralph Pourpin was talking to the government man, Lonald Guthrey. Who named their child, Lonald? She had never heard that one before. She had known some Lonnies. Maybe they were named Lonald but didn't want to tell anyone.

When they first started talking, Bea wasn't interested in what they were saying, so she heard only parts of it. Until Guthrey said, "Oh we'll build the bridge. But we will have to take his land to do it. And then we will take the timber cutting rights, which means the Corps of Engineers will build highways up the mountain." This caught Bea's attention, but what held it was where the conversation went next.

"What is of most importance is that the bridge is rebuilt," Pourpin said. "If that does not happen, you will see a revolt of sorts."

"You mean violence?" Guthrey asked.

"I would expect nothing less from this bunch of backwoods cretans."

"The bridge will be rebuilt. But not covered."

"That is fine. We just need a bridge. "

"We?"

"They will require one, Mr. Guthrey."

"And they will get one. A two lane asphalt. Very nice."

"And then, the German's land?"

"While the bridge is being built, we will need to exercise eminent domain. The road needs to be widened. That is the project I was sent here to do, so that will be done. "

Someone grunted at this point. It sounded like a grunt of approval. Pourpin most likely.

The next sounds were glasses and a bottle pouring. Bea began to fume. They were breaking her rule against drinking. She almost interrupted them and put them in their place. This was her house. Her rules. But the government man started talking again. "This is the part where we need your...assistance. Your knowledge of the people on the mountain. You know these people, correct? These are your friends and neighbors?"

"Yes, of course. I know all of them. Very well."

"Perhaps too well? Perhaps you won't like what I am about to tell you."

"Tell me," Pourpin said.

"All that timber land you told me about? Well I had one of my people look into it. That German has over 700 acres of timber rights."

"Seven hundred?" Pourpin repeated. Then the sound of him taking a drink. "I thought it was a lot, but not that much."

"Seven hundred. He's making tens of thousands off of land that isn't even his."

"I knew it. I knew he was crooked. Everyone around here acts like he's some kind of benevolent--"

"Oh he's not crooked. Not that we can tell. He's just another rich man getting richer. The American Dream, right?"

"Then why are you telling me about it? Rubbing it in? I don't care what that old Kraut owns."

"He only has one fire tower." Guthrie said.

"One what?"

"One fire tower. Virginia law requires one fire tower for every thousand acres of land. He only has one fire tower."

"He only needs one. You just told me that," Pourpin said.

"No. I said Virginia law requires one. Federal law says he needs one for every four hundred acres."

Pourpin grunted his approval again. "So he's breaking a Federal law. Is that a big deal? Can he go to jail over this?"

"No, but back at the end of February, I sent the violation back to my boss in D.C., and he showed it to his boss. Now his boss has it in the works to claim eminent domain on the timber land."

"Because he didn't have enough fire towers?"

"Nobody gives a damn about the fire towers, Pourpin. I'm tellin' you about them because that's what put this guy and all his land rights on the radar. Here's what no one else knows." The sound of glass on glass again. "The War Department has been looking for somewhere to build a special base...base isn't the word they used though...facility. And it has to be on a mountain. My boss passed along everything we had on that land. Maps. Surveying. Everything. So now they're gonna eminent domain about four thousand acres up there."

"They can just take it?"

"No, they can't just take it. They have to pay fair value for it. But they're gonna take every bit of that timber land for the new government..." He seemed to struggle for the word.

"Facility?" Pourpin offered quickly.

"Facility," Guthrey said. "Facility, yes." His words were already slurring. "They're building a giant government facility up there, and whoever actually owns land, is gonna be very rich."

"But that German is gonna be able to keep that big Estate of his?"

"Nope. No way will they let a German own land right next to a War Department facility. Not with all that's going on in Europe now."

Pourpin made a sound like he had just eaten something he liked the taste of. "So he loses his land?"

"Every damn acre," Guthrie said.

Bea didn't hear much after that. She could care less what that German lost. She thought America would be better off if that Hitler man took over Europe. She had been to Paris back in the twenties with Ben and those French people were rude and nasty. They looked at her like she didn't belong there. They were getting what they deserved.

What she cared about was the fact that the government was gonna be buying up land on the mountain. Land that she knew was now owned by the bank in forfeiture. Land that she could buy quickly from the bank and sell to the government for a profit. Or even better. She could buy land in the right location up there and make her dream of opening a hotel become a reality. If she acted quickly. Which she would.

As the wind shook the shutters of their boarding house on that bitter cold day, Ben Beaumont knew his wife was happy but he had no idea why.

Chapter 6

In the summer, when the breezes came down the mountain, through the pines and across the open fields, they carried the sounds and smells of life alive, and Nellie Morrissey filled her lungs with it, every chance she got. Those same breezes during the winter often brought cold and snow and though she liked these less, she still enjoyed them. The freshness of them, no matter how cold, revived her. When the breezes came as winter winds, they brought the memories of hard times. Of winters she didn't know if they would survive. Of frozen waters that swallowed what you loved. In a time of year when she should be feeling the warmth of spring, she felt like it was still winter.

When time had come to rebuild their little farm, she had almost asked Virgil to let it go and move away to somewhere warm. Yates had loved Texas and she knew she could convince him to go with them. They could start a farm out there and grow it into a ranch. She had read stories in Jeb's books about Texas and she thought, for several moments and several days, and eventually several months, that she wanted her family to go there. To leave behind the dark and cold memories of this mountain.

Though she had decided to stay and Virgil had rebuilt a beautiful home for them, on days like this one, where the cold winds came down off the mountain making vicious sounds like a monster hunting its prey, she felt sadness again and the yearning to go West crept back upon her. These feelings could always be erased quickly by Virgil. His presence calmed her. His words even more so. But he was not there. As the snow piled up around them, she wondered if he would be able to return as quickly as he had said he would when he left earlier that morning. It was nearing noon on the second day of this storm. Only Charlene and Little Virgil were there with her. Virgil had done all of the chores by flashlight and lantern. After that, he packed a horse and rode the path he had traveled repeatedly over the last several years. The Kaiser needed him. The Estate needed him. She needed him.

And Jeb had not come home yet. She had stopped expecting him every evening like she used to. But with the storm coming, she thought he would run home. And she would have at least the majority of her children with her. But he had not. And now the snow made certain he wouldn't be there for quite a long while.

She stared off towards Mercy Creek. Virgil was on the other side of it. He would come home because he said he would. But when?

Something brown cut through the snow filled air. She blinked to clear her eyes because whatever it was only appeared for a moment. Had she imagined it? Then several more, and a board landed a few feet from the front porch. Then chickens were everywhere. Some on the ground. Some in the air. She couldn't see the white ones, but the reds were all around her. The chicken coop must have blown over. She had asked Virgil to anchor it when she noticed one of the corner posts rotting, but he hadn't gotten a chance to fix it.

"Little Virgil!" She yelled while running off of the porch and towards the chickens. "Little Virgil!"

She called for her youngest son again as she grabbed two chickens and pulled them close to her. He emerged from the house, running. His limp appeared from time to time, but he hid it well. He tried to shout something to her as he grabbed three chickens, but she couldn't understand him. He was moving towards the barn, but she lost track of him and bumped against something like a wall. She thought it was the wall of the barn, but she pushed her face close to it and realized it was one of the boards from the fence to the left of the barn. She had gone too far. She turned around and walked towards where she thought the barn was, but the wind picked up and she lost both chickens before she could even fight to hold onto them.

She should be at the barn by now, but she couldn't see anything. She even waved her hand in front of her face but could barely see that. And now the snow was stinging her eyes, forcing them shut. She had left the porch so quickly, she wasn't dressed to be out in the storm. She had a light jacket and boots, but no gloves. Something brushed her leg. A chicken. She scooped it up, but then let it go as it fought her. She fell down on her right knee. Fought her way back up. Then back down on the same knee. And then onto her side. A chicken flew into her, or one of the boards from the coop. Her mind went

The World Comes To Mercy Creek

blank for a few moments but then one thought fought its way to the forefront of her mind. She needed to save herself now. That realization came upon her quickly, but with force. Along with that need for survival, that urge for self preservation, came the instinct to protect her child. Little Virgil was out there with her. Nellie planted a hand into the snow. It sank and then hit solid ground. She pushed herself up onto her knees and then lunged upwards to a standing position. The wind blew against her and something else was mixed with the snow now. Sleet. It pelted her face and stung her cheeks and eyes.

Behind her, she planted her foot and extended the other leg forward enough to find balance and stability. And then she lifted her face up. Not towards the sky, but towards where the rise of the mountain should be. Winds ripped at her face. She turned clockwise. Same harshness of the winds. She turned again. Less wind. The pines along the edge of the mountain made a whistling sound and she heard it. Faintly. Walking towards that sound and where she knew the mountain to be, she felt her hands touch block. Her porch. She began to shout Little Virgil's name over and over and she held onto the calmness she needed. If she panicked, the breath would leave her short. She needed to be able to yell. Which she did, over and over, calmly. And then he was there, holding onto her arm, his other hand holding one chicken.

Chapter 7

Joe and Jeb stacked wood like a fine-tuned and well-oiled machine. Though they hadn't stacked together for a few years now, the many years of doing it while growing up came back to them quickly. The snow was piling up and the low temperatures were causing them to burn wood at a much faster rate than normal. Jeb had cleared a place in the root cellar, and though Joe and Jeb had to split the wood out in the yard because the cellar ceiling was low, Jeb was throwing the split wood down into the root cellar. It was from that pile Jeb and Joe were pulling from and stacking next to the steps that led up to the kitchen. They had already filled the front porch and back porch, as well as a wall behind the stove in the dining room.

"Is this where you hide all your money?" Jeb asked as he looked around the root cellar. One shelf was half filled with jars of jams and apples and vegetables. The shelves on all the other walls were either empty or filled with empty jars.

"Yeah, it's buried under your feet. Once we stack this wood you can dig a hole and find it."

"You're trying to copy the Kaiser?" he said, laughing.

"He's got so much money, he's burying it now?" Joe asked.

Jeb sensed the edge to his brother's voice. "How is business?" he asked quietly as they stacked.

Silence - except for the sound of wood hitting the floor and tapping against the block wall.

Finally, Joe spoke. "Not great. We knew it would be tight at first, but we're losing money every week."

"No profit at all?" Jeb asked.

"What little we make, Frank eats," Joe said. Jeb laughed but Joe shook his head. "Not even joking, little brother. I don't know how one person eats so much. He isn't even that big. This week alone, I swear he's eaten thirty biscuits."

The World Comes To Mercy Creek

"It's only Tuesday," Jeb said, incredulously.

"Yep," Joe said. "He's trying to set a record, I guess."

"Is he a hard worker? Are y'all keeping him thin with all your projects he's working on?"

"You mean the list he keeps saying he's getting to, until I finally do it? No, that list ain't keeping him slim. Trust me."

"I thought you gave him free room and board," Jeb said.

"Yep, in exchange for work."

"But he isn't working."

"Right. He helped me hang a sign on our opening week. And then he fixed the pipes down in the bathroom next to the kitchen."

'Yeah, I tried to use that one," Jeb said, " but the door is locked."

"Yeah, well, we keep it locked because the pipes still aren't fixed," Joe said.

"Kick him out."

"Well, it isn't that easy," Joe said.

"I know you can't kick him out in the snow, but once this storm passes..." Jeb swung his foot as high up in the air as he could, and said, "Whammo!"

"Yeah, and then he goes around town talking bad about us," Joe said. "He sits at the table and goes on and on about how everyone did him wrong at some point in time. If I was keeping a list, it would be longer than the one Santa Claus has. And I can't afford to be on it."

"You can't afford not to be," Jeb said. "Does he drink? Maybe you can blame his drinking."

"He's been dry as a bone since he came here. And he keeps telling Emily he's sober because of us."

"Damn..." Jeb said. "What about the old lady? She looks loaded."

"Supposedly. But we aren't seeing any of it yet. She came here three weeks ago, after Old Lady Beaumont kicked her out to make room for that man who's surveying up at the creek. He stayed in a hotel over in Winchester at first. But then Mrs. Newberry said he came by the Beaumont's place and within a day, she was out and he was moving into her room. Something must have changed his plans and now he's staying a while."

"So why isn't she paying rent?"

"She claims she paid a month ahead and Bea kept her money when she kicked her out."

"How can she legally do that?"

"She claims Mrs. Newberry burned one of her rugs with a cigar, which broke her no smoking rule. That's supposedly why she kicked her out. The smoking. And she kept her rent money to pay for the damaged rug."

"Is that true? Did you ask Mrs. Newberry about it?"

"Emily did. And she told Emily it wasn't her. It was a gentleman caller who dropped his cigar."

"Well..." Jeb said. "That conjures an unsettling array of imagery."

Joe laughed as he picked up several small pieces from the floor and stacked them to the side for kindling.

"What about Esther? Is she a good tenant?" Jeb asked. Careful not to seem too curious.

"She's great. Pays early. And her room-mate came along shortly after she did. They share a room and pay full rate. We offered them two rooms, but they asked to share one."

"Okay, so you have two boarders paying full rate, but splitting a room, and you have one boarder taking up a whole room, but paying nothing," Jeb said. "You're a business genius, big brother."

"What's going on with you and Millie?" Joe asked suddenly, partly out of curiosity but more to change the subject. "She stopped by and gave Emily an earful about you the other day."

"I'm sure she did. Is Emily mad at me?"

"No. Why would she be?"

"I don't know."

"Well you asked for a reason. Did you do anything wrong?"

"I don't know."

"How could you not? If you did something wrong, you would know it."

"Not when it comes to whether or not a gal thought I was doing something wrong," Jeb said, sounding frustrated. The sound of wood hitting against each other filled the root cellar for several minutes. "But what did she say?"

"Who?"

"What do you mean, who?" Jeb asked, his voice cracking as his agitation showed. "Emily."

"I thought you meant Millie."

"I did. I meant what did Emily say Millie said?"

"About who?"

Jeb chucked a piece of wood at Joe who ducked out of the way and laughed. "She just said you only cared about yourself, little brother. And that you were too immature to have a girlfriend."

"Oh," Jeb said. More sounds of wood being stacked. "Well what did Emily say?"

"About what?"

"Dammit Joe!" Jeb said. Just give me the rundown and stop messin' with me!"

"Emily reminded her that you didn't date much. That she was your first girlfriend, and that you would never hurt anyone on purpose."

"You lucky bastard," Jeb said. "What in the world did Emily see in you? She should have waited on me to get a few years older." He barely finished speaking before a chunk of wood came flying at him from Joe's direction.

Chapter 8

The stress of trying to be in two places at once is bad enough but the stress of trying to make two different people happy is even worse. Up on the mountain, Virgil was learning that lesson first hand. If the Kaiser was pleased with his efforts, Nellie was not. But once he felt like Nellie was happy, he was worried the Kaiser was not. If he just had enough time, he could do everything everyone needed him to do, but he did not have enough time, and he was growing weary and exhausted.

At some point he knew he would need to sit Nellie down and confess to her. Tell her about the secrets he has kept from her. And more recently, the lies he has told. He will have to tell her what he has done. And he knows she will ask him to stop, but he cannot. So he has delayed telling her, not just from the pain it will cause for her to hear he has lied to her, but because she may look him in the eye and ask him to promise never to do it again, and he will not be able to do that, yet. He has to wait until he can. And at this point, he has no idea when that will be.

After finishing up with Leeza May and making sure she had everything she needed from his supply run to town, he stacked the other supplies in his office and locked the door and bolted it. Next to his office, behind a door no one else has a key to, he looked around, made sure no one was in eyesight and stepped in quietly.

When he re-emerged half an hour later, Virgil heard the sound of the Kaiser's new Mercedes churning its way through the snow where it stopped in front of the house. The Kaiser emerged quickly, dressed in a full length coat and a fur hat. He looked around and then began to make his way to the building where Virgil was standing. Virgil looked out the window and could barely see through the frosted panes. Across the pastures he couldn't see and across the creek was his home. He had been homesick during the War of course. But then he was thousands of miles away. How could a man be so homesick so close to home?

"Virgil?" the Kaiser's voice came up the stairs. "Virgil? We have much to discuss."

Virgil nodded and turned away from the window. "How was your trip?" he asked loudly, as he walked down the steps to meet the Kaiser.

"My trip was fine. A bit icey and dicey on the other side of the mountain near Snickersville, but isn't it always?" he said as he smiled at his own joke. "I received a call from this Pourpin fool. Did you?"

"Yes. He wants to meet with us about the eminent domain issue. He says he has a compromise to offer us."

"Who the hell is he to compromise?" the Kaiser asked. "The man who came here with the surveying crew - he is calling the shots, is he not? He is the man in charge. Why would we waste our time talking to a man we didn't want to talk to before when he was offering to be my attorney, now that he is the attorney for someone that has a whole government of attorneys? No. He is a carnival huckster, Virgil. That's all."

"I think we need to meet with him. Both of us."

"Oh god, Virgil. Why? Let us ignore him. Why don't we ignore him like the miserable little gnat he is. Why open our mouth and give him the opportunity to fly in?"

"If they take part of your land, they will follow the creek at some point. They will want to dam it up or build a bridge on it at the rear of the property. There are all kinds of things they could do to weasel themselves onto the property. And we cannot let them do that."

"We're not as vulnerable as you think we are, Virgil."

"No. Respectfully, I say this. We're not as secure as you think we are."

"Your brother says we are. He is head of security. He says no one will find out. No one will know.'

"He's speaking from the point of view of securing the Estate from someone invading or attacking or trying to rob us or something like that. I'm talking about having so much activity around us that someone bumps into the truth."

"It's fine, Virgil. You worry too much."

"You could go to prison, Wilhelm. And so could I. And so could Yates. And Uma. Federal Prison. Forever. I don't think there's such a thing as worrying too much," Virgil said. "Not even close. You know what it's like already."

"Virgil. You are my friend. My family. I do know what it's like. Why do you think I started this? Has it gone further than I calculated? Yes. Yes it has, Virgil. But now that we are in the woods, we must press on to the other side."

Virgil looked around the big empty room they were standing in and then looked up at the ceiling and back at the Kaiser. "You're right. We will finish what we started." And then, as he walked away, he said to himself, "God help us all."

Chapter 9

"The reason the world does not know what to do with him is because he is a man who does not value money. He values land. People think he values power. He values land. It is said that he values control. He values land," Pourpin said. "I'm not saying what he is doing is right, and I am not saying what he is doing is wrong. I am saying that no one understands why he is doing what he is doing. They have complicated it. He wants land."

"I think he wants money and power and control and he is getting all of that by taking land," Chip said. "He's going about it brilliantly. We are watching the modern Alexander the Great. And we've got a front row seat to it."

"We do not have a front row seat," Archie Feinstein said. His statement didn't just receive surprised looks from the other boarders at the table because of his tone, but because he rarely spoke except to ask for salt or pepper. He didn't even ask for seconds. He was a quiet man. "Everyone who occupies a front row seat dies. The Jews in Germany, in Austria, in Czechoslovakia, in Poland. Those men and women and children had front row seats and they are dead."

"I don't believe children are dying, Archie," Ralph Pourpin said calmly. "Maybe some women and kids got killed if they got in the way accidentally, but accidental is not the same as on purpose. There was no malice aforethought, to quote the requirements of the law."

"They are killing Jews over there," Archie said. "They go into houses and businesses and arrest entire families and take them to killing camps.

"Killing camps?" Mr. Guthrie asked. "I don't think that's true."

"Where are you getting your news from?" Chip asked.

"Not from your paper, that is for certain. Your paper should have a giant stamp across the banner, FUEHRER APPROVED,"

Archie slammed his hand down on the table. "I've seen what those Germans can do! I know what evil is capable of!"

"Don't be so senile," Chip said, while reaching for a dinner roll.

Archie stood up quickly. "I will show you what I am and I am not," he said as he began to walk around the table towards Chip.

"Gentlemen, Gentlemen," Bea Beaumont said from her chair. "Do sit back down, please." She looked over at Ben, but he continued to eat his meal and didn't even look up. "Gentlemen!" she shouted, causing everyone to stop and look at her. She calmed her voice and said, "Now Chip, you need to apologize to Mr. Feinstein. He was a Captain in the Great War and he's probably very passionate when it comes to this topic."

Archie looked around at everyone and said, "I'm sorry folks. I lost track of myself." With that, he turned and walked back to his chair, which he pushed under the table. "I think I should retire for the night, he said. "Goodnight everyone."

A few people said goodnight, but as his footsteps sounded from the chair, Bea Beaumont said, "Chip, for the record, I agree with you. That man over there in Europe has fed those Germans. He has raised them up from the dirt, and taken in his fellow countrymen from all over the world. Austria was begging to join his nation. And I've heard Poland was too. What do you think, Pratt?"

"I agree." Pratt Coalson agreed with everything Bea Beaumont said and everything she did. She was a retired school teacher and she had knowledge about current affairs because she spent the day reading newspapers and listening to the radio. If Bea didn't have an opinion, Pratt could talk for hours. But if Bea let her own stance be known, Pratt would adopt that stance and say nothing more on that topic, other than to state her agreement with her friend and landlord.

"Do you really think children are being killed over there? By Germany?" The man asking the question was the new preacher at the Baptist church in town.

"They most certainly are not," Mrs. Beaumont said.

"No!" Pratt Coalson said quickly.

"Do you think they are, Preacher Rawls?" Chip asked. He was staring the young man down, as if daring him to speak up.

The World Comes To Mercy Creek

"I don't know what to think, to tell you the truth," Matthew Rawls said. He picked at his lasagna with his fork. "I watch the news reels. I read the papers. I listen to the radio."

"I do all that!" Pratt Coalson said from across the table.

"As do I," Chip said. "And when you listen to all of that with not just an educated ear, which of course is important, but an ear for the truth," he tapped his right ear with his fork, leaving tomato sauce on the lobe, "you come away thinking this is a man who has rescued his country, and he is being vilified by all the other world leaders who couldn't do it."

"You don't think Roosevelt did a good job of bringing us out of the depression?" the pastor asked.

"I don't, thanks for asking," Chip said.

Mr. Guthrie spoke up. "Hitler has made bold moves, taking closed down stores and shops and revitalizing them, with the government's backing. He seized businesses which were being mishandled or run by greedy businessmen who could care less if their neighbors were starving. These same businessmen who were not even nationals of the nation they were milking for money and resources. He made bold moves. Moves that our government should be modeling."

"Our government should be looking at what he is doing, and of course not making the same mistakes, but doing what has worked," Ralph Pourpin said. "Has he used too much military power? Who defines too much? It would be too much over here. We are civilized. We would not need to be forced to do the right thing. To rise up and thrive. Look at how we have done already under weak leadership. Imagine if our government did what Mr. Guthrie is suggesting. The results would be staggering. We'd all be living in our own houses and driving our own cars."

Bea Beaumont made a grunting sound to show her disapproval of his last statement, but she clearly had agreed with everything else he was saying. "I do love how the dinner table, in businesses such as ours, can provide a place for education for those who may be...a bit naive as to the ways of the world." She was looking at the young pastor when she said it.

"If people are dying - if young children are being murdered - it falls to the rest of the world to speak up. To say this is wrong. And to say this will not be tolerated."

"Who are we to tell another country what is wrong or what is right?" Chip asked.

"We are the United States of America, that's who," the pastor said. "But more than that, it is important for each of us to remember that right and wrong, good and evil, has no geographical conditions upon it. What is wrong here in Virginia, is wrong in Berlin. What is wrong in Virginia is wrong in Tokyo."

"Now don't tell me you're one of those that think the Japanese are anything to worry about," Mrs. Beaumont said.

"I do believe they are," the pastor said. "They are snatching up land and resources at the same pace as Adolf Hitler. And with arguably more savagery. Though we haven't heard that they are transporting children to killing camps, I have heard that they are killing them where they stand when they invade a country."

The conversation paused when Mabel came in to remove any empty or dirty dishes. The look on her face did not reveal either way how she felt about what she might have heard from the kitchen. She quickly gathered what she was there for and went back through the swinging door.

"Do you hear what they're saying out there, Momma?" Abigail said.

"You hush. Hush now," Mabel said. "Mind your own business, for your own good. We're here to work. To work, girl. Not to have somethin' to say about every somethin' that's said."

"They saying Adolf Hitler is a good leader. A good President, or whatever he is. And Daddy says he is evil. Why would Daddy say he's like the Devil, but these people think he is like God?"

"Some people's Jesus is another people's Satan, that's why," Mabel said quickly.

Abigail looked to her momma and let those words move into her mind and plant seeds. "So what do we do? How do we know who is right and who is wrong?"

"You keep watchin' with your own eyes and you keep listenin' with your own ears. And you will know. I raised you to recognize what is good." Mabel looked at the swinging door and lowered her voice. "And to recognize what is evil."

Chapter 10

The dinner table at the Morrisseys was not crowded. Nellie sat in her seat. Charlene sat next to her on the bench that usually held three people. Little Virgil sat in a chair on the other side of his momma. On the table sat four boiled chickens and a side of potatoes, with a loaf of fresh bread.

The radio was on and they listened to it while they ate. The fireplace cracked and sparked occasionally, but there was not much other noise in the house. Charlene asked a few questions about the snow and about what people were saying on the radio, but mostly, the three of them sat in silence. They had talked a lot the first day of the blizzard, but by the end of the second day, they were all talked out. At the end of the meal, three of the chickens sat untouched. Nellie packed them up and put them in the icebox, while Charlene gathered the dishes and put them in the sink. The loaf of bread sat on the table. Little Virgil cut a small slice from it and ate it unbuttered before standing up and walking over to the wall where his coat and gloves were hanging. He had hoped his daddy would get home in time to help with the chores, but at this point, even if he made it home, he would be tired, and Little Virgil knew the right thing to do was go ahead and start. This way his momma wouldn't have to do it.

"Wait for me to finish up and we will run a rope out to the barn," Nellie said. "The snow is even worse than it was earlier. I don't want you out there without a lantern, and rope." She quickly took off her apron and hung it up.

Little Virgil nodded. "I'll tie the rope off to one of the porch posts and wait for you," Little Virgil said. He went out to the back porch and grabbed the longest coil of rope. This was the one his daddy used for this purpose. They rarely got blizzards, but whenever it snowed, Virgil tied off a rope from the house to the barn. He always worried a storm would come up they didn't expect and someone would go out to feed the cows and end up in the creek.

Little Virgil had long ago had enough of Mercy Creek in the winter time, so he tied the rope off to the corner post on the porch and went back inside to get a lantern and a flashlight. He lit the lantern and hung it on a corner of the porch where he could see it from the barn, or at least catch glimpses of it through the snow.

Nellie emerged from the front door, dressed in one of Virgil's heavy barn coats. She was wearing a hat and scarf and gloves. "Let's do it together. That way we finish faster." The wind swirled across the porch, stirring up snow around their feet, and dragging sheets of it across their bodies.

"Ma!" Little Virgil started to protest her help, but he knew his mother well enough to save his energy. He would need it over the next hour, and it would be wasted, arguing with his mother.

Little Virgil handed the flashlight to his momma and started down the steps. "Wait!" she called out over the wind. Quickly she tied a small length of rope she had through Little Virgil's belt and then looped it around her waist and tied it off. They could be no more than six feet apart. "Now we're ready!" She smiled as she said it, but no one could see it through the snow and her face was mostly wrapped in a scarf.

As Little Virgil stepped down into the snow he was shocked at how deep it had gotten. He expected to sink down to his knees, but he was waist deep. Hoping it was just a drift, he fought his way forward and found himself stepping up a bit to where the snow was just above his knees. He looked back and saw his momma fight her way through the same drift. Waving for her to come up alongside him, he shouted, "We need to walk shoulder to shoulder." She nodded but continued to walk behind him. "Shoulder to shoulder!" he shouted and then showed her with his hands what he meant. She quickly stepped up next to him and they walked forward step by step together. Another drift caused Little Virgil to trip and he went face down, but fought his way back up before his momma had to help him.

As they neared the barn, the snow became shallow, as there were no buildings or nearby trees on either side to block the wind, which swept the snow into drifts further down the property. Nellie started to unlatch the main barn door, but Little Virgil motioned for her to follow him to the smaller door on the side. Once they went

The World Comes To Mercy Creek

through it, he latched it shut behind them. "This one catches the wind less than that big one," he said.

"Smart," Nellie said, as she stomped her feet onto the straw floor.

Little Virgil laughed and asked, "Being careful not to track snow in?"

Nellie blushed, which of course wasn't apparent in the lantern lit barn, or under the scarf, or in contrast to the red of her cheeks from the cold. "Shush," she said as she stomped her feet again. "Let's get to this and get back to the house. I don't like leaving Charlene alone." The barn seemed even colder than the outside, though of course there was no wind.

"I'll muck the stalls, and put clean straw down if you don't mind tossing hay into each one for their feed," Virgil said.

"I will. How much does each one get?"

"A few flakes."

"What about water?" Nellie asked as she found a bale of alfalfa and went to each stall. They had five horses now. She could remember when they only had one. Nellie stopped in front of Soddy's stall and put a few extra flakes into her stall. The old horse walked over to her and nuzzled her. She could stand there all evening, soaking in the heat of that beautiful loyal horse, but she reminded herself that they had more to do at the back of the barn so she moved on quickly. "I have to bust through the top layer of ice on the big water barrel," Little Virgil said. "Daddy filled it up from the creek before he left."

" I'll help you after I finish with this," she called out. The next stall was empty. The door was open, so she moved past it and to the last one where their newest horse was stalled. He was still getting used to the farm and as the wind stirred up outside, Little Virgil called down for her to be careful.

"That one spooks easy," Little Virgil said from a few stalls down.

Nellie looked into the stall and saw a tall black horse move backwards and then push forward to the front of the stall, and then it repeated its backing up motion before moving in a half circle and butting up against the stall door. "I see that," Nellie said. She quickly tossed a few flakes of hay into the stall just as the wind shook the main door, right next to the stall, causing the big quarter horse to rear up and whinny. She heard Little Virgil react from the empty stall, like he had been startled by the horse. But then, further down the barn, she saw her son emerge from a stall opposite the one she heard the noise come from.

Backing up quickly with the lantern, Nellie moved to Little Virgil as quickly as she could. "Someone is in the stall next to Blackjack," she whispered as she pressed her face against his ear. She tried to fight back the fear she felt and balance it with the feeling of wanting to be protected, while letting her protective instinct for her son surge up at the same time.

Little Virgil didn't even ask for proof or explanation. The events of earlier in the year had left him ashamed and embarrassed and almost in a comatose state, though he knew what a real comatose state was like and he refused to slip back into one again. The need to rise up and show himself to be the son his father would approve of drove him to the tool room where he looked at the array of tools hanging on the wall and stacked in the corners. He grabbed a small hatchet, but then decided against it and pulled out the cutting bar they used for the small patch of tobacco they grew each year. It was longer and had a cutting edge at the end. He moved quickly past his mother, putting the bar in her hand before going quickly over to the truck they used to drive hay and feed and supplies into the upper field. He opened the door quickly and reached behind the seat. His hand was shaking until he felt the wooden stock. Clasping it, his grip steadied.

He backed up from the truck, leaving the door open. He motioned for his momma to climb into the truck. She shook her head vigorously in a way that immediately told him not to argue. He nodded and moved up next to her. Nellie hung the lantern on a hook. Its light shined to the edge of the stall, leaving the interior dark. Little Virgil handed his mother a flashlight and broke open the shotgun. Both barrels were loaded. He clicked it shut quietly and took a deep breath. The cold air filled his lungs and the smell of the barn, that familiar smell he grew up with, filled his nose.

As they moved closer to the stall, Nellie touched Little Virgil's shoulder and steered both of them out of the orb of light cast by the lantern. In the shadows Little Virgil remembered the rope tied to his belt. It could trip him if they had to run. Or it could be used against him if they had to fight. He tried to reach back and his momma was already untying it. She dropped the rope and it made a sound like a stone hitting the ground. The surprise of how loud it was caused Little

The World Comes To Mercy Creek

Virgil to breathe faster and he swore every living thing in the barn could hear it. His eyes went all over the area in front of him and then back to the open stall door.

He tried to calm himself and his momma moved beside him and whispered, "Let's take a second and think this through." He moved his eyes towards where her face would be. They stood in darkness for a full minute. Maybe two. He tried to draw peace from her, but instead, he felt an anger rise up within him. He asked himself why and towards who? Whoever was in the stall? For a brief moment it was his father he was angry with. But he quickly re-routed it to the stall. To the invader. To whoever was here to take what they--

"Poko ya vo!" was what Little Virgil heard come from the stall. Words he didn't recognize, but he raised the gun up and charged the stall as Nellie turned the flashlight on and pointed it at the door.

Little Virgil made a yelling sound as he threw open the door and again he heard "Poko ya vo" yelled by more than one voice this time. Two were standing and a third was in the corner lying down. The two standing had their hands out, defensively. The one lying down started to scream. A girl. Two girls. The one lying down was a girl, but one of the two standing up was a girl, too. The tallest of the two was the girl and she was yelling that same word over and over "Poko ya vo" and then "Sorry!" "Sorry!"

Little Virgil moved the shotgun from the two standing to the one on the ground and back to the one standing, which caused the shorter one, the boy, to yell "Pokoyavo! Pokoyavo!" over and over while the girl on the ground started screaming again. As he moved the shotgun quickly towards the screaming girl, he felt the barrel being pushed up towards the ceiling quickly. His momma was talking now and had moved the gun away from the people he now realized were kids. Scared ones.

"It's okay," Nellie was saying. "It's okay!" She pushed the gun barrel further up towards the ceiling and shouted "Son, it's okay." She seemed to be telling this to herself, just as much to the kids and her son. "It's okay," she said one last time as she moved towards them.

Chapter 11

"I'm not saying he should be fired. I'm saying he should quit. There's a difference." Frank said, as he finished his cigarette and rubbed his fingers in the air towards Jeb who chose to ignore him since this was the third Lucky Strike he had smoked from Jeb's already dwindling pack. That was as many as Jeb, Wallace and Esther had smoked, combined. Beth was smoking too but from her own pack.

Wallace, who had put on the leather jacket he kept protected in his backpack, was leaning forward towards the fire he and Jeb had built out back near the root cellar, in the area where Joe had cleared out to split wood. The conversation didn't seem to interest him like it did Jeb and Esther.

"So you're saying you told Sheriff Tyson this same story. And he didn't do anything about it?" Jeb asked. "That doesn't sound right."

"I don't care how it sounds," Frank said, reaching for the jar Wallace had next to him. "It's what happened." He took a long drink from the jar and sat it back down next to the log he was sitting on.

"You're telling us he didn't even care that a woman was walking back into town by herself, in the snow, on a night where two men were killed. One of which was a Deputy?" Jeb looked around the fire at the other faces near him. "What do you think Esther?" he asked.

"That sounds like bull crud to me," Esther said.

"Bull crud?" Jeb laughed and exhaled smoke into the cold air.

"What?" Esther looked around the fire quickly. "What's so funny?"

"That profanity coming out of your mouth," Jeb said as he laughed again.

"Aw. Go pound sand, why don't ya?," Esther said.

All of the men laughed again, with Jeb laughing so hard he fell back into the snow, which caused the other men to laugh even louder.

The World Comes To Mercy Creek

When Esther stood up and flicked her cigarette at Jeb, they all froze, until she yelled, "Fudge all you guys." Immediate silence was followed by Beth's low laughter, which was quickly joined by Esther and everyone else, the last of which being Jeb who laughed more from relief.

"I'm gonna go see if any more chicken is left from dinner," Jeb said. "I was writing through the meal and missed it."

"I wondered where you were," Esther said with a smile. She was forming snow into a ball about the size of a lemon.

"Did you write anything good?" Beth asked.

"I'm actually working on a bit of a mystery," Jeb said.

"Oh, really?" Esther said, as she lobbed the snowball into the fire. The fire hissed and a spray of steam spit into the night air. "I can't wait to read it."

Jeb smiled in the darkness as he walked inside.

"I'm surprised you aren't going in there to get some of that chicken," Beth said to Frank.

"No need," Frank said. "I finished it all off before I came out here with you all." Oblivious to the fact that no one else laughed or even said anything at all to his remark, Frank changed the subject back to the Sheriff. "Didn't the bank get robbed back around the same time as the killings?" Frank asked.

"Yes," Esther said. "On New Year's Eve."

"And they never caught that guy, either, did they?" Frank asked.

"No," Esther said. "They sure didn't."

"I'm telling you, maybe he should be fired, now that I think on it some," Frank said.

"The bank here in town got robbed?" Wallace asked.

"Yes," Beth said. Her voice had an edge to it. "She just said that. On New Year's Eve."

"I got here a few days after that," Wallace said. "But it makes sense of something I haven't been able to make sense of."

"What?" Beth asked. "Now you've got our curiosity up."

"Well, when I was working for this fellow up on the mountain, he had a small barn out in one of his fields. It was a new barn. And I mean brand new. Never had any horses in it. I assumed it was a winter barn for horses out in the cold in the back pastures, but there never was a horse in that barn that I saw. So one evening, the guy who runs the show, and his brother came to get a few of us from the barracks. That's what they call their bunk house. So they picked out a few of the guards that work there and told them to dress warm. Then they left. Well I got curious. I was so damn bored on that farm. I decided to see what they were doing. So I walked outside for a smoke, but they were all loading up a truck with these wooden boxes. I didn't think anything of it, but then they headed down the road that led to the back of the farm. And those boys didn't get back until early in the morning. And I acted like I was asleep, but I watched and I listened. They were covered with mud from head to foot. Tracked it all in the barracks and the next day they had to wash their clothes in a big barrel outside. So I heard one of the boys ask a guard where he had been. He said "The Kaiser is burying his money. Three months later and I still never saw a horse go in that barn in the back field. I figure that's where they buried it."

"I think you're just drunk and telling stories," Beth said.

"What if I told you I dug it all up and I'm on the run with it, now?" Wallace asked.

"I'd ask you to buy me a house in Florida," Beth said.

"Too many alligators down there for my liking," Jeb said from the darkness as he walked up and sat down. "What did I miss besides dinner and leftover chicken?" Jeb asked while cutting dangerous eyes at Frank who was sound asleep, still sitting up on the log.

"Just tall tales and boasting," Esther said as she stood up. "And it's time for me to turn in."

"No need for me to wake you up coming in later," Beth said. "I might as well do the same."

As Esther turned to go back into the house, she picked up Jeb's jar and poured the remaining contents into the fire, causing it to flame up so high it looked like the fire was exploding. Frank jumped up and yelled, "Call the brigade!" At that point, everyone lost it, and started laughing. When Frank realized they were laughing at him, he kicked at a log in the snow and cursed to himself while walking inside.

Beth and Esther said goodnight and followed him.

Jeb lit another cigarette and stared into the fire. He forgot for a moment that he wasn't out there alone until he heard Wallace's voice. "When do you think the roads will be open again?"

The World Comes To Mercy Creek

"Well, they will probably be open a few days after the snow stops. But then it depends on how deep the snow is before very many cars are out and about. And it depends first of all, when the snow stops."

Wallace began to count the fingers on his left hand.

"What are you doing?" Jeb asked.

"Oh, I'm just trying to calculate how many days equals a *depends*," Wallace said, as he kicked a piece of wood deeper into the fire. The flames leapt up and he leaned in towards the heat. "I'm used to Chicago where they clear the roads while it's still falling."

"Not here," Jeb said. "Usually it doesn't snow enough to justify the equipment it takes to do that. This winter has just been really bad for snow storms."

"And there are a lot less people needing to be out on the roads here," Wallace said. "So it makes sense that they don't make it a big priority to push the snow off."

"Right," Jeb said. "Around here, we keep our tractors in the fields."

Wallace stared into the fire and didn't respond to that. He dug into his pocket and pulled out a pack of Old Gold cigarettes and lit one. He offered the pack to Jeb. "I've been smoking yours all night. I forgot I had this pack in my jacket."

Jeb took one and thanked him. "Old Gold, huh? That's the brand my uncle smokes. He won't smoke anything else."

"I smoke whatever brand is in my hand," Wallace said as he puffed slowly on his cigarette and stared into the fire.

"You're in a hurry to get out of here?" Jeb asked.

"I just don't want to overstay my welcome," Wallace said.

"Hey if you're worried about that, don't. This is my family. We can stay here as long as we need to. The snow can't last forever."

"I don't want to be a burden. I just want to get back home. And try to start over. Find some job working for a grocer. Or a butcher maybe? Some place where no one's running a game."

"What's that mean?" Jeb asked. "Running a game?"

"Back home, someone's always got a hustle. They're working an angle. I used to get jazzed up about that stuff, man. I used to really get up on it. But now, I know it's time to settle down and build a life. Like my grandfather did. He worked in an icehouse all day. Came home to his family. Didn't run the risk of getting locked up. He played it straight."

"Can't you do that here, easier than Chicago?" Jeb asked. He took a short stick and poked at the fire while he spoke.

"I thought so," Wallace said. "But the place I've been at for the past couple of months? Out in the middle of nowhere. Working on a farm. Imagine if the boys back home knew I was shoveling horseshit all day. They'd never let me hear the end of it.'

"You didn't like it? Jeb asked. "I mean, I've done it all my life, so I get it."

"I didn't mind it, but that place? They had more angles and hustles going on there than my whole block back home." He lit another cigarette and held it in his fingers a long while before putting it to his mouth. After a long drag, he said, "If I got caught up there by the cops? Doing what they're doing? I'd be in prison 'til I'm old and gray. Til I'm my grandpa's age."

"Where were you working?" Jeb asked quickly. Part of it was the reporter in him, but most of it was the fact that someone, probably one of his neighbors it sounded like, had an illegal operation going on that scared a kid from the South side of Chicago who had probably seen more crime at his age than Jeb would see in his whole life.

"End of story," Wallace said as he stood up and walked back over to the back porch door. "I don't want any connection to whatever it is they've got going on up there." He pointed towards the mountain as he said it, and stomped his feet to free his boots of the snow and mud.

Chapter 12

Most likely it was the freezing temperatures and hunger, more than trusting Nellie and Little Virgil, that caused the three kids to come out of the horse stall and follow them to the house.

When Little Virgil tried to tie them all together with ropes for the walk back through the blizzard, the youngest immediately began to scream and the older two moved back quickly against a stall door. Nellie stopped him and made a show of throwing the rope across the barn. On the way back to the house, pulling herself along by the long rope tied to the house, part of her expected the children to let go and run off. She would try to stop them if they did, but the way the wind was blowing the snow into a blinding frenzy, the chances of catching them before they disappeared were virtually nonexistent.

The kids stayed between them on the rope, though. Little Virgil led the way, the oldest girl, who Nellie estimated to be around thirteen walked behind him, the boy, who wasn't much younger was next, and then, right in front of Nellie, was the youngest of the three. She couldn't be older than five or six. When they made it to the front porch, Nellie didn't want to waste time on the porch. The wind was mercilessly whipping snow at their little group. And the kids weren't dressed for it. She yelled for Little Virgil to open the door and they rushed in, startling Charlene who had stationed herself only a few feet from the door, sitting in her momma's rocking chair. She nearly flipped backwards at the sight of everyone exploding through the front door.

Nellie quickly dusted the younger girl off while the older two did the same to themselves. Each one was shuddering and their lips were blue with cold. When Little Virgil began to stomp his boots they became nervous again, but when Nellie showed them what to do, they quickly imitated her and stomped as much snow off as possible by the front door before moving as a group to the woodstove.

Nellie left them on the far side of the living room, near the stove, while she and Little Virgil and Charlene went into the kitchen to get heat from the cookstove, and to give their new guests room to get warm and adjust to their new situation, which Nellie, even in her height of humility, had to admit was a major step up from that horse stable. The kids moved to the living room, and when Nellie went to bed she left the chickens from dinner out on the table. By morning all that was left of the chickens were bones.

After cleaning up the table, Nellie had begun to make biscuits. Nellie loved making biscuits. It soothed her soul and when necessary, calmed her nerves. She started that morning making biscuits because she felt unsettled and needed to settle down. She was restless and worried and for some reason, scared. Not scared of the kids, but scared of whatever or whoever had caused them to hide like that.

Living through the depression, it had become almost commonplace to see families and sometimes only children, walking somewhere, or camped out somewhere away from their home. But this was different. Partly because they were in the Morrissey's barn. Right there on their farm. But there was more. Something in the way they acted, like they were running from something very bad. Something evil.

While the biscuits were baking, Nellie walked across the kitchen and into the living room. It was dark, but she could make out the figures of the three sleeping children on the other side of the stove. She had been concerned all night that the stove would go out, because she was afraid to add wood to it and wake them up. Instead, she kept the fireplace in the dining room and the cookstove in the kitchen going. Nellie was surprised to find the stove in the living room alive with heat. Someone had added wood during the night. She assumed it was the oldest girl, but as she turned to leave the living room, she saw Little Virgil asleep in an armchair with a stack of wood on the floor next to him. Her heart filled immediately at the sight of this. She had been worried about him lately. Joe had brought home a few horses that were loose on the mountain, probably from farms that had been foreclosed on. Most of the horses were older and beaten down and needed to be nursed back. Every now and then, though, Joe would bring in a young wild one and they would have a look in their eyes. Like they were ready to bolt at any moment. Over the past year, Little Virgil had had that look. Less in the last few months, but every now and then it was there again. But sitting there in that chair was her little boy. The one who would hide in her skirts when they were in a crowd. As she watched him sleep, she was even able to forgive him for piling that dirty wood on her living room rug.

A sound from the front of the house by the kitchen startled Nellie at first, but the familiar stomping of Virgil's boots caused her to exhale and smile. No matter how upset she was with him for staying over at the Kaiser's so long that he missed the chance to come home, she always knew she could assume the best about her husband.

"Nellie! I'm so sorry. I'm here finally. I am so sorry to be late," he called out as he stomped his boots by the door.

"We're in here, Virgil!" she called out as the sound of his boots came closer from the dining room. "Have we got a story to tell you." She realized she had woken the three children up by calling out so loud. She had been so relieved to have her husband home that she had forgotten they were sleeping.

"I would love to hear it," Virgil said. "Let me warm up next to this stove for a minute and then we can sit down," he said as he hugged Nellie.

A sound like a cat fighting off a predator sounded from the other side of the stove as the youngest girl began to scream from the floor. The boy slammed himself back against the wall while the oldest girl grabbed a poker from the rack next to the stove. She lifted the poker up and pointed it at Virgil and began to yell, "NO!" over and over.

Nellie began to say, "It's okay. It's okay," like she did back in the barn, hoping the kids would understand what she meant.

She knew they were startled and scared by the appearance of a man, so she began to repeat, "Good," when she pointed at Virgil. "Good," she said again, but as she looked at her husband, she saw a look on his face she had never seen before. Not when he was courting her and not one day in their marriage during the ups and downs and good and bad. This was a face she had never seen, and it caused chills to roll across her body.

From behind her, Nellie heard the girl say, "Bad," and as Nellie turned around she saw the girl point the poker at Virgil and yell "Bad man! Bad! Bad man!"

Part 3

Chapter 1

The line of trucks slowly made their way through the countryside of Loudoun county. Grass. Trees. Farms mostly. A few scattered businesses pushed their way to the edge of the highway as the convoy crossed the mountain and made its way down towards the Shenandoah river. At the river, the lead truck, carrying two surveyors, a project foreman, and a load of surveying equipment turned left and down Bridge Road. The men in the first truck barely had time to enjoy the view of the river to their right due to the fact that they were the lead vehicle and they had to watch ahead for their turn because turning around a convoy of nine trucks, four of which were pulling trailers with earth movers on them, would prove quite difficult.

The driver of the lead truck slowed down enough to catch a few quick glimpses of the river. The sun was shining off of it and even that early in the morning, campers were in tents on the river lots and a few boats were already in the current. The Fourth of July was only a few days away, and people were getting a head start on the holiday. No one in this convoy would be enjoying an early holiday. If they pushed hard, they could get to a point where they could take part of the day off and enjoy it. The government men who were already at the construction sites would head home in a day or two. Their holiday was protected. For the rest of the crew, they would work from sunrise to sunset, making the most of the time. The quicker the project was completed, the quicker they could go back to their families in Arlington and Alexandria.

Part of their project was just ahead of them. A small portion of the crew, once they reached the Robertson farm and set up their base of operations, would come back and work on re-building the bridge they were about to cross. Another crew had been there in June to demo the bridge and lay steel plating and beams across to form a temporary bridge. The Army Corps of Engineers had taken care of the temporary bridge because they were the ones who tore down the previous structure. The roof of the old covered bridge didn't allow for the equipment the government needed to clear the structure and pass through.

This crew would be building a bridge a bit further up the stream so it could be completed while the temporary bridge allowed local traffic to still flow without having to go all the way up the mountain and wind their way across several miles of roads which were currently barely better than logging roads. That would all change soon of course. The roads all across the mountain would be widened and straightened and paved.

As the lead truck crossed the creek, listed as Morrissey Creek on the map they were given, the driver slowed down to a crawl as he crossed the steel structure. He looked quickly to his left and couldn't help but admire the beauty of the green trees and the flowing water. To their right was a better view of the river. Large rocks broke the surface of the water and gave the appearance that the river had its own bridge of sorts. It seemed possible that someone could cross from large rock to large rock without getting their boots wet.

Behind the lead truck was a much larger truck, which pulled a trailer with a bulldozer loaded on it. The truck and trailer crossed the creek with no problem. The next truck and trailer also had a bulldozer on it, but this trailer and dozer was smaller. The truck and trailer after that was hauling a tractor with a front end loader attachment. The last truck and trailer had two tractors and two front end loader attachments on the trailer. As it approached the creek crossing, the driver, perhaps operating off of an increased confidence level fueled by the successful crossings of the drivers before him, accelerated and his wheels went onto the steel panels at a higher rate of speed than those before him. The driver, feeling nothing of concern, accelerated while on the temporary bridge and crossed successfully.

It was not until the next vehicle, a 1938 GMC bus, crossed the bridge that the damage done by the truck and trailer before it became evident. As soon as the bus was leaving the bridge, the right side of the steel panel slipped and dropped four feet, causing the rear wheels of the bus to spin against the creek bank, fighting for traction. A spray of gravel was followed by a flume of dirt, which was followed by a splattering of mud and clay. The top of the bus slowly tilted towards the river and for a moment stopped in the air. The heat of the day and

The World Comes To Mercy Creek

the mountain breezes mixed with the humidity coming from the road on either side of the creek created a vividness to the day, capturing the bus with driver's side wheels up, like a photograph. And then it toppled back down onto all of its tires with a thud and a bounce, followed by a loud groaning sound as one end of the bridge collapsed and then crashed along the creek bank before slamming against the rocks and water with what sounded like a series of short explosions.

The passenger of the last vehicle climbed out. He was the foreman in charge of the bridge. Only a few of the laborers and one piece of equipment were under his supervision, as the rest of the team would be working up on the mountain. His job was to rebuild the Mercy Creek bridge. He locked his jaw and shook his head. His job had just gotten harder and he would be in this backwater county a lot longer than he had hoped.

Chapter 2

No one ever wondered who tied the rope to the high limb of the sycamore tree. It was probably the same person who tied the loop at the bottom which had originally been tied around a tire, according to some of the older stories told about the swing. Over time it had held another tire and at some point, a long piece of wood people would stand on before letting go when the swing was out over the river. Virgy Morrissey had his foot in a knot at the bottom of the rope that looked like a noose knot, but it was just big enough to slip a foot in and out of. Whoever had tied that knot had done so with skilled intentionality. It was big enough to slip a foot out of at just the right time, but not so big that the foot would slip out too soon.

As he swung out over the Shenandoah, Virgy let the breeze sweep past him, cooling the sweat on his face and down his arms and chest and legs. He always closed his eyes on the swing, not because he was scared, but out of a desire to feel like he was flying. He hit the water sooner than he liked and kept his eyes closed for a moment as he floated on his back and let the current carry him. Behind him on the riverbank he heard shouts and laughter and all the things he loved about his friends and this river and this time of year.

"Come on in!" he yelled at the top of his voice as he opened his eyes and swam towards a large rock downstream from the swing. He climbed up onto the rock in time to see Randy Mulkey, a boy who lived upriver, launch from the rope swing. At the same time, several boys and a few of the girls began to swim out towards Virgy. He stood up on the rock, feeling the heat soak through his feet and up throughout his legs and as he took in a deep breath of the summer mountain air, he knew he was where he wanted to be for the rest of his life. All around him, his friends talked about getting out and moving away and leaving the mountain behind, but he knew he didn't want to do that and he wouldn't.

The World Comes To Mercy Creek

One of the girls pointed up at a flock of geese flying over and Virgy followed them with his eyes. They were headed straight towards the Kaiser's estate. His father was probably up there now. He was always there. When he wasn't traveling to take care of something for the Kaiser. As he watched the geese flying in formation, following the other, going where the other was going, following the lead of just one, Virgy moved his eyes in the opposite direction towards the far riverbank. Directly across from them was an open field, but just a bit further up river, was a large hillside full of rocks and past that hillside was an upward slope and at the top of that slope was a large granite rock and anyone who walked out on that rock would be almost a hundred feet above the river.

"I'm jumpin' off Hawk's Ledge," Virgy said, staring upriver at the rock peak barely visible in the distance. Around him, for just a moment was silence. One of the girls made a sound like they didn't believe him. So he looked around at the small group around him and said it again. "It's a good day to do it. I'm jumpin' off of Hawk's Ledge."

"Damn right," Davey Gray said and then in a louder voice, "Virgy and I are jumpin' off of Hawk's Ledge!"

As Virgy and the rest of his friends made their way back to the rope swing, his body felt alive with electricity and excitement. The same way he felt when he and Ellis first decided to run across Bridge road, dressed like a monster. Similar to how he felt when he and his momma found those Polish kids in the barn during the blizzard back in April. He pushed that memory aside and pulled himself out of the river by grabbing hold of a small sapling. His feet sank into the mud and he lifted his knees higher to break free. Once onto the grass he heard someone ask him a question, but he was busy looking for his boots.

Davey answered for him. "Yep, we're doin' it. Wanna do it?" A chorus of "No" and "No way" filled the air around them.

The easiest way to get to Hawk's ledge was to drive to it. Everyone began to pile into cars and trucks in no particular order with Virgy in the lead as he pulled his car up to the Bridge road from where they were parked on the long patch of grass along the river. Before he could pull out onto the road he looked up and saw several horses coming his way, so he cut his engine off quickly and yelled back, "Kill your engines! Don't wanna spook the horses." And behind him, one and two at a time, the car motors were cut off.

The clopping of horses' hooves echoed along the country road. Virgy heard his name and looked for who was saying it. Millie Robertson. "Sorry to slow you boys down," she said, loud enough for at least half of the group to hear her.

Behind him, Virgy heard a girl's voice say something negative, but Millie didn't react.

"My daddy wants to talk to you, Virgil," Millie said.

In his haste to answer her, he almost missed the fact that she didn't use the "Little" part of his name. He liked the sound of it coming from her mouth. "I'll stop by this evening," Virgy said.

"That should be fine," Millie said. "Don't forget to say hello to my sister." She lifted her chin slightly and nodded in the direction behind her.

Virgy looked past Millie and saw Fern Robertson. He hadn't seen her since the accident and just the sight of her brought a wave of guilt over him. But then she smiled and all that guilt was replaced by something else. "Hello Virgy," Fern said.

"Hey," he said. And then the group of horses and riders, as well as the opportunity to say anything more than "Hey", passed.

Next to him, Davey Gray shouted, "Let's go!" and Virgy started his car and pulled onto the road. Behind them was the Mercy Creek bridge. It was half collapsed and barely passable. When they made it out to the main road, they could go right to cross over the mountain and into Loudoun County, but they all went left and crossed over the long bridge that crossed over the Shenandoah. Once over the river, they made a left and went down the road that paralleled the bridge road. Virgy accelerated, stirring up a cloud of dust. He and Davey laughed as they looked back as their friends, swallowed up in the grey dust of the hottest day of the year so far.

"Right there!" Davey shouted and Virgy had to slam on his brakes and jerk the little car to the left and down a road that only declared itself a road by two red tracks straddling a long bright patch of green grass. Virgy accelerated down that trail but no dust stirred up. The Virginia clay was brick red and packed tightly. The clay trail led the long line of cars and trucks through a field of green. No fences. No gates. No cattle. Whoever owned it didn't use it, or someone had forgotten about it. As they all parked, Virgy let his eyes move along the green grass, almost at the height to be cut for hay, and up the slope of the hill where it turned to brush and small rocks, and then past that, where they couldn't see, was Hawk's Ledge.

The group of teenagers made their way up with laughter and talking and bragging until they came out onto the ledge. The view from up there silenced most of the noise as they all looked out over the river and towards the mountain. Though the mountain still loomed up over them, this view gave them a line of sight not many of them had ever had before. One that could have made them feel almost equal to the mountain, but the effect was the opposite. The mountain and the river were both even more awe inspiring.

Virgy let his eyes follow the river, it curved to his right and crawled among the green of the tops of the trees until it was lost in the blue of the sky. To his left it flowed straight to the bridge which he could see if he squinted his eyes. He quickly shifted his focus back up to the mountain, and then down to the water below. They were close to seventy-five feet in the air. Everyone around him said it was over a hundred feet to the water below and he let them think and say that, but it wasn't. Seventy-five feet was plenty high enough though. High enough to hurt him badly if he landed wrong. Three big rocks formed a crooked triangle in the water below and he realized being hurt wasn't the full extent of the risk. Those larger rocks could kill him instantly if he jumped out too far. And where there were big rocks jutting out like that, there were almost definitely smaller rocks, right below the surface of the water, waiting for him. He looked around and saw a few girls who lived further up the mountain.

Dani, a girl whose family had just moved there from New York, walked quickly over to the edge of the rock and then looked back with big eyes. "This is like being in the Empire State Building," she said with an accent that made her seem like she was from a foreign country. She looked at Davey first. "Are you jumpin'?"

Davey was almost ten feet back from the edge and he didn't come any closer. "Hayell naw," he said, in an accent that probably made Dani think *he* was the one from a foreign country. "I'm just here for moral support." He opened up a Ball jar of clear liquid, took a quick gulp, shook his body, danced in a small circle, and then held the jar out towards Virgy, who took it and sipped some of it before passing it to a boy who lived over near Cully's Tavern on the horseshoe.

Virgy Morrissey was a boy who had gotten more attention in the past several months than he ever actually wanted, but he found himself there again, in the center of it at the top of the rock. At some point he would slow himself down to figure out why he kept putting himself in the center of something he didn't desire or need, but at that point in his life, towering above the river he loved and looking at the mountain that raised him, he knew there was only one thing he needed to concentrate on. Jumping.

That time between his foot leaving the ledge and his body hitting the water made him feel like a bird and he liked the feeling. This was his first time at the river that summer and he needed the air and the water to wash the winter off of him. As his right elbow cut through the surface of the river, the rest of his body followed and when his head went under, he opened his eyes and exhaled a stream of bubbles, breathing out the winter air he had held in all spring.

The embarrassment and fear of the mountain monster fiasco. The angst and anger he had towards his father for always working. The shame of the limp he tried so hard to conceal. All of that had been wrapped and covered and surrounded by what his father had been doing for over a year now. Right up on the mountain that was currently reflecting on the surface he was sinking under. He had listened to his father explain it all that day in April, back during the blizzard. He had even helped him take those three kids back to the Kaiser's estate. When asked about it, he lied and said he understood, but he didn't.

His momma agreed, but she always agreed with that man. Or at least she always seemed to. They never showed any form of disagreement in front of the rest of the family. That day, though, Little Virgil had looked in the eyes of his mother and he saw that she agreed with him and she was with him. Even as he asked hard questions of his father, his momma would quickly interject or answer. She wasn't only justifying his actions, she was endorsing them.

When Virgy's face broke the surface of the water, he felt the heat and brightness of the sun and heard faint cheering from above him. He squinted and waved his hands to more cheers. As he pulled himself up onto one of the rocks that could have killed him, he looked across the river and saw the line of horses heading back up the bridge road. One horse was stopped while the rest of them moved along. On that horse was Margaret, and as Little Virgil watched her from across the river, he remembered his Daddy teaching him how to ride a horse back when he was young. "Follow my path, son," he had told Little Virgil. "Look where I go and come along. That way you don't get into a bad spot." As Virgy looked across the river and then moved his eyes to all of his friends coming down from the Hawk's Ledge, he resolved to move away from the path his dad was walking and find his own way.

Chapter 3

The Kaiser knew how to enjoy himself, but alone, as he was now, walking through the pines above his Estate, he admitted to himself that he had never truly known happiness. That didn't mean he had never smiled or laughed or found pleasure in his surroundings or those around him. It simply meant he had often heard others describe happiness and he had watched people like Virgil Morrissey walk through life obviously happy, even in the worst of times, and he knew he had never felt that emotion. The thought of Virgil, the man whom he considered his closest friend, brought him sadness as he walked along that afternoon a few days before the Fourth of July, which was his favorite holiday of the year. Sadness he had felt many times in his life and he had replaced the search for happiness that many men and women spent their time towards with the goal of simply not being sad. He had found great success over the years in not being sad and that was what he considered a good life.

He had never concerned himself much with the sadness of others. He, of course, had tried to help others when he could. Pull or push them out of bad situations. Come alongside them in times of need. But never on an emotional level. Yet, over the past year, emotions had dictated much of what he had done. And now, as he walked in the woods near his beautiful home, he felt sadness and guilt for bringing Virgil into this so deeply. It had started so slowly. Yet it had gained momentum like a landslide. And the Kaiser could not help but to feel like they were about to be buried.

First, there was the letter. It had come from a man in New York who did business with the Kaiser occasionally but was also close friends with men who did business with the Kaiser regularly. He had asked if he could visit. It was no more than that. A salutation. A sentence or two of formality. And then the question. "Would it be too bold of me as to request an invitation from you to visit your home for

The World Comes To Mercy Creek

a few hours this summer?" The Kaiser loved having visitors so he responded succinctly but in the affirmative. This happened in May of 1940.

A month passed and a letter was received announcing the man's intention, unless he received notice otherwise, to arrive in Virginia the second Monday in July. And he did. Bright and early on the second Monday in July, a car pulled up to the gate of the Kaiser's Estate, and after the gate guards confirmed he was who he said he was, he was given entry.

During lunch, after the visitor was given a brief tour of the Estate, a story was told of a child who had been rescued from Germany. A boy. Twelve years old. He was from the same city as the Kaiser. The story then turned into a story the child had told to his rescuers. One night, after he had been asleep for quite some time, he awoke to shouting and fighting. Frightened, he pulled his blanket over his head and waited for his father to come tell him that everything was fine. That did not happen. Instead, a man in a uniform had ripped the cover off of the bed and dragged him down to the street where he was herded into a large warehouse for the night. In the morning he was loaded into the back of a truck. The truck took him on a long trip to a railyard where crowds of men and women and children were being loaded onto the trains. One man tried to run but he was shot. Several men then tried to fight but they were shot as well. The boy had crawled up under the straw that was in the back of the truck and tried to hold his breath and close his eyes in hopes that he would go to sleep and never wake up. But he did wake up. When the truck pulled away from the railyard, the boy woke up. He did not think he had fallen asleep, but rather, he had passed out. And when he came to, the truck was on a road, leaving the railyard. When the truck came to a stop, the boy jumped from the back and ran into the woods.In the woods he spent two nights with no food and no fire. He climbed a tree on the second night to protect himself from animals and soldiers who had passed by his hiding spot during the day. On the third day he saw a group of men pass by beneath his tree, and he heard them say things that let him know they had escaped the same thing he had. So he ran to them and they helped him. One week later he was out of Germany. Several months later he was brought to New York.

After telling the boy's story, the visitor asked the Kaiser if he had heard anything like that before. The Kaiser had replied that he had. Not about children, but it was implied. If families were being arrested, something was happening to the children. He was not surprised by this story. He expressed to his guest that he had known for several years that the current leader of Germany was a bad man, and bad men do bad things. Once they feel comfortable enough, they begin to do the bad things on such a scale that their badness is undeniable. The Kaiser expressed that this story was just the tip of the iceberg. He predicted many more. His visitor had apologized but expressed that he was compelled to ask a very imposing question of the Kaiser. The Kaiser gave him permission to ask and the question was this: What are you going to do about this?

    The visit had ended with exchanged formalities and compliments from the man regarding the beauty of the Estate and the efficiency of Uma and the staff. The question was not asked again. As the man was departing he asked if he could give something to the Kaiser and the Kaiser affirmed that he could. The man reached into his car and from the passenger seat withdrew a small wrapped package. The man then drove back to the gate. The gate was opened for him. And he left.

    The package contained a book. Brave New World by Aldous Huxley. The Kaiser read the book over the course of one day. At the end of the book was a photograph of a young boy, which had been slipped in between the final pages by someone. The Kaiser surmised this was the boy who had told the story which was told to him by his visitor. The picture annoyed him. It was obviously a ploy by his visitor to emotionally manipulate him. He did not like manipulation of any form and emotional manipulation was particularly loathsome. The book was also an attempt to manipulate him, but intellectually. This did not annoy or frustrate the Kaiser because he viewed life as intellect attempting to influence intellect. When done correctly, a symphony can be formed. His visitor had been too blunt and too obvious with both of his attempts at manipulation, but after several days, the Kaiser admitted to himself that the manipulation had been successful.

    On the Sunday morning following the visit, he went into his library and withdrew two volumes from the shelves. Mein Kampf, the original volumes 1 and 2. He read them again with the end in mind, and when he was done, it was Monday afternoon. He had slept between volumes and taken his meals in the library. He had read the first volume before and of course saw it at the time for what it was, the autobiography of a man filled with hatred. He had read the second volume through the lens of the first, which led him to see it as the political plan of a man filled with hatred. This time, however, he noticed and grasped the concept of Lebensraum, which translates into "living space". The concept of Lebensraum is what led the original Kaiser to dispatch the other Kaisers throughout the world. That Kaiser wanted living space, and he gave the means to the other Kaisers to find living space as well. And as the Kaiser looked out at his Lebensraum, from the window of his library, he did something he had not done much of in his life. He had done very little of this in his adult life, actually. He wept. Throughout the afternoon of that third Monday in July, he sat in his most uncomfortable chair and cried the tears of a man who realizes he has been placed in a time and space and position to do something good. And very simply put, he stood up in the orange glow of that summer sunrise, intent to do so.

A year later, up on the ridgeline above his home, he stood among the pines and felt good about what they were doing. Good about the progress they had made. The kids they had saved. But he knew this was not sustainable. He looked at the weight Virgil carried on his shoulders everyday and he knew this was more than anyone and even any small group could bear for long.

Chapter 4

Nellie's peace emanated from her kitchen. When she was frustrated, or worried, or just out of sorts, she always gravitated to her kitchen. She would then clean it, even if it did not need to be cleaned. Next, she would prepare food in it. She would knead and roll and slice. She would bake and fry and roast. Sauces would boil and simmer. Cakes would be frosted. Meat would be marinated. Biscuits would be buttered. Whatever was missing would most often be found. Everything that was scattered would be regathered.

Since the blizzard in April, Nellie had stayed in her kitchen for the most part. She did not want to be anywhere else. She rarely went anywhere else. She told others she was busy. She told Virgil she was just figuring things out. While both of those facts were true, she had to be honest with herself and admit that she was worried and frightened and confused as to what should happen next for her and for her family. When she was brutally honest with herself, she knew she had to admit that she had let these feelings take her very low. And she had been low for weeks, which had recently become months.

It was cornbread, and Charlene, that began to lead her back home. One morning in early July, while cleaning up from a breakfast that none of her sons were present for, she heard Charlene's voice from the staircase. "How come you don't make cornbread anymore?"

"What's that?" Nellie asked as she turned from the sink.

"I love your cornbread. Remember when you used to ask me when I wanted you to make me some, and I would say, 'Why not tonight?'"

"I do remember that," Nellie said. She felt a warmth inside her that she hadn't felt in a while as she took time to look at her daughter. She was growing up so fast. They all had, of course. Her blue eyes seemed so big that morning and they were staring at her. Nellie allowed the emotions to return to her as she said softly, "Charlene, when would you like me to make you some cornbread?"

"Why not tonight?" Charlene said. A smile slowly spread across her face and she hugged her momma as hard as she could and stayed there for a long time.

"Do you want to help me make it?" Nellie asked.

"Yes, please!" Charlene said.

Nellie's kitchen swallowed the two of them for an hour or more after that, as they measured and mixed and poured and baked.

After they made cornbread, they prepared a roast for the oven. And to be served with the roast, they peeled potatoes, glazed carrots and spiced apples.

There is always a time in a kitchen, amidst all of the things that have been done, when one realizes that the only thing left to do is to wait. When that point in time came, Nellie looked at Charlene and asked, "Do you want to go with me to see your Daddy?"

Charlene jumped up and ran to the door to put on her shoes. It was a simple question which received a simple answer, as far as Charlene was concerned. For Nellie, of course, it was a much more complicated question. After sitting for hours by the stove that day of the blizzard and listening to Virgil talk to her and tell the story of what was happening at the Kaiser's Estate, her mind began to accept it and she understood why they were doing it. She knew it was a very good and very right thing to do. She knew it was a very Virgil thing to do. And she was proud of him.

But mixed in with all of that were feelings she didn't know what to do with. Fear. She was no stranger to fear, but it had not come around her doorstep as much in the past few years as it had for many years before. Confusion. So much had been happening without her knowing it. Big things. She always considered herself to be someone who knew the world around her. It may have been a small one, but she knew every inch of it and understood those who walked around in it. But she clearly didn't. Betrayal. That was a word and a feeling that had never existed in her life before. Not while growing up. Not while married. Not while raising a family. That was a big word. A dangerous one. That word had the power to slaughter. Had she been betrayed? She had been lied to. She had been misled. She felt betrayed. She did. She didn't want to feel that way, but there it was. She had to figure that out. She had to figure it all out.

In the kitchen, with Charlene, Nellie had not found all the answers or figured much out, but what she had found was the peace she needed to get moving. To see for herself what was going on over there, and to help. And just like cooking and baking and cleaning and working in her kitchen, it was in the taking of action that all the chaos around her began to shape into something a home can be built around.

On the walk over to the Kaiser's house, Nellie and Charlene took their time. Nellie had walked this road many times and most of those times she had assumed a quick pace, hoping to get where she was going quickly. That day she strolled. They stopped to watch birds, and pick flowers, and smell honeysuckle. Charlene chased a bee. And then a different bee chased her.

Their shadows were short in the bright sun when they finally arrived at the Kaiser's house. The guards knew Nellie well, of course, so she received only welcomes from them. Josh, her son-in-law came towards them at a brisk pace and seemed very nervous. "Did Virgil know you were coming, Mrs. Morrissey? I mean--Good afternoon, Mrs. Morrissey. Did Virgil know you were coming?"

"No, but everything is fine, Josh," Nellie said. "I'm here to see the children."

For a moment Josh said nothing. In fact, he did nothing. Nellie didn't even think his eyes blinked. But then he quickly said, "Of course. Wait right here. I'll get your husband."

"Wait right here in the middle of the lawn, Josh?" Nellie asked with a smile.

"Of course not," Josh said. "No. I'm sorry. Follow me to the front porch.

On the front porch, Charlene began to walk along one of the railing shadows, pretending she was in the circus on a high wire. Nellie could relate to the balancing act she was trying to pull off.

"Nellie, my dear darling," the Kaiser's voice echoed across the long porch. He spoke over his boot steps as he walked quickly towards them. His words didn't only compete for volume, they also competed with his quick pace. "Your husband is not here right now. I know, as you know, that if he had known you were coming, he would have made sure to be here, but as he did not know, he did not make provision to be here, as he is currently up the mountain talking to a man who seems determined to tie ribbons to my trees and drive painted pieces of wood into my ground."

The World Comes To Mercy Creek

"I hope you will forgive us for showing up unannounced," Nellie said. She had not seen the Kaiser for months, but it had not affected how they interacted. She had always liked him and even loved him as family, but she also never felt completely close to him. He didn't seem to let anyone close.

"Oh there is nothing to forgive, Nellie. You are welcome here anytime. I am simply explaining why your husband is not here to greet you. So, alas, you are stuck with me. What can I do for you? Are you here to see Ginny?"

"No, Wilhem." She lowered her voice. "I am here to see the children."

The Kaiser looked at her and then to Charlene. "Would you like to come with me to see my birds?" he asked.

"Can I Momma?" Charlene asked.

"Of course," Nellie said.

"I will have Josh take you to them, if you do not mind waiting here. This bench is nice." He pointed to an iron and wood bench, the kind Nellie had seen in parks in Richmond. This one was flanked by two tall plants. She thanked him and told Charlene to behave as they walked towards the bird sanctuary.

Nellie let the late Spring breezes comfort her and remind her to breathe.

After a moment, Josh appeared again. He was coming from the direction the Kaiser and Charlene had just gone.

"You're here to see the kids?" he asked.

"I am," she said. "I'm sorry you're stuck being my tour guide. I could get Ginny to do it, if that helps you get back to your work."

"My work is whatever the Kaiser tells me to do," Josh said. "What makes you want to see them?" he asked.

"Well, curiosity, I guess," she said. "And to see if I can help whoever is in charge of taking care of them, maybe?"

"Oh," he said, making a confused face. "Well, you probably need to know that no one is in charge of them, really. We just take food to them and watch them in case they start fighting."

"Really? What is the age range with these kids?" Nellie asked.

"I...I'm sorry. I'm not really sure to be honest with you," he said.

"Well how many are there? Back in April, Virgil said there were almost thirty."

"Oh," Josh said. His eyes had gotten big quickly and he looked nervous. "Mrs. Morrissey there are almost a hundred kids here now."

It took Nellie a moment to catch her breath and find her words. After a moment, she said, "Take me to them now, please, Josh. I'm beginning to suspect that I should have come a lot sooner."

Chapter 5

When he broke up with Millie, Jeb didn't cry. Neither did Millie. He had cried before in front of Millie, so it wasn't embarrassment holding him back. She had cried a few times as well, but considerably less than he had over the duration of their eighteen month courtship. It didn't surprise him when she didn't cry, but he had to admit, he had expected to shed a few tears. Neither one of them did, though, and when they parted, Millicent Robertson stuck out her right hand and said, "We will have to see each other quite a bit around the two towns, and I would like for us to remain civil. I will not speak ill of you. And I expect you to only speak positive words about me." This was not presented as a question, offer, or deal. It was presented as an action plan. She then added, "And also, we should wait a socially acceptable length of time before either of us dates anyone else."

After he shook her hand, Jeb drove away and saw her continuing to brush her horse. That had been back in January. Throughout spring he had been trying to figure out just how long "socially acceptable" was.

Jeb had planned to go by the house to see his parents or at least his momma. He had barely been at the house during daylight hours. He usually arrived late at night and left early in the morning. So he knew he needed to spend some time there, but instead he was headed to Joe's house. He had volunteered to help Joe by mowing the lawn and digging up two stumps in the front yard, so he planned to drop by for lunch, under the premise of checking out the yard and seeing what tools he would need to bring the next day.

When he arrived at Joe's his timing was perfect. Everyone was already at the table and Joe seemed to already know why he was there since he had already shown him everything he needed to know about the lawn and the stumps the day before. "Hey here's an idea. Why don't you come on in for dinner, little brother," Joe had said, as he walked back to the table.

At the table, Esther called out, "Jeb Morrissey. You must hide all of your money in a coffee can."

"What brand?" Beth asked. "Sanka? Faust?"

"No, no. He's a Maxwell house boy," Esther said.

Jeb looked back and forth and smiled like he understood the joke but he didn't. "I drink Maxwell House," Jeb said.

Both ladies laughed, and Emily said, "They're saying you don't come by the bank, so you must hide your money in a coffee can," she said with a gentle smile.

"Oh," Jeb said, laughing nervously. "I know someone who did that. Buried their money, I mean. Not in a coffee can, though." As he sat down next to Emily, he heard Joe make a noise as he walked in from the kitchen.

"You wanna sit in my seat Jebby boy?" Joe asked.

Jeb stood up quickly and moved to another seat. Frank laughed and said, "Jebby boy," through a mouth full of mashed potatoes.

"I'm still looking for your articles," Mrs. Newberry said. "Are you writing under a pen name? I've heard people do that. Mark Twain wrote under a pen name."

"Mark Twain was his pen name," Beth said. "His real name was Samuel Clements."

"I don't think so," Mrs. Newberry said.

"She's right," Esther said.

"I taught school for twenty years," Mrs. Newberry said.

"What subject?" Esther asked.

"Math, but school is school. His real name was Mark Twain."

"I went to the Mark Twain museum when I was a kid," Beth said. "The Clements family home was part of the museum. Not the Twain family home."

"Well, I never liked his writing anyway," Mrs. Newberry said. "And I don't know if I like your writing," she said as she pointed her corn on the cob at Jeb. "Because you've never written anything."

"Would you write something for me, Jeb?" Esther asked.

The table grew silent and Jeb felt his face go hot. The room was already hot. And the heat of the food combined with the heat of the day and he could feel sweat on his ears. Such an odd place to feel it, he thought to himself. No sweat on his forehead, but his large ears, his ears which had always been too big, were now sweating. He knew he should have worn his cap.

"Sure," he said, as he reached for the plate of corn. He didn't realize until it was too late that the plate piled up with corn wasn't a serving plate. It was Frank's plate. And it was Frank's fork that was promptly stuck into Jeb's hand, by a less than generous looking Frank. It took Jeb a second to feel the pain, but he saw the fork go into his hand and in his shock he let go of the plate which slammed down on the edge of the serving bowl of mashed potatoes. The mashed potatoes didn't exactly fly through the air. It was more like they flopped. But they flopped a further distance than one might have imagined they could, and they landed on the face and blouse of Esther. Esther sat still for a moment with mashed potatoes dripping down her cheek (she had somehow managed to turn her face to avoid the full splash of the potatoes) and then laughed. It was a small laugh at first. Low in volume and not projected at all. But the fullness of it grew quickly as Beth joined in.

Jeb, not sure what to say, didn't. Instead he jumped up and fled the room. Emily was busy trying to assist Esther while Esther and Beth continued to laugh, so she didn't see Jeb leave in time to stop him. Joe was distracted by Frank who was demanding a clean fork, as the one he was originally given currently had Jeb's blood on it.

On his way back to the mountain, Jeb realized no one was ever going to take him seriously unless he found a big story and wrote it himself, with his own name on it. The hardest part was going to be figuring out just what that story could be.

Chapter 6

Nellie was not sure what she expected to see when she went into the barn, but what she saw shocked her. Perhaps she expected to walk into a school classroom setting. Or an orphanage she had seen pictures of in Look magazine. Maybe even the children's wing of a hospital like Little Virgil was in when he fell through the ice. But this looked like none of that. There was no organization. There was no supervision. There were kids everywhere. Some were running around and climbing on the loft ladders. Others were sitting on blankets or bales of straw and hay. They weren't outrageously loud. But they weren't quiet either. Chaos would have made sense. But this wasn't chaos. It was just a massive crowd of kids.

A small girl ran up to her, followed by a boy. They grabbed hold of her legs in a big hug and then ran back to the crowd of kids they were playing with. Those were the children she had found in their barn. The kids were dressed well. What clothes they were wearing weren't worn out or torn. They all had shoes it seemed, though not all of them were wearing them.

The boys were mostly separated from the girls but it seemed more like this was a social consequence and not the result of any intentional organization. Nellie walked down one wing of the barn and noticed that the stalls and walkways were very clean. She found out later that Virgil had the guards rotating cleaning duties. By the time she was done looking around, she had spotted a few girls and boys that were probably teenagers. The youngest ones were most likely six or seven. So they had mostly school aged children there. More girls than boys. More older than younger. If she had to pick an average age, she would say ten.

"Who keeps track of their ages?" she asked.

"I think Miss Uma does," Josh said. "But I'm not positive."

"So there really isn't anyone in charge here," she said.

The World Comes To Mercy Creek

"Well...I think we're all just focused on saving their lives over there, and keeping them alive here."

"But do they have a life here? Is this a life?" she asked, pointing around her.

"I guess we're looking at it like it's better than the alternative," Josh said.

Nellie started to respond, but instead just looked around. She knew he had a point, but she still didn't have to like it. "Where is Ginny?" she asked.

"In our room," Josh said. And then added, "In the house." He made a face like he realized that "in the house" was an unnecessary addition.

"And what does she do all day?" Nellie asked.

"She keeps pretty busy," Josh said.

"Doing what?" Nellie asked, staring her son in law in the eye as she asked it.

"Reading," he finally said. "She reads a lot."

"She's upstairs right now?" she asked.

"Yes," he said.

"I'll be right back, she said."

"Should I come with you?" he asked.

"No, Josh. That won't be necessary."

As Nellie left the barn, she saw a line of kids drinking from a ladle at the water pipe. The older kids seemed to help the younger ones with most everything.

Near the door, standing at a window was the oldest girl who had been so scared of Virgil in their house. Nellie stopped and waved at the girl. Virgil had told her he found out from Uma that the girl's name was Agata. Agata slowly raised her hand and waved back. Nellie stared for a long moment and felt her heart pounding a beat inside of her.

She turned and left the barn at a fast stride. As she crossed the yard, Yates came towards her diagonally from his office. "Hey there, Sis," he called out as he got closer.

"Yates Morrissey, you haven't been by the house in weeks," she said while not slowing her pace.

"I know. Things have been crazy lately. I'll be by, though. For dinner soon?" Yates found himself walking faster to keep up with her.

"You know there's always a place for you at the table. It isn't very crowded, lately. And what has kept you so busy lately?" she asked, stopping so sudden that he had to turn his shoulder to the right to avoid clipping her.

"Keeping this place safe and secure," Yates said. He was always the heroic young man around town to everyone else, but to Nellie, he was the little boy who hid behind his mother's stove whenever Virgil brought Nellie to his house when they were courting. "It's more than a full time job. You know that, Nellie."

"I know that, but I also know that no one is in charge of all of those children. It's appalling."

"Well, the priority was to get them here alive," he said.

"And it seems no one thought of what to do with them once they got here."

"Now that's not fair, Nellie. It's not as simple as that."

"Oh it is," Nellie said, as she started towards the house. "And just so you don't get your feelings hurt, Yates Morrissey, I don't blame you."

"Oh, well...thank you," Yates said. "But don't be too hard on Virgil, neither. He's spreading himself thin trying to make all of this work."

"You and your brother are off the hook for now. I understand the parts you and Virgil are playing in this. There's someone else over here who clearly doesn't know her role yet."

"Well, I'll leave you to that, sis," Yates said. "I just remembered I need to patrol the grounds."

"Be careful," Nellie said, without looking at Yates. She was determined again to get where she was going. As she walked up on the porch she started to knock and heard noise on the step behind her as Yates ran to open the door for her. "Thank you," she said quickly.

"You look like you might kick the door down, so I figured I would save some of the boys the work of fixing it," he said with a smile.

She smiled but fought the smile away because she was upset and hated how Yates could always make her smile. "Go on and check the property and keep everybody safe, Yates," she said as she walked through the grand hallway and up the stairs to her daughter's room.

Ginny opened the door on the third knock. Her look of surprise when she saw her mother became a worried look when she read her mother's face. "Momma, what are you doing here?" she asked.

The World Comes To Mercy Creek

"That's what I'm here to ask you," Nellie said. "May I come in?"

"Of course," Ginny said. She led them over to a small table by one of the windows. Nellie had been in her room before and always marveled at the size of it. Nearly the size of their old house. The curtains were all closed except for the one near the table. An open book was on the table, along with three other books stacked next to it.

"How have you been filling your time lately?" Nellie asked as they each sat down. "Reading?"

"Yes," Ginny said. "I've been reading quite a bit."

"You used to do that all winter long when you were home," Nellie said. "After your chores were done and there was nothing left to do."

"That's right," Ginny said. "I've loved to read for as long as I can remember."

"Yes," Nellie said. "I have too. I don't often have time to read, but when I do, I love how books can take me away, to a different place and time."

Ginny smiled. Her face didn't seem used to smiles. "That's what I love about them too. They can be a wonderful escape."

"And what are you escaping here?" Nellie asked.

"I don't know," Ginny said.

"Well I don't either," Nellie said. "You've got it made here. You live in a fancy, giant room, in a fancy giant house, on beautiful grounds. You have a staff waiting on you, doing whatever you need. Cooking, cleaning."

"I don't want all of that done for me. I want to do it. For me and for my husband."

Nellie looked at her daughter for a long time and saw the sadness there. "You don't like it here, do you?"

"It's not that I'm ungrateful. I'm so thankful to have all of this, but I don't need it. I don't. And I don't really want it. Does that make me awful? I'm sure it does. But I don't need this."

"What do you need?"

"I need Josh. And my family."

"And what else? Why can't you just have Josh and have us and be happy here? You have everything you need on this Estate."

"Because this Estate doesn't need me," Ginny said. Then, soft crying. "There is absolutely nothing for me to do here. Nothing of purpose. Nothing of meaning."

"Virginia," Nellie said as she stood up and walked over to one of the covered windows. "You are sitting here every day, reading, escaping, searching. While a barn full of purpose sits right over there." Nellie opened up the curtains and the sun came through in a wave of light. Outside, the barn stood on the horizon.

"I want you to take a walk with me over there," Nellie said.

"Why?" Ginny asked.

"You already know why," she said. "And you are going to stand up. Stop feeling sorry for yourself. And walk over there with me. Then you're going to figure out what you can do to help those children. Do you know how many people have risked their lives to get those boys and girls here? Do you know how much the Kaiser has risked and spent to bring them here? And all these men have done everything they can do. They have done everything they know to do. It's your turn to do your part."

"What if I mess up? What if I can't do it?"

"Girl, you've been taking care of kids and teaching them and helping them since you were a little girl yourself. You need to stop worrying about how you will feel if you can't do this, and start worrying about how you will feel if you *don't* do this."

Chapter 7

"Just remember to let me start out doing all the talking. When we get to the part where the government wants to put a road through his land, I will let you get into all of that," Pourpin said. "I know how to talk to these people. We have to build up slowly and work our way up to the ask. Or in this case, we should present it as a tell. Because we aren't asking him to do anything. We are telling him what we can do." Pourpin was in front of the door, but wanted to sort out business before he knocked.

"He needs to know he doesn't have much of a choice," Guthrie said.

"You haven't dealt with many mountain people in your life, have you Guthrie? Making it seem like it's his idea will make this easier on everyone, and if he signs today, I get a signing bonus."

"I haven't cleared that with my supervisor yet," Guthrie said.

"You'll clear it," Pourpin said with confidence. "Or you'll cover it. These people love me. They will do anything I tell them to do." Pourpin leaned in close to Guthrie, hoping to emphasize his words. "Or not to do."

"We need this road system or the facility doesn't get built. So do what you need to do to make it happen the easy way. But only because the easy way is quicker. And more efficient. That's all I care about," Guthrie said. "Efficiency is key."

As Guthrie was speaking, the door opened but only an inch or two at the most. "Come around to the front door," a man's voice said from the other side.

"What's that?" Pourpin said as he pushed on the door. It opened a few more inches and a small dog ran out, followed by a second one right behind it.

"Catch them!" the man behind the door yelled.

Pourpin turned and watched both dogs run to the front yard gate where they began to follow the fence, seemingly looking for a hole through which to escape. Guthrie followed the dogs, but only made a minimal effort as he walked slowly across the yard.

"They won't go far," Pourpin said as he pushed on the door again and started to walk in the house. The butler, who was as wide as Pourpin but not from obesity, put both of his long arms forward and grasped the lawyer hard by the shoulders. With little effort he turned him around and then gave him a quick shove off of the porch.

Pourpin landed on his feet, but barely kept his balance. When he spun around to confront the man, he realized he was wearing a butler's uniform.

"Catch the dogs you just let out," the butler said, withdrawing what appeared to be a short but stout club from his jacket.

Pourpin was a man who normally loved to debate. He became a lawyer because of it. But the butler's tone, and the club he was now brandishing, told him this was not the time or place for debating or arguing. Instead, he turned around and started chasing the dogs along the picket fence.

"Turn around!" Guthrie yelled. "Run opposite from me. We'll pancake 'em!"

Pourpin wasn't sure what Guthrie meant by using the word "pancake" as a verb, but he caught on quickly when he rounded the corner of the yard and saw the big government man running straight at him with the two little dogs caught in between them. Right before trapping the dogs, someone whistled sharply from the front porch and the dogs cut sharply to the right and ran towards the whistle. At that point, Pourpin realized much too late that he was running too fast to stop, so he didn't even try. To try to stop might cause him to hurt himself. Instead, he quickly reasoned in his mind, if he kept running at the same speed, when he collided with Guthrie, it would most likely be the other man who was injured.

Pourpin was correct. His stomach collided with Guthrie's hip due to the fact that Guthrie was stopping and turning to form a defensive stance. Pourpin's forearm, which was lifted and thrust outwardly, hit Guthrie squarely in the mouth. A tooth flew up in the air in an arc away from Guthrie's lips. It almost seemed to pause in the early afternoon sun, before it fell to the ground to be swallowed up by the bright green grass. Guthrie's body found a similar trajectory as his tooth, except when he hit the ground, the grass was swallowed up by him.

Pourpin emerged from the collision uninjured. His face was the color of an eggplant and his breathing sounded like a wounded sea animal, but he had managed to stay on his feet, which was no small feat given the circumstances. At this point, Pourpin realized he needed to help Guthrie up so they could get inside the house and have the meeting. While Guthrie was not a big man, he was not moving. It is very hard to help a motionless man up. He is at that point the very definition of dead weight. The attorney, breathing in squeals and squeaks, walked around Guthrie in a small circle and decided to leave him. The meeting was important enough to Guthrie to cause him to pick himself up at some point.

Stepping over Guthrie, Pourpin made his way over to the front porch where the Butler was standing at the door. "This is the door we use, Sir. Using any other door runs the risk of the dogs escaping. And once the dogs escape, I have to whistle for them. We like to use the whistle only when necessary."

Pourpin wanted to hit the man. He even picked out the portion of the butler's face, right above and slightly to the left of his mustache, where he thought a landed punch would do the most satisfactory amount of damage. However, a quick survey of the man's overall stature discouraged any physical aggression on the point of Pourpin so the attorney at that point simply said, "My name is Ralph Pourpin. My associate and I have a Noon appointment with Mr. Robertson." Casting a glance diagonally across the yard, Pourpin added. "My associate may be tardy. We should probably start the meeting without him."

Inside, at a small table on the back porch, Ralph Pourpin and Vance Robertson ate a small lunch of fruit and roasted chicken served cold. Vance listened while Pourpin ate and laid out the reasons he had requested the meeting. He concluded with, "You see, Robertson, we can take what we need and choose our own path right down the middle of your farm, or you can work with us and choose which land you will sell us as a right of way from the facility on the mountain to the rear of that German's property. It's not important to us where the road hits his property. So you can choose the path which does the least amount of harm, and the United States government will pay you a fair price for your land."

"You said you can take my land. Talk to me more about that," Robertson said.

"It's called eminent domain. I brought a book. I will leave it with you. I will need it back, but I will leave it with you for you to read. It sets forth the laws by which the government can seize your land and pay you the fair market value for it. But in that case, they choose what land they take and essentially what they pay. If you do so voluntarily, as a patriot of sorts, you can name your price, and even negotiate some other services that the government must provide, including a paved front driveway, an irrigation system, or anything like that."

"What's the Kaiser going to do?" Robertson asked.

Pourpin stared at Robertson while finishing his chicken. He moved around a few pieces of fruit on his plate and then pointed at the plate which sat in front of an empty chair. "May I have that chicken?"

"It's for your associate, once he arrives."

Pourpin pulled the plate over and said, "I would hate to see it go to waste." Between bites and swallows of the chicken, Pourpin managed to communicate the plan to seize the Kaiser's estate. "With our European allies at war with Germany, and our fool of a President just a few decisions away from joining in, there is not a chance in Dante's Hell, that the Department of Defense will build its facility within spitting distance of a Nazi sympathizer."

"Is he a Nazi sympathizer?" Robertson asked. "I had heard the opposite. The man flies more American flags over his property than they do at the White House. Virgil Morrissey manages the German's property and timber rights. They don't come more patriotic than Virgil. He was in the Great War. A Sergeant I believe. No matter what I think of the German, I have to say, it speaks volumes that Virgil Morrissey works for him"

"Managed."

"Pardon me?"

"Managed. Past tense. By the end of the week, there will be nothing left to manage. We will seize those rights immediately, and the Estate soon thereafter. He's been getting rich off of all that timber, while our country so desperately needs it to help with the European war effort."

"So what will happen to the Kaiser's house?" Robertson asked.

The sound of a door opening was followed by muffled talking from the front of the house. The next set of sounds was someone shuffling down the hallway. It was Lonald Guthrie. "Please forgive me," Guthrie said. His words were slurred and jumbled, most likely due to the fact that his bottom lip looked more like an ear. And he seemed to have lost more than the one tooth. Pourpin wondered if maybe one was swallowed during the collision.

Guthrie looked from Pourpin to the two empty plates in front of the attorney and back to Pourpin before turning to Robertson and laboring through a short statement. "We can take your land. Every damn inch of it. But we don't want to have to do that because it would take a few months longer. Select a tract of land for our right of way and name your price." Guthrie made several loud swallowing sounds before picking up a glass of water he assumed was meant for him. He drained it slowly, making even louder swallowing sounds and grimacing from apparent pain. "I will return tomorrow. Alone. And bring documents for you to read and sign."

Robertson sat for a long moment and then got up and walked over to a bar along the far wall of the room. He poured himself a bourbon and drank it at the bar. He poured a second one and sipped it on his way back to the table. When he sat down, he spoke softly. "I will give you a right of way that runs along the western edge of this farm. The side opposite the creek. It will then run along the same side of the Kaiser's estate. I will give that to you with no monetary charge for the land."

Pourpin gasped and Guthrie swallowed noisily again.

"But in exchange," Robertson said as he took a slow sip of bourbon, "I want the deed to the Kaiser's estate transferred to me after it is seized from him."

"I will bring the documents by tomorrow," Guthrie said, between swallows.

Chapter 8

Agata turned thirteen on July 2, 1941, and did not even know it. She had lost track of days and even months since arriving in America. Those first few days had been a culmination of the scariest time of her life. She had last seen her father as he nailed a coffin lid closed above her. He had tried to prepare her for what was about to happen. He had spent hours explaining *why* it had to happen. But the reality of her six hour trip in the back of a truck sealed up in a wooden casket was beyond her worst nightmares.

Agata moved to the window of the barn and looked out across the green pastures and breathed in deep breaths of the mountain air. She spent much of her time on the Kaiser's Estate as close to windows as she could. She even tried to sleep outside when it was possible. Since reaching America, she had treasured air and the ability to breathe it.

She had tried to stay awake for as many hours as possible before her trip in the casket. This, in her mind, would serve a dual purpose. It would give her more time with her parents, and it would also increase her chances of falling asleep during the trip while inside the wooden box. The first goal had been accomplished. The second one had not. She was wide awake the entire time.

For the first hour, she tried to get used to being in such a cramped space but most of her time was spent missing her parents and battling the fear that she would never see them again. The second hour had brought with it muscle cramps. She struggled to take deep breaths and her eyes had begun to itch from all of the crying she had done. By the end of the third hour, every inch of her body itched and needed to be scratched, but she could barely move. Her father had told her not to move, but she found that an impossible promise to keep. By the fourth hour she ached with an intensity she had never felt before and the heat had begun to cause her to hallucinate. During the fifth hour she felt like someone was pushing her down against the bottom of the casket.

The World Comes To Mercy Creek

She feared she was not alone inside the death box. She wanted to scream but she lacked the breath. She was suffocating. And she began to fear she had already died.

A voice called out her name from the other end of the barn and she had to remind herself that she was free of that box and free of anyone who would want to hurt her. The man she had been so scared of when she first arrived at the Estate was walking towards her with Uma. Agata knew Uma and trusted her. At first, it was only because Uma spoke her language and to hear words she recognized but over time, she knew that there was kindness inside this tall woman who told men what to do and they ran to do it.

"Agata, Mr. Morrissey would like you to tell all of the children that school will start next week," Uma said in German.

"Yes ma'am," Agata said.

"Please tell everyone that they will begin to learn English and skills which will be helpful to you in this country."

"I will," Agata said.

"And please tell them that classes will be taught by Mr. Morrissey's daughter."

Agata looked at the man who had scared her so badly within minutes of arriving on the farm, that she had run with the two children she had traveled to Virginia with. She had run as fast as she could into the darkness, expecting to be chased, but the snow had started falling so quickly that the only person who had come was the man she later came to know as Mr. Morrissey. He had driven around in his truck and had almost come upon them when he stopped and picked up a lady who Agata came to know later was his daughter.

She had since apologized for behaving the way she had in his house that day during the snowstorm. She had been afraid he had come to hurt her. After being scared for so long, it took her many weeks to realize she was in a place where she could feel safe. A place where she could breathe again.

Chapter 9

Little Virgil arrived at the Robertson home later than he had anticipated, due entirely to the fact that the Mercy Creek bridge had now, for the second time that year, been rendered unpassable due to construction. In Little Virgil's mind, construction was meant to build things, but these construction crews had now twice torn down the little bridge which had survived a century turn, a great war, a great depression, and two river floods. It had not, however, survived progress.

As a result of the bridge being down, Little Virgil had to circle around the back end of the mountain, passing through Hickory Hollow, and then up the mountain on a steep grade, followed by a winding descent to a one lane gravel road which led to the Robertsons' road. In order to make up for lost time, Little Virgil accelerated up the hill at a higher rate of speed than he normally used when approaching a house, or especially a horse farm.

He had gotten the little Austin 7 as a result of the previous owner crashing it into the Kaiser's guard shack, and then fleeing the scene of the crash, followed by two guards, both of which stopped and emptied their rifles in his general direction. Little Virgil traded a summer of work for the remains of the car. Interestingly, while banging the dents out of the body, he had found two bullet holes. He never mentioned what he found to anyone, but he always drove the car past the Kaiser's guard shack with additional caution.

Rounding the last curve before arriving at the Robertsons house, a black Ford nearly slammed into him. He jerked the wheel quickly to the right while braking, and then accelerated while steering left, in order to avoid crashing into the black four board fence which ran around the entire Robertson farm.

The horses in the field to his right were spooked and began to run. The memory of the night at Baker's pond came up in his mind and Little Virgil felt sweat form on his forehead. He wiped it away, only for it to reappear.

Just as the house appeared in his windshield, Little Virgil slowed down to a stop so he could take a moment to get control of his nerves. He contemplated making a u-turn and driving home, but the lane was too narrow.

"You're leaving us already Virgy?" a voice called out.

Little Virgil pushed the clutch back down and looked around quickly but couldn't see who had been speaking. To his left, a tree shook and some leaves fell, before a boot appeared, followed by a leg and then the rest of Fern Robertson stepped out of the tree and down onto the ground.

Little Virgil wasn't sure what to say. His mouth felt dry and his tongue was asleep.

"I didn't mean to run you off," Fern said, as she walked over to his car. He watched the slight drag of her foot and felt as small as a gnat.

"I just didn't expect you to be climbing trees, is all," Little Virgil said.

"What did you expect? I'd be laid up in a bed after riding horses this morning?"

"No. I... No," Little Virgil said. "I just. I'm sorry you got hurt."

"Oh it's not your fault. One minute you're getting ready to go ice skating, and the next minute, a buffalo spooks your horse. Welcome to country living, right? At least I'm not in some preparatory school. Father sent Millie there, and then Angela, but he didn't send me. He said if he had, I wouldn't have gotten hurt, but I know that's not necessarily true. I could've been hit by one of those New York City taxi cabs."

"I don't know about all that," Little Virgil said. "I just wish it hadn't happened. None of it. You could've died." Little Virgil felt his hands start to shake a little, so he made fists. This made his hands stop shaking, but then he felt the sadness of it all up into his chest.

"You made sure I didn't," she said.

"Does it hurt?" he asked, pointing to her leg. It was a stupid thing to ask, but he was trying to change the subject and he said the first thing that he could think to say.

"Sometimes, but not as bad as it did. Does yours?"

"Not really," he said. "Least not in a way that gets my attention much. Only when I run a lot. Or I jump and land on it. Stuff like that."

"I think mine will mostly go away, too," she said. "The pain I mean. I might limp some for a while."

"I hope it all goes away," Little Virgil said.

"Well, if it doesn't I guess I will just have to always walk beside you. You've got a bad left leg, and my right one is hurt. Between the two of us, we've got two good ones."

Little Virgil tried to smile, but the guilt of it all rose up in his throat again.

"I'd better let you go," she said. "My father is waiting on you."

He nodded and tried to say something but couldn't.

"Hey," she said. "I know that buffalo didn't mean to scare my horse like that. He was just out having fun. I know he didn't mean any harm to me." Little Virgil looked down quickly. He could feel her watching him, but he couldn't lift his eyes to meet hers.

After a few moments, Fern said, "Now don't you keep my father waiting, Virgy Morrissey. Go on now." Before he could say anything, she was back up in the tree. He squinted into the sunlight and tried to see her through all of the leaves, but it was no use.

"I'll see you later," Little Virgil said, as he put his car back into gear and drove to the house. When he walked towards the front porch, he saw someone sitting in a rocking chair at the far end of the porch.

"Come on up and have a seat Mr. Morrissey," Vance Robertson said.

Little Virgil walked over and sat across from the man in the only chair that wasn't a rocker. "Thank you sir," he said.

"I should be thanking you," Robertson said. "I never had the chance to say it after you got my baby girl to the hospital. She could have died, you know?"

Little Virgil just looked down at his boots.

"Well, I know your father, and your brother, Jeb, but I don't know you well, and you don't know me," he said. "But the thing you need to know about me is that I don't mess around. I don't beat around the bush. I've got a lot of things happening at this farm and all around us over the next few months, and I need some help. Millie and Fern vouch for you, and that's enough for me. So I'm offering you a job, Mr. Morrissey."

The World Comes To Mercy Creek

"What all do you need me to do, Mr. Robertson? I don't want you expecting something I can't give you. I'm not good at building, like my daddy is, or my brother Joe. But I'm good at general farm work, and paintin' and such."

"I just need you to do whatever is needed," Robertson said. "And if there is something needed which you don't know how to do, I'll teach you."

"When do you want me to start?"

"Why not right now?" Robertson asked, as he stood slowly from the rocking chair. "I can take you on a tour of the place and show you what needs to be done."

Little Virgil looked down for a long time. He knew his father would need him to help with the garden and the animals for the rest of the summer, especially since Jeb seemed to always be busy and Joe was spending more and more time at the boarding house. The thought of it made him feel like he did under the ice. Only for a second. And then he looked up and took in the view of the farm from the front porch and felt the air move past him the way it did when he jumped from Hawk's Ledge. "I'd like that, Mr. Robertson. I believe that sounds like a good idea."

Chapter 10

Jeb used his anger towards Frank as fuel, and within an hour after starting work on the stumps, he had managed to dig three of them out of the ground of Joe and Emily's front yard.

"We'll have the prettiest lawn in town before too long," Joe said, as he handed Jeb a glass of iced water. The sun was hot and high above them and Jeb's shirt was muddy from the dirt and sweat he was covered in. Joe had hoped they could dig out at least four stumps by the end of the day, which would only leave two to be dealt with later in the week, after the holiday.

For the most part, Jeb was going to be working alone and he was fine with that. He had hoped this would give him time to think about some articles he wanted to write, and he always thought best while working. Frank passed by him twice, and each time he did, Jeb would work harder and faster, because he found himself more and more angry with how self centered the man was, and how he was taking advantage of Joe and Emily.

"Hey Frank," he said, the third time the man passed by him. This time he was carrying a brown paper bag and Jeb could hear the bottles clinking against themselves.

"Good Morning Jebby boy," Frank said. "How can I help you?"

"Are you living here for free now?" Jeb asked. "Because it looks like you're the only one living in this boarding house who isn't paying anything."

"I'm helping out whenever Joe says he needs something," Frank said. "I'm not living here for free. You're saying I'm a freeloader? I'm no freeloader."

"What's the last thing you helped Joe and Emily do around here?" Jeb asked.

The World Comes To Mercy Creek

"Well, Joe hasn't asked me to do anything for him in a long time," Frank said. "But when he does, I will do whatever he needs."

"Let's start now," Jeb said. "He needs you to help me dig these stumps out."

"He never said anything to me about no stumps," Frank said. "And now I've got plans today. Stuff to do."

"This was one of the first jobs he asked you to do," Jeb said. "And now I'm doing it, because you haven't."

"He hasn't said anything to me about doing it. Not since the first of the year."

"Grab a shovel and start digging, or grab a bag and start packing," Jeb said, as he held out a shovel towards Frank, stared at him for a few moments before walking on into the house.

Jeb smiled to himself and tried to control his anger. He knew Joe would be back soon and he would talk to him about it then.

The third stump was stubborn and did not want to be free of the ground around it. Jeb dug all around the biggest end and he used a digging iron to try to pry it up but it wouldn't move. Not even an inch or two. Jeb pictured Frank eating all of Joe's food, which made him dig harder and faster. Finally, when he grabbed the digging iron this time, he was able to force most of the stump out of the dirt, exposing the roots he needed to cut. While he was doing that, Esther came out of the house and sat down on the front steps.

Jeb said hello to her but kept digging. He hoped she would see how strong he was as he dug and cut and pried the big stump free.

"Bravo!" she said. "Now I won't have to worry about tripping over that thing when I come home at night."

"Nope, but you have to worry about falling in this big hole, I've created."

"I can jump over it," Esther said. "This is gonna look so much better once it's done."

"Yeah," Jeb said. "I might miss these old stumps though. They gave the yard character."

Esther laughed and asked, "Growing up, did y'all have a big front lawn?"

"We did. But we didn't call it a lawn."

"Tell me about the farm you grew up on," Esther said. "I wanna know what it looks like."

Jeb sat down next to her without thinking, and spent a few minutes telling her how the farm had changed from when he was younger, because of the flood. He described the flood and then told her about how they had rebuilt the place.

"You still live there?" she asked.

"Yeah," Jeb said, as he picked up a small clod of dirt from the ground and broke it in his fingers. "I pretty much just sleep there. Life is so busy. But it will slow down. I'm just trying to work my way up at the paper right now. But it won't always be this way."

They were quiet for a while, and Jeb was enjoying having Esther sitting next to him. She made him feel content to sit for a while. Usually he felt like he had to be on the go, but she made him feel like he could sit and talk for hours.

"Your dad takes care of the farm behind the farm you grew up on?"

"Close. It's the farm next to us. Right across the creek."

"Is it a big farm?" Esther asked.

"Oh yeah," Jeb said. "Ten times the size of it. So big, they call it an Estate," he said with a smile.

She smiled too and Jeb looked at her for a long time. No one had ever made him feel content like this. Millie had a great smile, but she rarely used it. Esther always seemed to be smiling.

"Did you spend much time on the Kaiser's farm? On his Estate I mean?" she said with a laugh.

"No, not that much," Jeb said. "I always wanted to, though. I went there any time I could. The place was like some magical empire I read about in books. At least that's how it was in my twelve year old mind."

"Tell me about it," she said. "Describe it to me. Pretend you're writing me a story about it. The first chapter always describes the setting, doesn't it?"

"I guess, you're right," Jeb said. "The classics used to do that."

"I'm gonna close my eyes and I want you to tell me about it. Use that writer's mind of yours."

Jeb stammered a bit at first. He felt his face flush and his mouth went dry on him. He took a big gulp from the glass of water Joe had brought him. The water was warm but wet enough to help him talk a bit better. He started out by telling the story of how he visited the farm one night before Thanksgiving, describing with detail how he felt and what he saw as he went through the gate with the guard, and met Leeza May.

"So the whole place is protected by gates?" she asked. "Is there a wall or fence around the place?"

"A gate at the front entrance," he said. "But no wall. Just a wooden fence. We call it four board fence. It's built for the cows and horses. My brother Joe painted that fence one summer. Every bit of it. He started some time in May and finished in August."

"So are there all these secret paths all over the property?" Esther asked.

"Not that I know about. Just a road leading from one end to the other. The creek runs all along one side. From the Bridge road, all the way to the back road, which is an old logging road. You can't drive a normal car on that part of the road, though."

"It sounds wonderful," Esther said. "Is it still wild wilderness and forest up there or is it covered in buildings?"

"It's built like a little village at the front part. Lots of buildings. But as you walk towards the back, there is one shed. For the horses, I think. That's at the part of the farm where it starts to get wild like you asked. Where it climbs a steep slope up the mountain."

"Oh well at least he hasn't ruined the whole farm by building on it. Just most of it."

Jeb gave her a look like he didn't understand what she meant. "No. Not at all. Past that horse barn, over half of the Kaiser's land is undeveloped. It's wild and beautiful."

"I would love to see it soon," she said.

"We can take a hike up the mountain soon," Jeb said.

"Could we have a picnic?" Esther asked.

"We sure could," Jeb said.

"Well then," Esther said. "It's a date." And with that she stood up and walked back into the house, leaving Jeb sitting there smiling.

Within an hour, he had all of the stumps dug out, and the holes filled in.

Chapter 11

Bea Beaumont left the Lyttle's Mill bank with a smile on her face. Ben was with her and noticed the smile again, because his wife had smiled more times in 1941 than she had throughout the entire 1930's. She had made a down payment which allowed her to purchase what had, up until the afternoon of July 3rd, been referred to as "the old Baker farm". The bank had owned it for seven years, yet had referred to it by that name the entire time. Bea Beaumont informed her husband, as they pulled out of the bank parking lot and turned onto Main Street, that the property would immediately begin to be referred to as "Valley Vista".

Bea had also been extended a line of credit by the bank, which would allow a full construction crew to arrive on the property the week after the holiday to begin building a thirty-six room hotel. This had been her dream for the past twenty years. She had planned on building one in Lyttle's Mill back in '31, but the depression hit and changed her plans. Instead, she continued to rent rooms at her boarding house, waiting impatiently for the day she could build the largest boarding house in the state. At some point in the thirties, she had gone to New York with a friend, and she realized what she really wanted to build was called a hotel.

The reason she moved her dream to the mountain was because she had overheard from the conversation between Pourpin and Guthrie that night back in April, that a military building was being built on the mountain, which of course would raise the value of housing on the mountain, and since there was no boarding house within fifteen miles of where the facility would be built, her hotel would be in high demand as families and workers traveled to the area.

On the drive to the mountain, her husband said nothing, and Bea didn't mind that at all. He was angry with her of course. Most likely because she had not included him in the planning or the purchasing of the property. He considered their money partly his, but she did not. Even though they had used his inheritance to buy the boarding house, it had been her management of the business which had made the boarding house into a profitable business.

Ben Beaumont had never been a driven man and he lacked the motivation to do anything with his inheritance except for plopping it down in a bank somewhere and letting it earn low interest. It had been Bea's ambition which drove them from lower middle class to among the wealthy of Lyttle's Mill. His paltry inheritance had been dwarfed many times over by the money she had piled on top of it over the years, which caused her not to consult him on anything regarding her plans for expansion. She wouldn't have brought him along in any capacity, had it not been for the fact that the loan officer at the bank told her his signature was necessary in order for the sale and line of credit to go forward.

She suspected he was also sore about the conversation she had carried on with the loan officer. They had both been in agreement that the things Aldolf Hitler was doing in Germany would drastically change the financial structure of Europe, and the United States would soon cease to be as powerful as it currently was. In fact, it might even need to ally itself with Germany within the next few years. At the end of the conversation, Bea had requested that a portion of their savings be converted to Reichsmarks, just in case. She had of course noticed the look on her husband's face, but she chose not to acknowledge it. In fact, she was determined to never acknowledge his disapproval of her business decisions. She did not put any value on his approval, which rendered his disapproval completely devoid of worth.

Bea spoke when they finally pulled onto the property. "Park there," she said, pointing to an open clearing next to a dilapidated structure which had once been the house. "No not next to the old chimney. It could fall on us!"

Ben, showing just how angry he was, did not reply. Instead, he just moved the car out of the shadow of the old chimney. Usually he would respond to being yelled at. Not defensively, but with apologies. He was making no apologies at that moment, though. He was clearly fuming. His face was red and his fingers were drumming on the steering wheel. He had one foot on the brake and the other on the clutch, while taking the car in and out of gear. The metal clicking sound annoyed Bea and she finally grabbed his hand and shouted, "Put the damn car in first and leave it there!"

After Bea departed the car, Ben began to shift the car in and out of gear again. He watched her as she walked around the old house, looking at it the way one would look at a dead possum along the highway. The property was shaped like a wide triangle pointed at a slight angle down the mountain. The view of the valley was beautiful, but the property also had a view of Mercy Creek to the left, the Kaiser's estate past that, still slightly to the left, and a pine forest to the right, which bordered a side of the Morrissey farm. The back end, which would be the wide part of the triangle, was next door to the Robertson farm, and ran along the new road the government men were building.

Ben had to admit one thing about this whole mess. Bea had chosen a great location for her hotel. It was smack dab in the middle of some of the most prominent land on the mountain. And it was central to all of the new construction going on. All around them, Ben could hear the sounds of machines. He could also hear trees crashing to the ground, either pushed down by bulldozers or cut down by chainsaws.

After walking for several minutes in the opposite direction from the old house, Ben came across the pond where locals on the mountain like to skate when the temperatures stayed below freezing long enough. That was also a place where the mountain monster had been spotted. Of course, the Morrissey brothers had captured a buffalo they claimed was the monster, but Ben wasn't so sure. He hoped maybe the mountain monster would resurface and prove to be a tourist attraction. Or maybe there was a second buffalo roaming around, which would attract hunters who might stay in the hotel.

When he returned to the car, Bea was already waiting inside, complaining about how hot it was. When he shared his thoughts about the monster and the buffalo being good for business, she just stared at him and didn't respond.

Chapter 12

Millie Robertson's horse was a black mare. She had not a hint of any other color on her body. When the sun was at its brightest, and she was galloping, she looked like liquid moving through the air. Her name was Caligo. Copper was Angela's horse - a stallion the color of his name. Fern's horse was named Low Winter Sun. He was a palomino, and she called him Sunny.

Sunny always followed Caligo, no matter where she decided to go. If she walked in giant circles, Sunny walked in circles. If she climbed a hill, sunny climbed it right behind her. When Caligo ran, Sunny tried his best to keep up. He followed Caligo wherever she went. At night, they were usually put in stalls next to each other because Sunny would spend the night pacing and sniffing the air unless he could bed down next to Caligo's stall. Caligo would probably walk and live alone if she could, but Sunny wouldn't let her.

Copper was always surrounded by other horses. The others followed him and he assumed the role of leader naturally. When the Robertson's horses weren't with their riders, they were predictable in their movements and actions and even locations. They had places they preferred to run, or stand, or lie down.

The sounds of the trucks and earth movers changed all of that. The roars and rumblings caused the horses to scatter and move across the fields. Some moved along the fenceline, rubbing against the rough boards and posts. Others plunged deep into the trees, moving in the darkness of the shade. None stayed out in the open fields. None were still.

Caligo was especially spooked by the sounds. Her ears stayed turned backwards, and she would angle her head from side to side in a way that might make an observer think she was trying to hear the sounds more clearly. But anyone who knew the beautiful black mare, knew she was moving her head the same way she did when she was trying to avoid flies and shoo them away.

The appearance of the machines, after a few days at the back of the property, threw the horses into total chaos. They no longer stayed in one place for longer than a few minutes, and they seemed to constantly be moving in sets of circles. Some wide, and some very narrow.

As the air began to change, the horses became even more agitated and their behavior was no longer predictable in any way, other than the fact that they could be expected to be erratic. The dust was thin at first, but as the bulldozers and tractors went deeper below the surface, the dust became red and thick. Black smoke layered on top of the red dust, forming a ceiling over the heads of the horses. A ceiling which provided difficulty in their breathing as opposed to security and safety.

The smells of exhaust and burning fuel and oil drifted through the air, pushing against, and covering over, the smells of honeysuckle and wildflowers.

The horses, which normally could be attracted by the mere appearance of one of the Robertson daughters carrying a lead rope, had to be sought out now. They moved from clumped up to spread out, seemingly at random, but most likely in tune with the rhythmic invasion of the sights and sounds and smells of the machines.

As the evening of July 3rd surrendered to the darkness of summer, the machines began to shut down in one long line on the Robertsons' property. They had been pushed to the edge of their manufactured purpose in order to finish the first section of right of way before the holiday. As their engines cooled and the steel machines popped and crackled and settled in for the night, their blades were pointed towards the boundary markers of the Kaiser's Estate.

Chapter 13

The giant white tent was set up in the same place it had been set up back in 1933, and again in 1934. Once by a traveling preacher. The second time by the Kaiser himself, who had kept the tent packed up in a shed. It had not seen the light of day for almost seven years. The majority of the Fourth of July celebration was set to take place in the town square, but the tent was set up at the last minute just in case the dark clouds on the horizon were bringing rain.

The Fourth of July at Mercy Creek always meant a gigantic celebration at the Kaiser's Estate complete with fireworks, flags, roasted meats of every sort, and games of competition like foot races and, in recent years, baseball out on the back lawn. Over the past twenty years, there was only one year the Kaiser didn't host the annual event. 1941 would be the second year. He had begun to let neighbors know back at the New Year's Eve party, but most everyone thought he would reconsider. By Memorial Day weekend, word had gotten out all over the mountain and down in Lyttle's Mill that there would be no Fourth Of July party at the Kaiser's Estate that year.

In response, the Mayor of Lyttle's Mill had gathered a group of townspeople together and delegated the job of creating a town hosted Fourth of July celebration. The heads of the committee, Mac and Penelope MacBatten dove headfirst into the preparations. Mac's main motivation was to bring as many people to town as possible, as his Trading Post would be open for any last minute picnic needs, since everyone would be providing their own food. Penelope's motivation was to keep her mind off of the loss of her brother and the fact that the killer was never captured.

The committee had focused on decorating the town and by July 1st, every utility pole in town was connected by red, white and blue bunting and the street signs had patriotic ribbons tied to them.

There was also a "Most Patriotic" house contest. The Beaumont Boarding house had won, as Bea had made Ben and Chip and Ralph cover the entire house with bunting and flags. She had joked about flying a German flag as a prank, but of course she would never do that. Mostly because she hated the Kaiser and wouldn't want him to misunderstand her German flag as any nod towards him. She considered him a fence sitter and she hated fence sitters. She had once asked his opinion about the Fuehrer and his answer was filled with too many words at too fast a pace to track. It seemed he had no opinion. If he had, he would have expressed it more succinctly. She had formed the opinion that anyone who talked a lot about a subject did not usually feel as strongly about it as their verbosity implied.

Even though the day started with gray skies full of storm clouds, it seemed like most of the county came to town for the celebration.

Nellie and Charlene arrived alone. Jeb had promised to meet them at noon outside of Mac's Trading Post.

Inside the Trading Post, a line had formed at Mac's new butcher counter. Behind the counter were the twins, dressed in matching khaki pants, khaki shirts and white aprons. A line had already formed.

"Next!" Pete called out as an elderly lady stepped up.

"One pound of ground beef," she said.

"Pound of ground, Patty!" Pete yelled. "Just step over there ma'am and we will have that right out to you." Pete pointed to an area he had cleared near the section where his father had put the outdoor cooking equipment. This was intended to give the customers something to be tempted by while waiting for their meat choices.

Deputy Morton stepped up next.

"What can I get for you Deputy?" Pete asked. He knew John well. They had played football together. "Hey you guys never caught the guy who shot my uncle," Pat said from the butcher's table where he was running slabs of beef through the new grinder Mac had bought.

"Nope," the Deputy said. "And the Sheriff closed the case." Morton was clearly not happy about the closing of the case or having to tell his friend's nephews that the case to solve his murder was now just a box with no lid, sitting in the Sheriff's office in a corner.

"What the hell?" Pat said, coming around from the butcher's table to the counter. "You guys should be stinking ashamed of yourselves. Might as well close the whole office down if you guys can't even catch a guy who shot one of your own."

Pete, who was usually the hot headed one of the twins wasn't sure how to handle the situation, so he looked past Deputy Morton and said, "Next!"

"You're not gonna take my order, Petey?" Morton asked.

Pete, realizing he had skipped the Deputy without meaning to, quickly decided to make it seem like he fully meant to. "Go find somewhere else to buy your meat," Pete said.

"Yeah, get the hell out of here, Sherlock Worthless," Pat said.

As the Deputy moved out of the line and stood near the grills for a minute, trying to figure out what to do next, Pat moved back to the butcher's table and while wrapping the lady's pound of ground beef, called out to Pete, "Did you hear what I called him? Sherlock Worthless."

"Good one, Patty," Pete said, while keeping one of his eyes focused on the Deputy, who slowly walked out of the store.

"Happy Fourth of July, everybody!" Pete called out to the line of customers which was now out the door. "We got good fresh meat for you! None of it horse," he added.

Across the store, his father, who had been helping a customer load their car outside, gave his son a look that could have dropped a horse and shook his head. Pete, thinking he had just coined a great marketing phrase, turned back to the line of customers and said softly, "Who's next?"

Outside, where Main and Church streets cross, a large empty lot which had held a blacksmith shop before the depression, was filling up with people.

"Gather 'round! Gather 'round!" The man sang into the microphone. "Gather your kids and grab a seat. Grab your girl and grab a seat. Grab a seat. The final two matches of the day are just minutes away. "We've had an exciting day of professional wrestling here in...Little Town, Virginia!" Several voices from the crow yelled out, "Lyttle's Mill!" One of the men who yelled was Brian. He lived up on the mountain near Mercy Creek and was Joe's brother-in-law by marriage to Emily's sister, Faith.

Brian called out to Jeb and Anthony as they walked past, and said, "Boys! You've gotta watch this. This is the best thing I've seen in my whole life at least!"

By the time the announcer was introducing the wrestlers for the next match, Brian was surrounded by Jeb, Anthony, and Joe. Joe called over to Emily who approached with Esther and Beth.

"We were just about to leave," Esther said.

"Oh, you have to stay for the fireworks," Emily said quickly. "It's going to be even better than the New Year's Eve show."

"I do love fireworks," Beth said.

Esther gave Beth a confused look. "I thought you weren't feeling well."

"I think I just need something to drink," Beth said. "Walk with me to get some lemonade and then let's watch this wrestling match. I used to watch them in Tampa," she said.

"Tampa?" Emily asked. "In Florida? Tampa Bay?"

"No, dear," Beth said. "Hampton. There were matches there all the time when I was a child and my father would take me."

Emily laughed. "I'm sorry. This crowd is so loud, I misheard."

"It's okay. We'll be right back!" Beth shouted over the announcer who was now even louder and seemed to be competing with the volume of the growing crowd.

"Now entering the ring, wearing the black mask, please allow me to introduce to you, from the mountains of Tennessee, "The Grappler!" Most of the crowd cheered. At this point they didn't know if he was the good guy or the bad guy, so most of the audience gave him the benefit of the doubt and shouted his name.

"And now our champion, hailing from Houston, Texas. Blackjack Donovan!"

The Grappler began to shake his fists at the crowd, which caused the men nearest the ring to begin yelling back at him and shaking their fists in return. Boom! Blackjack hit The Grappler with an outstretched arm, sending the masked man backwards onto the mat. The crowd roared.

The Grappler stood up quickly only to be hit by Blackjack bouncing off the ropes. As the crowd cheered, Blackjack stood over the body of his opponent, lined up a fist with the masked face, and BOOM! Blackjack's fist pounded The Grappler's face as the Texan dropped to his knees with a loud banging sound.

The crowd was growing now, as friends waved other friends over to the ring area, while neighbors shouted to neighbors who were walking by.

The World Comes To Mercy Creek

As Blackjack took a moment to wave to the crowd and shout out how thankful he was that they stopped to watch the match, The Grappler slowly got back onto his feet behind Blackjack and menacingly began to climb to the top of the turnbuckle. The crowd began to yell as one, and several men shouted statements like, "He's behind you!" and "Watch yourself!"

Just as The Grappler made it to the top rope, he put out his hands as if he were about to fly like a plane, and his landing field was Blackjack Donovan. Just in time, the big Texan ran to the turnbuckle and grabbed The Grappler by his legs, causing the masked man to beg for mercy from the top rope. Mercy was not given by Blackjack, who did a slow slashing motion across his own throat, using his thumb to represent a big knife. The crowd went crazy in response and Blackjack pulled the masked man off of the top rope and onto his own big shoulders. The Texan then spun him around several times as the crowd counted, "One, two, three, four, five..." and on the sixth time around, Blackjack unceremoniously dumped The Grappler onto the mat with a splattering sound. Blackjack responded to the crowd's cheers by standing over his opponent and placing his boot onto the chest of The Grappler, as the referee slid into the ring and slammed his hand down onto the mat three times. Blackjack Donovan was announced as the winner and the crowd began to chant his name!

While the crowd was cheering for Blackjack, the announcer began to talk again over his microphone and speakers. "Who is this, ladies and gentlemen? Who? Is? This?"

People in the crowd began to look around to see who the announcer meant. Jeb spotted a tall man coming from the far side of the crowd, pushing people out of his way as the crowd split open like the red sea. A tall man with a shaved head and bronze colored skin made his way to the ring. He was wearing loose black pants and no shirt or shoes. He had big hoops in both of his ear lobes. When he got close to the ring, he ran in and punched Blackjack in the face, knocking him down. When Blackjack pulled himself back up, using the ring ropes, the bald man held his right hand out to the crowd and formed a claw, while the announcer screamed, "It's the terror of the Pacific Islands, Taika!"

Taika turned to Blackjack and grabbed his right side with the hand that he had formed into a claw. "Oh my God!" the announcer yelled. "Taika must be planning on having ribs for dinner!"

The gasps of the crowd were both individual and collective at the same time as Taika lifted the tall Texan by the rib cage and slammed him to the mat. The horror continued as Blackjack screamed from pain and the crowd went silent.

The announcer filled the silence with this ominous statement as Taika began to walk around the ring while wiping the drool from his lips and looking menacingly at the crowd. "I speak now only to the Gentlemen in the audience. Taika has no opponent to face today because none of these fine wrestlers will even agree to wrestle him. Blackjack, our champion, has avoided Taika The Terrible all across this fine nation. That is why Taika has attacked him today." The crowd made some oohs and ahhs but seemed to be listening closely. "That's where you fine people can help me. I need one volunteer to step into the ring with Taika so that he will have an opponent and not attack his fellow wrestling troupe as we travel tonight by train."

"Who will it be folks?"

Silence. Some laughter as men pushed other men towards the ring and friends began to goad each other. One man, a tobacco cropper from near the county line raised his hand, but his wife pulled it down and gave him a look that would have made Taika The Terrible run from the ring.

After almost a full minute of silence, the announcer said, "I haven't told you about the reward yet folks." The crowd grew quiet again.

"Anyone who can last three minutes in the ring with Taika will win FIFTY DOLLARS. That's right friends. I didn't misspeak! FIFTY DOLLARS. AMERICAN CURRENCY!"

Around the ring men began to line up and as quick as they jumped into the ring, Taika would throw them out or chase them out.

"Folks! Folks! Folks!" the announcer shouted. "You don't even know the rules yet. You must stay in the ring for three whole minutes without being thrown out or chased out. You must wait for the bell. Folks! Folks! Folks!"

"What about your Uncle?" Beth asked quickly.

"What?" Jeb asked.

"Your uncle," Beth said. "Yates. Everyone says he's quite the fighter. Maybe he could win."

Jeb looked surprised. "How do you know my uncle?" he asked.

The World Comes To Mercy Creek

Beth looked around and pointed at Joe who was several feet away. "Your brother told us about him. He talked about him at dinner once or twice." She turned to Esther and asked, "Do you remember that?"

"Oh yes," Esther said. "He told some story of brawling, and your brother was the star."

Jeb laughed. "That sounds about right."

"Is he here?" Beth asked. "Let's find him!"

Joe walked up as Beth was speaking. "This guy is gonna wrestle locals all day or until someone beats him. Maybe one of us should fight him once it gets dark and he's wore out."

"We think Yates should wrestle him," Jeb said.

"Yates?" Joe asked. "Well, he's right over there with that buffalo the Kaiser has. There's a line across the street with people wanting to see it."

"Folks, we will be taking an intermission break for one hour. One hour. We will see you all back here with your friends, family, and neighbors. Ten men have already tried today and failed. Will you be the one who wins the FIFTY DOLLAR prize?"

As the announcer continued to build up the show for later that afternoon, Jeb, Joe, Emily, Beth and Esther all walked over to the lot where Yates had the buffalo. The crowd was walking away, and Yates was leading the big animal back up onto the trailer.

"Are you leaving already?" Joe asked.

"Yep," Yates said as he looked around the small group. "Hey there everybody." He closed the rear gate on the trailer and told Joe, "There's only a few guys up on the Estate, and the Kaiser is here now, somewhere, so I figured I would take the horses back and relieve the guards so they can enjoy the evening. Leon hasn't seen anything like this before in America, so I'd like him to be able to come down and see it."

"We've all decided you need to wrestle over there," Beth said while turning and pointing at the wrestling ring.

"Oh you've all decided it?" Yates asked. He smiled at Beth and introduced himself. "Yates Morrissey," he said as he shook her hand.

"It's nice to finally meet the hero of so many stories," Beth said.

A father with two small boys passed by and called over, "Are the clydesdales gone?"

"I just loaded them onto the trailer," Yates called back.

"There's a big guy over there challenging locals to a wrestling match," Jeb said quickly.

"Wait one second Jeb," Yates said, as he looked towards the father who was now consoling the two disappointed boys. "Hey, I'll bring one of them back out for your boys." And then to Joe and Emily, "There's no way you two are in on this are you? Surely you know this is a con these wrestling boys do from town to town. They circulate a guy around the ring to take bets."

"We're just an old married couple hoping to see some entertainment, Uncle," Joe said with a smile. "Do I think you can beat him? Of course I do. Do I think you will try? Probably not."

"I thought you were the bravest of the brave," Beth said.

"Bravery's got nothing to do with not jumping into a fight against a professional fighter who travels around the country picking fights," Yates said.

Beth looked disappointed and then turned to Esther and said, "Well, he's no fun."

As Yates turned to open up the trailer. "I'll stop by your place later this week, Joe," Yates said. And then to Beth, Esther and Jeb. "I hope to see you all there as well."

Esther quickly spoke up. "Jeb why don't you try it?"

"Me?" Jeb asked, his face turning red as he forced a smile. "I'm not the fighter my Uncle is."

"You don't have to be," Esther said. "Now hear me out. The contest is to see who can stay in the ring for three minutes without getting thrown out or chased out by that Terrible man, right?"

"Right," Jeb said. "And to avoid being killed."

"And that's exactly what you will be doing," Esther said.

"Esther, you're a scholar among scholars," Beth said. "Great plan."

"Well someone needs to fill me in, because I'm not following you," Jeb said.

"You're gonna spend the whole three minutes avoiding him. You run and duck and jump and whatever you need to do to keep him from even touching you."

Behind Jeb, Virgil and Nellie walked up to Yates. Nellie handed him an ice cream cone. "With three scoops, just how you like it," she said. "Except the top scoop has pretty much melted all over my hand."

"You sure you didn't help it along," Yates asked with a smile as he took the cone. "Thank you both. I was just packing up."

A woman with three small children came up and asked, "Are the horses gone? My kids were hoping to see them."

"Hey Uncle Yates, I'm gonna wrestle that big guy. Will you come watch? Daddy? Momma?" Jeb called over and then started walking towards them with Esther and Beth following him. Joe and Emily had decided to go get ice cream.

"Do we know you, young man?" Nellie asked. "You look a lot like my son, but he hasn't been home long enough lately for me to even remember what he looks like."

"Very funny," Jeb said. "I promise I will be by this week. I've got an idea on how to beat this wrestler over there by the bank. I could win fifty dollars. And have a story to write about. This time I wouldn't just be watching something happen. I'd be making it happen by fighting this guy."

"Wait? You're fighting someone?"

"It's just a wrestling match. It's not even real."

"Yates, I want you to go with him," Nellie said.

"I can't do it," Yates said. I've got to take this buffalo back to the farm and let some of my men come back here for the day."

"We'll do it for you, right Virgil?" Nellie said as she watched Jeb and the girls walk slowly away and across the street.

"We can do that," Virgil said. "And we can let the buffalo out again because it seems like people are lining up again for it. And that way you can make sure the boy doesn't get his back broken by this wrestler he's gonna fight just to impress one of those young ladies."

"It's the brunette," Yates said.

"Vance Robertson's daughter was a brunette wasn't she?" Virgil asked Nellie.

"Yes," Nellie said. "Millie is her name. She was at the house an awful lot last year. But it wasn't meant to be, I suppose."

"I suppose not," Virgil said. "I always preferred strawberry blondes," he said as he smiled at Nellie.

Nellie blushed and laughed as she tusked a loose lock of her hair behind her ear."

Yates nodded, thanked them for the ice cream cone and set out to find his nephew and get him ready for this fight. He was sure Jeb didn't know what he was getting himself into.

Chapter 14

The two thieves knew they only had a limited amount of time to walk up the creek from the bridge, cut across the Kaiser's property, find the new barn, dig up the money, and carry as much of it as they could back down the creek and to the car they had waiting further down Bridge Road. The two thieves had discussed the timing extensively. They estimated thirty minutes to walk up the creek, another thirty to locate the new barn, and at least thirty minutes to an hour to dig up the money. Then it would take them at least forty-five minutes to walk off of the farm and to the car they had parked down near the bridge. They had argued a bit about what to do with the car, but they eventually agreed on simply parking it near Mercy Creek, like so many other cars parked along the river for holiday camping or fishing or floating.

The two partners had known each other since they were very young, though they had lived in separate parts of the country for over a decade and had communicated only by correspondence until their reunion a bit over six months earlier. They had not planned on robbing the Kaiser.

Their original plan was to lay low in plain sight until they could leave town with the $14,000.00 they had stolen from the bank on New Year's Eve once spring came and they could pull one more job at the bank. Beth was supposed to arrive a few days earlier, but she had decided to stop at a few more banks along the way to Lyttle's Mill. After quickly robbing the bank while no one else was in the lobby, Beth returned to the orchard to eliminate the last of her traveling companions.

It was during the blizzard that they had decided to switch the plan from robbing the bank again to robbing the Kaiser. The had all been sitting outside and the boy from Chicago had mentioned his boss burying money on his property. They had wondered for a while who

Wallace's boss was, but it didn't take long to make the connection. Jeb had confirmed it without meaning to when he said one of his neighbors buried their money. They had originally planned to somehow take the money while on the property for the Fourth of July celebration, but when the Kaiser had announced he wasn't having one, they changed their plans again, and decided to still try for the money while the town was celebrating the holiday fifteen miles away from the Estate. They knew the Estate would still be staffed but they were gambling it would be greatly diminished.

As they made their way up the creek, Beth kept slipping on the rocks and when she tried to switch to the creek bank, she kept getting snagged by the thorns. "Dammit to hell!" she yelled as she fought her way free of the latest briar bush to attack her. She tried to swing her shovel at the thorns but ended up tangling the handle as well as her arms in the vines and weeds.

"I told you we should have hiked the creek a few times to prepare for this," Esther said. She was trying to hide the fact that she was already out of breath, but with each step, that was becoming more and more difficult to conceal. As was her anger.

This plan had been Beth's all along. The original plan was to steal the old money from the bank. It was supposed to be a one time deal. Then it became a two time deal, but then the second time changed to this plan, which Esther had thought was too risky, but she went along with it. She had always gone along with Beth, but she had been regretting that choice for months. She just hadn't known how to stop the whole thing, once the wheels were in motion.

Beth slipped again and this time went down into the water. The shovel made a loud clanging noise on the rocks and she screamed out and then stood up and stomped down on the water as hard as she could, which threw her off balance again and she had to hop to keep from falling.

Esther didn't even try to hold back her laughter. She had been so worried for so long about what they were about to do, that all of the stress came out in the form of laughter. She stood on the muddy creek bank and leaned on her shovel and just let the laughter roll out of her.

This made Beth angrier and she shouted, "Shut up!"

Esther immediately stopped laughing and said, "Don't talk to me like that. We don't do that. I don't like that at all."

The World Comes To Mercy Creek

Beth was quiet for the rest of the hike out of the creek and up the hill except for several times she cursed briar bushes or rocks or sticks that looked like snakes.

When they reached the edge of the woods, Beth spoke up quickly. "No damn barn, Esther. Where's the damn barn?"

"Calm down!" Esther shouted. "I told you not to talk to me like that. I didn't like it when we were kids and I still don't. It's right across that gravel road." Esther pointed across the short field of deep green grass which almost hid from view the road that cut through the field. "If we were taller, we could see the roof of it. We're close."

"If you're wrong, we're gonna be walking around in the sunlight. With shovels over our shoulders."

Esther didn't reply. Instead she walked out into the open. At first, she was ducked down, but by the time she reached the road, she realized it wouldn't make a difference if she was ducked down and someone spotted them. They would both immediately be recognized as trespassers, even if they were stooped down trespassers.

Esther decided instead to just walk steadily towards the top of the hill and she heard Beth behind her. When she looked back, Beth was also walking at a steady pace with her shovel held low like she was prepared to drop it and run if necessary. Esther decided to do the same thing, so she switched from carrying it slung over her shoulder to holding it low, just below her hips.

At the top of the hill, Esther became nervous as she second guessed her understanding of Jeb's description. But there it was. A small shed with a metal roof and new boards, barely weathered. Beth started to run and Esther decided there was no reason not to so she followed her and they made it to the shed quickly. Beth looked around quickly and Esther did the same. The barn was small. It was more like a shed. There were two horse stalls and a small area outside the stalls. The floors were covered in clean straw and the whole building was clean. Wallace had been right. The stalls looked like they had never been used.

"Where do we dig?" Beth asked.

Esther pointed to one of the stalls. "You try that one. I will try this one. Start in the middle." Esther drove her shovel down into the straw and she was met with a loud clanging sound as the shovel bounced. "What the hell?" she said, as she heard the same clanging sound from the stall Beth was in. Esther kicked the straw with her feet and revealed concrete. She ran to the corner and moved that straw with her foot and saw more concrete.

"Dammit!" yelled Beth. "The floor is made of cement!"

Esther looked around and then ran out to the small area outside the stalls. She dragged the shovel in a big circle. "Everywhere is," she said. "Everywhere is." She looked frantically around. "We just need to go. We take what we have already and go."

"It's here somewhere," Beth said. "It makes no sense to have this place out here like this. That guy said it. And then Jeb said it." She jammed the shovel down against the concrete again and again.

"Stop it!" Esther shouted. "Just stop it. We need to slow down and think this through." Esther took a deep breath and looked around the room. Piles of straw. "Check the straw bales," she said quickly. "Cut them open. Do you need something to cut the string with?"

"No," Beth said, pulling a small folding knife from her pocket. She opened it quickly and started cutting the strings on the bales stacked against the wall. As she pulled one down, she would cut it, and spread the straw out. She counted quickly. "There's about twenty bales."

"I'll help," she said, as she grabbed a bale and started shaking it free of its strings.

"Hey!" Beth said sharply. "Hey listen!"

A buzzing sound just outside the barn wall was getting louder. "Hornets?" Esther asked. "It sounds like bees or hornets."

Before Beth could say anything, the noise became louder and sharper. It was a motor and it was on the road because the sound of gravel popping mixed with the roar of the engine.

"A motorcycle!" Esther yelled. She moved back into one of the stalls, but then came back out because there was nothing in there to hide behind. The roar of the motor was right outside the barn so she dropped down and tried to crawl under the pile of loose straw as Beth ran past her, with the shovel held back like baseball players hold a bat right before the pitch. She swung before Esther could even speak or fully comprehend what was happening.

The engine dropped down in volume as if it was slowing as Beth jumped forward and yelled so loud she could be heard over the idling engine. Beth's swing of the shovel was wide and fast and Esther realized that someone was on a motorcycle which Beth could see more clearly because of where she was standing. The man on the motorcycle screamed out and tumbled sideways as the shovel connected with his upper chest and an arm he had lifted in an attempt to block the object coming at him.

Esther saw the motorcycle hit Beth and knock her down but she didn't know where the rider was after he had been hit by the shovel. Esther jumped up and tried to lift the heavy motorcycle up but she couldn't even budge it. Beth, with a line of blood running down her left cheek, yelled out for Esther to help her as she pushed against the rear tire which was across her lap.

Esther pulled while Beth pushed with her legs and the bike was off of her and still running.

"Let's go!" Esther yelled.

"I'm not leaving without the money," Beth said.

Behind her, a young man stood up and took two steps into the barn and leaned against a support beam. His mouth was bleeding and he had a dark purple mark across the left side of his face. "I can't let you take it," he said, as he moved to the entrance of the stall farthest from the door.

His accent was so thick Esther had trouble understanding him at first, but when he spoke again, she realized it wasn't just his accent. He was spitting blood and his jaw was swelling up like it might be broken.

Leonid looked behind him at the wall with the water and feed buckets hanging from it and then back to Esther and Beth. "You don't understand." He took a deep breath and moved back against the wall. "I can't let you do it," he said.

"We've already got it," Beth said.

Leonid's eyes narrowed and he tried to say something as he turned and ran his hand against one of the boards. He turned quickly and started to say, "No--" but his words were cut off when Beth connected with the shovel again, knocking him to the ground where he lay still.

"Give me something to pull this board off with," Beth yelled.

Esther looked at the man on the ground and then ran to the wall where she found a small hatchet. Running back into the stall, she had to step over the man on the ground as she swung the little axe at the board above the feed bucket. The board cracked but didn't split. She hit it again and it cracked a bit more. Beth stepped up next to her and wedged the shovel point between the split in the board and pulled down on the shovel handle. The board made a cracking sound as a large piece of it split off and fell to the ground. Esther quickly reached in the gap and felt fabric. "I think it's burlap," she said. Beth took the little hatchet and swung up against the board below the hole they had created. After three hits, that board split, and Esther grabbed it and pulled as hard as she could. The board came loose so quickly that Esther almost lost her balance and fell.

"Help me," Beth said as she put the shovel point in the crack between the next two boards. Esther grabbed the handle with her and together, they pulled down on it and popped the next board loose. They repeated the process on two more boards until several small burlap bags were exposed.

Esther pulled a bag loose and opened it. She smiled and said, "Money!"

Beth pulled several more loose. And as they opened each one, they realized there were thousands of dollars in each sack. Esther and Beth worked together to pull as many of the burlap bags free as they could. In all, by the time they were done, they had over forty bags. "Can we carry all of this?" Beth asked.

"Each bag weighs about ten pounds," Esther said, "So, no, I don't think so. There's no way we can get all of this down to the creek and then to the car."

Beth looked around the barn and found a larger burlap feed sack. Tossing it to Esther, she said, "fill that sack with the smaller bags." She found another sack on the floor at the back of the barn. "Fill this one too," she said, as she dropped it next to Esther.

Next, Beth moved quickly outside and after several attempts, finally picked the motorcycle up off of its side. She had ridden one before but she had never been the driver. She got it started by repeating what she had seen other people do to start their motorcycles. Esther dragged a full sack of money out to the motorcycle. "Do you know how to drive that thing?" she asked.

"No, but I'm figuring it out," she said. After a few failed attempts, she got the motorcycle moving and rode it in a circle. "Do you know how to get out of here the back way?" she asked.

"I do," Esther said. "But we will have to circle back to the car. And to do that we have to go all the way back across the mountain."

"Well, we just need to make it to the car," Beth said. "So we'd better start strapping those bags to the bike."

The World Comes To Mercy Creek

The hardest part for Esther was finding ropes, until she thought of the baling twine they had cut loose from the straw. She grabbed the small pile of twine and together, she and Beth tied the two big bags of money to the back of the motorcycle. As they climbed onto the bike and Beth got it moving slowly, Leonid stumbled out of the barn and tried to chase them. After only a few steps he fell down to his knees and watched helplessly as the two women rode away.

Chapter 15

A brass band was playing patriotic songs across the street from where the wrestling ring was set up. This provided a soundtrack to Jeb's match with the giant wrestler and made Jeb feel like he was representing his country and his flag on Independence Day. It was with that attitude that he ran into the ring. He would help rid his American town of this foreign menace. But right before the bell rang, the big Pacific Warrior, Terrible Taika leaned forward and whispered in a voice completely devoid of accent. "Hey are the fireworks gonna be good? Or are they just a quick show? I really love fireworks."

To which, Jeb could only force a reply of, "They're pretty good." And then the bell rang and Taika smashed a forearm into Jeb's chest, knocking the wind out of him and putting him on the mat. Jeb jumped up and began running along the edge of the ring, staying as far away from the other wrestler as possible.

The announcer was marking the time every ten seconds. Half a minute had passed before Jeb realized he couldn't effectively stay away from Terrible Taika and search the crowd for Esther at the same time. The first time he looked for her, Taika caught him in the jaw with an outstretched hand and smacked him to the mat. He hit the mat and looked for Esther again and it earned him a foot stomp from Taika. By the time the announcer marked the passing of forty seconds, Jeb told himself Esther was stuck in the back of the crowd and would be waiting for him at the end of the three minutes.

Up until that point, Jeb had back pedaled and moved sideways while dodging the big man. At fifty seconds, he started running around Taika, hoping to stay just out of reach. It didn't work. Taika smacked him again and this time Jeb went sailing through the air and hit the ropes. It was then that Jeb realized just how bad an idea this was, as Taika picked him up and pressed him high into the evening air. A breeze was blowing, Jeb remembered that much. He also remembered hearing his wrist snap like a dead tree branch.

Jeb tried to ignore the pain as he forced himself up. He knew he couldn't let the big wrestler pick him up again or he was going to be hurt even worse than he already was.

"Look out, Jeb! He's behind you," a woman's voice called out.

Jeb looked around for Esther but he couldn't see her. The same voice said, "Duck your head!" so he did, just as the big wrestler tried to hit him with an outstretched forearm.

In the back of his mind he knew he recognized the voice as the same person yelled, "Stop turning your back on him. Use the ropes to bounce away from him!" It was Millicent. She was on the opposite side of the ring from Jeb's family and she was with her sisters and Little Virgil.

"Stay away from him, Jeb!" Little Virgil yelled.

He was up in the air again before he knew how he got there and then he was on the mat again. This time, his landing brought sharp pains to his ribs. He heard the announcer say eighty seconds while Taika hugged him so tight he felt the air rush out of his lungs. "Time to say night night," the big man whispered to Jeb. By the time he heard ninety seconds he blacked out as he felt another sharp pain run through his ribs.

The next time Jeb opened his eyes, he heard a bell ringing. At first he thought he had won the match, but he saw boots near his face and realized he had been thrown from the ring. Above him, on the edge of the ring, stood Taika. Jeb could barely see him because of the sharp glare from the sun, but he braced himself for the inevitable pain that would follow once the big wrestler jumped down on top of him.

But he didn't jump down on top of Jeb. Instead, he fell sideways onto the ground after Yates slammed into him from the other side of the ropes. When he got back up, Yates was waiting for him and landed two shots to the big man's stomach. The first one caused Taika to shout out but it wasn't in pain. It was anger. And he reached out a hand and smacked Yates in his shoulder, knocking him sideways. Yates steadied himself and charged the wrestler, spearing him to the ground. He rolled up quickly and backed up to put himself between the wrestler and Jeb, as other wrestlers ran in and made a big show of pulling Terrible Taika away from the locals.

Joe and Emily were helping Jeb up as Yates turned around once he was satisfied that Taika was no longer a threat. The announcer was telling everyone how disappointed he was that none of the local men could put Taika the Terrible in his place as the crowd began to disperse. Most were heading out to the field near town to begin to cook their dinner and prepare for the fireworks to start.

"Are you hurt, Jeb?" Yates asked, as Jeb leaned on Joe and was looking around like he was lost.

"Where's Esther?" he asked.

They all looked around, and Joe said, "I haven't seen her for hours. She wasn't here for the match."

"Are you alright, Jeb?" Millie Robertson asked as she walked by in a large group of friends. She slowed a bit, a look of concern was on her face.

"I'll be okay," Jeb said. "Are you alright?"

"I'll be alright," she said. "Be careful."

"I will be," Jeb said. "You too."

And then Little Virgil was there. "My big brother, the wrestler," he said. "There's easier ways to earn money, you know."

"I'll figure that out one of these days," Jeb said. "Where have you been lately? Momma said you aren't even staying at the house."

"I'm bunking at the Robertson's," Little Virgil said. "They need me over there."

"Daddy needs you at the house," Joe said.

Little Virgil started to reply but a man's voice calling for Yates interrupted them. It was Otto, one of the Kaiser's head guards.

When Yates made his way to him through the crowd, Otto spoke quickly and Yates yelled back over to Joe, "Can you all take Jeb to the doctor without me? We've got an emergency."

"Sure thing," Joe said, but Yates was already running with Otto to one of the Kaiser's cars. They jumped in quickly and the car sped away.

Chapter 16

The meeting was held in Virgil's office with little fanfare. None of the normal pomp and circumstance which gatherings on the Kaiser's Estate normally exhibited. Just a group of people gathered in the room lit by one lamp. Ginny sat in a chair with Josh next to her on a stool. Nellie had a chair, but she was standing. Uma was in a corner, standing. Leeza May was there, wringing her hands. Otto, the lead guard. They were both standing. Virgil was standing next to Nellie. He kept asking everyone there if they needed a chair, or anything. He started out standing next to Nellie, but kept moving to the window and back to Nellie again.

Behind Virgil's desk, staring out the same window Virgil walked back and forth from, the Kaiser stood. He had been quiet for several minutes as everyone else came into the room.

"Are we waiting on Yates?" Leeza May whispered to Virgil.

He shook his head and said, "No," quietly.

"When I was a boy. Very young. Eight, perhaps? Possibly younger. Not older. My family had a mantle clock in the parlor of our house. For some reason I was allowed to do my school work in that room. It makes no logical sense that I was put there for that purpose because my family used that room in a very limited fashion. Very limited. Regardless, that is where I did my school work when I was home each evening."

He was still staring out the window, and he was speaking at a pace much slower than was normal. "I mentioned the mantle clock. It made a sound. We would wind it with a key periodically and when it ran it made a sound. This sound undeniably marked the passing of time not only in that room, but throughout the lower level of that house. But within that room especially.

While I did my homework, I heard it. The ticking was constant and loud and undeniable. My mother told me, when I complained to her about the noise and claimed that it was distracting, that I should let the sound motivate me. She said I should use it to establish a rhythm within my mind which propelled me forward in my work and helped me accomplish my goal. I tried that. I really did. But instead, the sound reminded me that time was passing, and my life was being spent doing school work while it could have been spent playing outside or doing something I enjoyed. The ticking of that clock. The passing of time. Haunted me then." He paused abruptly as if he saw something outside the window which captured his attention. And then he turned to face everyone.

"It haunts me now," he said. "The passing of time. I hear that ticking so loud. So loud within my head right now. Reminding me that time is passing, and it is passing quickly." He paused again. This time he seemed to be searching for the right words. This was not normal for him. Uma leaned forward, as if she wanted to help him. But she stayed where she was and she listened. After a few moments he began to speak again.

"It was with this ticking in my head, this ever-present awareness of the passing of time, which drove me to begin this endeavor which we gather today to discuss. There is no need to surmise. Everyone here knows what we are doing and much of why we are doing it. A mad man is in power across the world in a place which must feel so far away to some of you here, but for some of us, Uma...Otto... we know how close it is, do we not?"

Otto nodded. He was a man of little emotion and now he had allowed a look of concern to creep across his face.

The Kaiser continued. "This mad man has begun to do things that our human minds do not have the ability to fully comprehend. It is why so many are in denial. But doubt not, friends, he is doing what the very worst rumors say he is doing. And beyond, I'm saddened to say. Beyond our worst imaginations. I know this because people I know and trust have told me and I believe them."

"For a while, I sat back and did nothing. My goodness, it hurts to admit, but I did nothing. Then I wasted time, that precious time, wondering what I could do. But then an opportunity to help presented itself and we all stepped forward to take it. And the results...my goodness the results are right outside this building. In fact, some are in this building, aren't they, Ginny? You have them everywhere don't you?"

"Yes," she said with a quick and guarded smile. "Pretty much."

"I hope no one doubts my knowledge of how much has been sacrificed to make this happen. To bring these children here. To bring more and more of them here. Virgil. You and Nellie. I... I can never say how sorry I am for the toll this has taken on you and your family."

Virgil locked eyes with the Kaiser and nodded. They each held the gaze for several moments and then the Kaiser said, "But yesterday, something happened on this property, and combined with something that happened earlier this week on the borders of our property, and the result of these events has been devastating to our plans here. To what we have been doing here. Devastating is not an exaggeration my friends. I'm sorry to say it is not. Yesterday we were robbed of nearly all of the money we have left. We converted all of our gold, due to the current gold standard laws, into paper currency, and then, due to the many bank robberies throughout our state, we made the decision... I made the decision to protect our own money right here. And that did not work. We were robbed of most of our money. Yates and Leonid have gone after the thieves. I'm afraid it will be like finding a needle in a haystack, but Yates believes they made a mistake in taking the motorcycle. He will track the motorcycle as far as they take it. And maybe he will get the money back. We need every bill back in order to keep this going."

The Kaiser looked around the room slowly. "We have some money reserves across the estate. But earlier this week we learned that the government has seized our right to cut timber on the land across the mountain. That is our source of income which has been funding what we have been doing for the past year. I will spare you the legalities of this but that is over for now. Also, we are being told that I am no longer allowed to own this property, as a military base or outpost or something of the sort is being placed near here, and as a German, my owning land so close is considered a strategic mistake for our government."

"They can just take your land?" Josh asked. "Just like that?"

"Well they would be buying it from me," the Kaiser said. "The government has the right to buy it and I have the right to accept it and go somewhere else. I do not have the right to keep this property. According to the government." The Kasier nodded towards Uma. "Uma has been meeting with friends in New York. These same friends are the ones bringing these children into the country. They have an attorney who is helping us delay this seizure. This theft of my land. But delay is the most we can hope for. To be blunt, we have until the end of this year to vacate the property. Completely."

"This thing we've been doing. I lack the words to know what to call it. I can only speak for myself right now, but this...has and will cost me everything. But I tell you with complete lucidity and soundness of mind. It is worth it. I walked among these children the other day, for the first time, and I watched as Ginny led them in lessons and I can tell you, it will all be worth it."

But for each of you, right now, I offer a way out. A chance to leave with something and some chance at rebuilding away from here. I can't offer much, but I still have some money. And I have automobiles. I will give you a vehicle and some money and you can go with no shame or regret. You have served this endeavor well."

"For anyone who chooses to stay, the best we can do is see this through to the very end. And then it is over."

"What happens to the kids?" Nellie asked.

The kids will be sent all over the country. Foster homes. Children's homes. I'm not sure. They may be sent to Europe. England maybe. There are orphanages there. You see, folks, some of what we did here...what I did here...is not legal. We are not allowed to do this. Bring Polish young people into this country without the proper procedures being followed? That is why we had to keep this secret. Why we tried to keep the surveyors and construction crews away from the property. And we didn't tell people in town, because we have seen all over the country where refugees are not accepted into local communities. The results were often violent and disastrous. People worry that they will be right back to where they were five years ago. They do not want to be hungry again, and they will do whatever it takes not to be in that position again."

"This is what I brought you here to say. If you choose to leave, you will leave with our blessing. If you choose to stay, all we can hope to do is see this through to the end."

"We're with you until the end," Virgil said. He and Nellie were holding hands and moved over next to the Kaiser.

Otto snapped a salute and said, "I will stay on duty as long as you will have me, Sir."

The World Comes To Mercy Creek

"Who else would I cook for?" Leeza May said. "I've gotten used to your strange food requests."

Uma walked over to the Kaiser and hesitated. But then hugged him. The silence in the room was measurable and then the Kaiser whispered something to her and she nodded and smiled and stayed next to him after she ended the hug.

"There is something more we can do," Ginny said. "It might not sound like much, but we can teach the kids English. Make sure they speak the language as well as they possibly can. It will help them have just that much more of a chance of success here."

"I love that idea," Nellie said.

"I will help," Uma said.

"So will I," Josh said.

"Ginny, dear, I think that is the best idea. We can do that. It's the one tangible thing we can do before we lose them." His voice broke while saying the last few words and he turned to look out the window again.

"We can make it. We are fighting this in court. We are selling everything we can. We are bringing in every child we can bring. Teach them English. They will then be sent all over the country. But they will be alive, and they will know the language. "That's how this ends. The kids are alive. We have to be satisfied with that."

Chapter 17

Sheriff Tyson and Deputy Dale searched Bea Beaumont's car by themselves. There were other deputies there, but the Sheriff only wanted them to check the area around the car for evidence. The Sheriff had known Bea for most of his life. They went to school together and Bea had dated the Sheriff's best friend until he had gone off to War and never came back. Tyson knew Bea could be nearly impossible to deal with, and the fact that her car was now part of a murder investigation made this a case he wanted to take the lead on.

"When do I get it back?" Bea yelled from the edge of the road where she had been stopped by Deputy Morton. "Dicky Tyson you need to answer me! Dicky?"

Sheriff Tyson took a deep breath, locked eyes with Dale, shook his head slowly, and then turned around to wave Bea down to her car.

"Now, Bea, keep in mind this is a crime scene," Sheriff Tyson said.

"No crime has been committed here," Bea said. "So how can it be a crime scene?"

"We're calling it a crime scene because a weapon possibly used in a crime was found in it," the Sheriff said.

"Weapon? Nonsense. What weapon?"

"This one." Dale said, holding a shotgun up with a gloved hand. The barrel was cut off and the stock was cut down as well. "And this one," Dale said, holding up a revolver.

"Those don't belong to me," Bea said. "But the car does. I'm taking my car."

"We also found money that we believe was robbed from the bank last year," Sheriff Tyson said.

"Well, I didn't do it. You two rednecks think I did it?" she asked.

The World Comes To Mercy Creek

"No, Bea. If we did, we wouldn't be showing all of this to you." The Sheriff lowered his voice. "We know you called in the stolen vehicle last night."

"Right. And it took you a whole 'nother day to find it."

"Well, the good news is, we found it, but now we need your help finding the people who stole it."

"Well this is a fine way of asking for my help," Bea said. "Holding my property hostage."

"Do you have any idea who would have taken your car?" Dale said. "This isn't just a bank robbery, Bea. These are most likely murder weapons. Do you have any idea who might have taken your car?"

"No. And whoever it is, they didn't take my keys," Bea said.

From the road, one of the Deputies called down, "Sheriff? Virgil Morrissey wants to talk to you."

The Sheriff looked quickly up the hill and yelled back, "Send him down."

"Do you think they were trying to drive it into the river?" Bea asked Dale, while the Sheriff walked towards Virgil.

"I doubt it, "Dale said.

"Well, the river is right there," she said.

"Right, so they could have just pushed it in, if that was their intention."

"Well, I think they were trying to ditch it in the river and destroy all this evidence. Maybe I should be the investigator. You wanna hire me, so I can close this case for you all?"

"Then why would they leave all that money in there?" Dale asked.

Bea looked at the car, then at Dale, and then back to the car before looking at Dale and saying, "How should I know? We pay you all to figure that stuff out." With that said, Bea turned to walk over to where the Sheriff was talking to Virgil Morrissey.

"So the only thing taken was the motorcycle?" the Sheriff had just asked.

"That's all we are reporting stolen," Virgil said.

"And this guard you have that saw them, can I talk to him?"

"He's not here, unfortunately. He left with Yates to try to catch them."

"Damn, Virgil. There is more to this than you understand right now." Sheriff Tyson turned to Bea as she walked up and said, "I'm gonna have to ask you to give us some privacy, Bea."

"Why? He's giving you information about my stolen car. Was it one of your Germans who took it?" she asked Virgil. "Why in the world would you work for that man? He's a disgrace to his country. And a traitor."

"How is he a traitor?" Virgil asked quickly. "Be careful saying things you can't prove. We've seen not that many years ago how that can go wrong quickly."

"I mean he is a traitor to his homeland," Bea said. "You know we're gonna be neighbors, Mr. Morrissey?" she asked. "I already live next to your son, down in town. And now my new hotel will be right behind your land. It would make sense if we all learned to get along."

Virgil didn't say anything until she walked away. "What's she mean about a hotel?" he asked Sheriff Tyson.

"I have no idea, Virgil. I try to deal with her as little as possible. She's like a snapping turtle. She moves slow in her daily doings, but when she attacks, she moves fast and hangs on til the other side gives up."

"Wonderful," Virgil said, shaking his head.

"I'm gonna be honest with you, Virgil. I need to come up and see the crime scene. And I need to talk to anyone who can identify these two suspects. Based on the clothes in the car, at least one of them is a woman."

"Both are, Sheriff," Virgil said. "My son Joe had them both as boarders." Virgil opened up the little notebook he carried for to-do lists and read their names. Esther Hausen and Beth St. Clair. We know the first name is real. She grew up around here. Her momma and daddy left back in '29 maybe? Moved to California. She moved back here just a few years ago. Esther I mean. This other lady, I don't know. Joe said he will meet you at the Station and answer any questions you have and take you to their room. They left a few things behind."

"Thank you, Virgil," Sheriff Tyson said, as he wrote the names down and took some more notes. "Virgil?" Sheriff Tyson said as Dale walked up. "I'm gonna need any help you and the Kaiser can give me on this one. I think we are looking at our prime suspects for the murder of Monte Montgomery."

The World Comes To Mercy Creek

"Let's head on up to the property," Virgil said. "I give you my word this has nothing to do with your investigation, but I'm gonna have to ask if I can take you in the back way."

Part 4

Chapter 1

On maps, the stream of water which flowed from a spring at the top of the mountain and down into the Shenandoah River was named Morrissey Creek, after the first family who registered land as their own with the local government. Before that, it may have had a name, but no one knew it. As homes began to be built along the river, a road was needed and as the road was being built along the river, a bridge was needed where Morrissey Creek flowed into the river. That original bridge had been built by neighbors working together.

At some point, the name Mercy Creek became what everyone called it, and along that same time, the county grew tired of repairing the bridge the community had built, and decided to build a new one. The covered bridge was finished some time around the turn of the century, and it had stood for four decades.

By November of 1941, there was no bridge over Mercy Creek. Work crews had moved their resources higher up the mountain to create and connect roads to the construction site of the military facility and surrounding properties. They left behind a large steel culvert, through which most of the creek flowed. Soil and rock and gravel had been dumped on top of it and pushed down around the pipe, burying it but also leveling off the surface so vehicles could pass safely as long as the passing was slow.

The mountain side of the creek had been flattened and pushed back by bulldozers which scarred the trees and land and left behind trenches and holes which marked the forest and caused most of the locals to shake their heads when they drove by. Fewer people passed by though, compared to years past.

After construction had started in July, more and more traffic had started to flow higher up the mountain or on the other side of the river to a bridge which crossed the river further upstream. When cars crossed the Mercy Creek bridge, they did so slowly and with caution as the dirt and gravel and stone around the culvert had begun to compact and erode.

Out on the main highway, near the beginning of Bridge Road, several large signs advertised many of the exciting building projects which were occurring on the mountain. One of the signs proclaimed, "Progress Is A Beautiful Thing."

Chapter 2

"Caviar?" the Kaiser asked as he surveyed the table. "No caviar?" His tone was humorous, but it was a dark humor lost on Leeza May who had worked hard to provide a Thanksgiving meal for the Kaiser while still feeding over one hundred people with food supplies which were slowly running out. Uma had told her that the Kaiser had sold his last car in order to purchase groceries enough to last until Christmas.

The children would be gone by mid-December. The house and land would be "sold" by the end of the year. When Leeza May had asked Uma what the Kaiser planned to do after that, she said she didn't know. He only talked about the children and what could be done to help them. She supposed he would begin to plan his own future once the kids were dispersed. Leeza May had grimaced at the sound of that last word and Uma had apologized for it. She said she had not allowed herself to grow fond of or bond with any of the children. She had to view everything in terms of credits and debits, and assets and liabilities. Leeza May had told her that was a sad way to view life, and Uma had agreed.

Thanksgiving had always been a time of celebration on the mountain, and Leeza May had worked hard to make this one as nice as possible. She cooked on every burner and every stove in the kitchen and was even cooking outside in order to make sure everyone had food.

The Kaiser and Uma ate alone at the large table in the Great Room. They shared a turkey, boiled potatoes, spiced apples, and pecan pie. The Kaiser knew that Uma loved pecan pie and he had asked Leeza May to surprise her with it.

Uma did not speak of the future or the present with the Kaiser while they ate and neither did he. Instead, they talked of Thanksgivings past and smiled and even laughed at the memories they shared.

Out in the building which had been Virgil's office, but now served as the main area where the kids gathered, a meal of turkey, chickens, and duck was served with mashed potatoes and gravy, corn on the cob, yeast rolls and pumpkin pie. Leeza May dined with the children as Ginny and Josh and Helmut served, along with the other guards and their families.

As the children ate with glee, Ginny, fought with emotions ranging from sadness, to desperation, to anger, and finally, resignation She found herself looking from child to child, memorizing their faces and voices. The ticking of the clock the Kaiser had talked about back in July had started that day for her, and she continued to hear it every day since.

They had stopped receiving children in September. They currently had ninety-four. Forty-one boys. Fifty-three girls. The rescuers in Europe had found somewhere else to send the children they were rescuing, and the Kaiser had worked to help them find other connections in the States. Josh said he had heard it was other Kaisers that were now helping, but Ginny never knew if that were true or not. It sure would make a wonderful story someday, she thought. As would the story of what they were doing right there in Virginia in this barn. But Ginny could not help but worry the ending would be bad for many of these children. Would they go to families that took them only for the money the Kaiser was sending with them? He had planned his finances so that they would each have some money to take with them. Would they go somewhere, have their money taken and then be kicked out on the streets? What if someone hated them as much as Hitler did? There were Nazis all over the cities of America. Why wouldn't they pose as helpers, just to finish what they had tried to do in Europe? These questions haunted Ginny, as did every smile and sound of laughter. Even those very beautiful things caused her fear and worry and sadness. Fear that the smiles would end. Worry that the laughter would echo no more across the Kaiser's Estate. Sadness that this story would ultimately not have a happy ending. "But they are alive," Ginny's father would say. "They have a chance at least," Josh told her many times.

"You can't control what others do. You can only make sure you do the right thing," her mother had said.

The World Comes To Mercy Creek

But no matter what others told her, Ginny could not get past the ticking in her head or the thought that this would be one story without a happy ending.

Across the fields and Mercy Creek, the Morrisseys gathered for Virgil's favorite holiday. For the first time in all of her Thanksgivings with Virgil, Nellie prepared a Thanksgiving meal without a turkey. He delivered one to Emily's mother, as he did every year. He delivered the other two to Leeza May the day before, along with every one of their chickens and some geese he and Joe shot while hunting.

"What's your favorite Thanksgiving memory, Momma?" Jeb asked. He had caught her staring out the window, so he was trying to distract her.

"Oh, that's a hard question," she said as she looked over at Virgil. "Why don't you answer, while I think of one?"

Virgil smiled. He looked tired and his face was wrinkled more than Jeb remembered. "Can I say every Thanksgiving memory is my favorite Thanksgiving memory?" he asked with a laugh.

"My favorite memory was from Thanksgiving the year before last," Charlene said. "Ginny and Josh and Joe and Emily were here." She looked at Jeb. "Jeb, you were here all the time, not just at night or running in to change clothes after work." And then she pointed at the empty chair across from where she sat. "And Little Virgil was here, too. It was before Daddy was tired all the time and before he and Little Virgil argued all the time. It wasn't just my favorite Thanksgiving. It was the last good one, if you ask me."

The sound of an engine coming closer caused Charlene to jump up and run to the window. "It's Uncle Yates," she shouted.

"He always seems to know when I'm serving a meal," Nellie said, smiling for the first time that day. The house had been so quiet and empty, and Yates filled any space he walked into with something more positive than what was there when he came in.

"I thought he was gonna celebrate over at the Tavern," Virgil said, as he stood up and walked to the door. Charlene and Jeb followed him and they descended the porch steps as Yates was climbing off of his motorcycle. He had found the bike deserted in North Carolina. The two ladies had run it off the road and into a tree. The State Patrolman that called him had said someone had seen the two women climb into a truck with Mississippi tags. The truck had been heading South but only a few miles from there was a junction where he could have gone in at least three different directions. Yates had checked around as long as he could, but the trail had grown cold. After having the motorcycle repaired, he loaded it into the back of his truck and went on back home.

He had gone down to Florida twice to follow leads. After that he went to Mempis and then New Orleans, but found nothing. Yates had no doubt Esther and Beth would eventually be caught. But he knew by the time it happened, the Kaiser's money would be long gone, and so would the children.

Sheriff Tyson had sent out an alert to all the other Sheriff's in the country, but those things took time to circulate. The Sheriff had issued a reward for their arrest, since one of them had murdered a Deputy, and Mac had matched the amount, hoping Beth being brought to justice would bring some comfort to his wife, who had felt like her brother had died for nothing. In his mind, Mac had to agree she was right, and though he was never fond of Monte, Mac was grieved that the man was killed for no reason other than he had crossed paths with the wrong person at the wrong time. He found himself thinking about Monte a lot, and he listened to the radio more closely when reports about the war in Europe came across the airwaves. While he listened, he watched his sons and allowed his heart and mind to begin to worry.

"Look at this spread," Yates said, as he walked in the door.

"You're just in time, Uncle Yates," Charlene said. "We were telling each other about our favorite Thanksgiving memories."

"Can I share?" he asked. "Is it my turn?"

"You sure can," Virgil said. He was glad his brother was there. Yates had a way of bringing life to a room and they needed him.

"Well, Yates said, as he sat down next to the stove, which put him directly in Nellie's way. She didn't mind working around him. "I was young, probably about your age, Charlene, maybe younger. I remember my ma had put all of this food out on the table and we had cousins and friends and neighbors all there. Pa had gone hunting and he took me with him. We killed a big old buck. I mean a monster with a rack. Golly, it had to be fifteen points? Maybe more." Yates reached for a yeast roll quickly, expecting Nellie to smack his hand. Instead she offered him a pat of fresh butter.

He smiled and put it on his roll and let it melt while he talked. "It was a great day. I mean everything was in place for it to be the best

The World Comes To Mercy Creek

day. But there was an empty chair. One empty chair. And because of that chair, there was a sadness in the room. Even I picked up on it. And I felt it, too. You see," Yates said, looking at Charlene and then to Jeb who was leaning in. He had not heard this story before either. "You see, the Great War had ended two weeks earlier. Or thereabouts. And Virgil had not come home. He had written us to tell us when he would be home. But that date had come and passed. Nellie, you were there."

"I was," Nellie said. "And so were Ginny and Joe. We were there. Waiting." She quickly brushed a tear away and untied and retied her apron and turned to the counter where she began to slice a pie.

"What you kids don't know is, your Daddy didn't care much for Thanksgiving back then. Did you Virgil? You just used it as a day to go hunting all day. Pa would come back by Noon, but Virgil usually missed the meal. He didn't care about it. But secretly, we all knew something would need to be very wrong for him to not be there on that Thanksgiving. With his wife and two kids waiting on him." Yates paused to eat his roll. After he finished it, everyone was still quiet and listening.

"So, we all sat down to eat. And that chair was still empty. Ma asked me to say grace but I didn't want to do it. So, Nellie asked if she could. She was technically a guest in that house, but our parents loved her like family. Didn't they Virgil?"

"They sure did," Virgil said. He was staring at the fire and listening.

"So Nellie started saying this prayer. And in our house, the blessing was Grace. A prayer from a book. But Nellie starts asking God for Virgil to be safe somewhere. Not hurt, or worse. Not stuck in some lonely train station. But she asked, and I remember this like it was yesterday. She asked that he be somewhere he could feel God's love and be thankful." Yates looked around and continued, "Then she stopped. She stopped asking. Well, I didn't hear Amen so I was too scared of Ma to open my eyes, so I kept them shut until I heard chairs scraping the floor and people crying so I opened my eyes and looked up, and there he was," Yates said. He looked over at his brother and said, "There he was." He sipped from his glass of buttermilk and said, "And since that day, your daddy has loved Thanksgiving like no man I've ever known."

"I think we're ready to eat now," Nellie said, wiping her eyes again. "I hope you all don't miss the turkey too much."

A bird doesn't make Thanksgiving, Thanksgiving, Nellie. This looks like a very fine meal."

"Family makes Thanksgiving, Thanksgiving," Charlene said. "Where is Little Virgil? He's gonna eat Thanksgiving with some other family? That makes no sense!"

"Your brother is figuring some things out," Nellie said, looking towards Virgil.

"I will go by the Robertsons next week," Virgil said. "And talk to him."

Nellie nodded and asked who wanted to say Grace. When no one responded, she said, "Jeb?"

Jeb shook his head. "Sorry, Momma."

"You and the Lord are not on speaking terms right now, son?" Nellie asked.

"Yeah, but it's not his fault," Jeb said quickly.

"Oh, I don't doubt that," Nellie said. "What's going on?"

"I just haven't seen Him doing much God work lately, which is His right. But it's just...I guess I'm just not in the mood to ask him for anything right now."

"Well, why don't you try thanking him, instead of asking," Virgil said.

"I guess I don't much feel like that, either," Jeb said.

"Is that why we haven't seen you in church lately?" Nellie asked.

"Yes ma'am, I guess it is," Jeb said.

The front door opened and Joe's voice called in, "We heard a rumor that the Morrissey family up on the mountain was trying to have Thanksgiving dinner without a turkey."

Emily quickly said, "So the Morrissey family from down in town got to thinking we should go up there and join them, since my momma has a Virgil Morrissey raised turkey at her house and not enough people to help her eat it."

The room immediately filled with Emily's mother, followed by Brian and his family.

"My goodness, you all didn't have to do this," Nellie said.

"Yes you did!" Yates said. "I was starting to get depressed, thinking about no turkey on turkey day."

After everyone sat down at the table, Virgil asked if anyone would like to say what they were thankful for.

Brian spoke up and said, "I'd like to say I'm thankful my mother got to meet her grandson before she passed this year. And I'm thankful for my wife and son and my mother-in-law."

"I'm thankful for our President," Laura. Rhodes said. "That he is wise enough to keep us out of another War over in Europe. I'm thankful because these boys here won't have to see what Virgil saw, or my Sam."

"I'm thankful for that chocolate cake Emily just brought into this house," Charlene said. Everyone laughed.

Yates asked, "Can we slice into that now or do we have to wait?"

"You have to wait," Emily said. "Joe tried to eat some all last night, and I just about had to guard it with my shotgun." Everyone laughed again.

"I'm thankful for laughter," Virgil said. "Especially the laughter of children. It's becoming more and more rare these days, and I'm thankful to hear it here in my home."

"I'm thankful my true love is back home safe and sound," Yates said.

"Who's the lucky lady?" Laura Rhodes asked.

"Yeah, tell us who, Uncle Yates," Charlene said.

"He's talking about his motorcycle," Virgil said, shaking his head.

"Yates, you're not!" Nellie said, with a gasp.

"Indeed I am," he said. "And I've almost got Jeb here convinced to give up girls and buy a motorcycle."

"I've already got the giving up on girls part of it done," Jeb said. "I'll have to save up for the bike."

"I knew you would be a bad influence on my boys, Yates, but I never thought it would be Jeb," Virgil said.

"Speaking of your sons, I hear Little Virgil is running Vance Robertson's stables," Yates said. "He's making more than I did when I was delivering mail and painting houses."

"What in the world is he doing to make that kind of money?" Nellie asked.

"He's really good with the horses," Joe said. "I was over there helping him build some jumps. He's a natural, Daddy."

Virgil nodded. "Well I'm glad he's found something he likes doing," Virgil said. "Let's carve this turkey here and dig in."

As the food was passed, everyone began to talk and share and ask questions like one big family.

Virgil walked over to Jeb's chair and leaned in and asked, "Are you still writing articles for the paper?"

"Well, sort of. I write some stuff for the local section."

"Can I talk to you about an article idea I have?" Virgil asked.

"Yes sir," Jeb said. "Now?"

"After dinner. Okay?'

"Yes sir," he said. "Okay."

Virgil patted Jeb on the arm and then walked back to his seat and sat down. "So what's next Joe?" Virgil asked.

"I guess I could ask you the same question," Joe said. "With Beaumont's hotel opening up in a few weeks, I can't compete with it, even though it's up here on the mountain. She's moving all of her boarders, and the one I had left."

"She took your maintenance guy, too?" Virgil asked.

"You mean Frank? No, I fired him three weeks ago, when he ate the first slice of Emily's birthday cake."

"The day before my birthday!" Emily said, laughing. "You should have seen your son. It was the best birthday present I've ever gotten, seeing Joe pack his bags for him."

"And now he's working in the dining hall of the new hotel," Joe said, shaking his head and laughing.

"Maybe we can figure out something both of us can do, together?" Virgil asked.

"I would like that, Daddy," Joe said. "I'd like that a lot."

"I got a letter from Anthony," Jeb said. "He said to say hello to everybody."

"Oh, how nice," Nellie said. "Where is he now?"

"He just finished his flight training," Jeb said. "He just got sent to somewhere in Hawaii. Can you believe that guy's luck? He said it was seventy degrees the day he wrote me. In late October."

"Momma, you never shared your favorite memory," Charlene said.

Nellie looked across the table to Little Virgil's empty seat. "I'm still hoping it's this one," she said.

Chapter 3

"I'm not running this," Jim Marbling said.

"What don't you like? I'd be happy to rewrite it. As many times as you want me to. This is important."

"It's contentious. And pretentious. It will upset half of our readers to know this kind of thing was happening right under their noses. And I wonder if it's even legal, what they did up there. We could be complicit in a crime."

"What kind of crime? Come on, Chief."

"Kidnapping. The taking and holding of hostages. They could be breaking child labor laws. And then you get into Federal stuff. They are illegal aliens. I have no idea how many immigration laws have been broken." Marbling looked past Jeb like he was hoping someone would come in and rescue him from the conversation. "I'm not running it."

"Chief, there's a hundred kids up there on that mountain that are gonna be shipped off to God knows what situations and we have the chance to keep them local. To keep them where they can still be taught by the same teachers. They would have each other. If they get shipped out, they get all split up. Probably families will be split up even more than they already have."

"I'm not doing it, and if you ask me again, I'm firing you."

"Chief, what if I--"

"Get the hell out of my office," Marbling said, calling out the door to his secretary, "Lissa, honey? Get Ralph Pourpin on the line for me. Tell him I have a legal issue here I want to run past him."

Jeb's eyes lit up again when he heard this. "If it turns out they're not breaking any laws, will you do it?"

"No!" Marbling shouted. "If you must know, I'm trying to find out what my legal responsibility is as far as reporting all of this to the authorities."

Jason L. Queen

It took everything Jeb had not to go across the desk and break a few picture frames over his head, but he calmed himself down enough to walk out of the Chief's office and across the street to his building.

Sitting at his desk, Jeb began to think of another way to get the word out. After several minutes, he stood up and walked out onto the preparation floor. After looking to see who was working that day, Jeb smiled to himself and went back into his office. He had a lot to do and a lot of people to talk to before the next edition ran.

That night, a one time run of "The Mercy Creek Courier" was tucked into every edition of the paper and sent out across the town and county. After three years of working at the newspaper, Jeb had made many friends and every typesetter, printer and processor did what he asked without hesitation. Earlier in the afternoon, when Jeb had presented the plan to him, Artie Fox had lit a Lucky Strike and said, "What's the bastard gonna do, fire all of us?"

The Mercy Creek Courier. Volume 1 of 1. Edition 1 of 1. December 1, 1941.

This year, many articles were printed regarding the construction projects occurring on the mountain near Mercy Creek. From Bridge Road to Mountain View Road, two United States Government construction crews have been working since July, building roads, rights of way, and a new military facility, which will potentially employ hundreds of local civilian workers and military personnel. In addition, a crew began construction on a new hotel in August.

Many stories were printed about these projects, however, many were not. Here are some of the stories local citizens were never told:

The Mercy Creek Bridge, once considered a local landmark, was destroyed twice, with the third and current version of the bridge a remnant of what once was. Additionally, a historic covered bridge is now a pile of debris, leaving that section of the road washed-out and unreliable.

The World Comes To Mercy Creek

Directly above that bridge, on property scarred by bulldozers, another story unfolds. Over a year ago, while Germany invaded countries in Eastern Europe, one of our neighbors, Wilhelm Viktor, known locally as the Kaiser, learned of atrocities previously unheard of in times of peace. He learned of families being ripped from their homes at night, stripped and separated in the streets, and relocated to camps where they labored and died. Across our country, Americans dismiss these stories as rumors or lies and refuse to believe these first hand accounts which are only now beginning to trickle into the United States.

I have heard these stories directly from children who witnessed and survived these atrocities. These children were rescued by a contingent of mercy-minded British, French, German, and Polish men and women who smuggled them out of Warsaw and the surrounding villages. Many were concealed and transported in livestock grain crates and even burial caskets.

When these children reached America, many questions arose. What do we do with them? Where do we house them? Who will feed and clothe them? For over a year, Wilhelm Viktor provided everything these children needed, including an education in the English language. He is now unable to continue providing for these children. He has given all he has.

The dilemma is this: Who will take care of these children until the War in Europe ends and they can return to their homeland? If you are able, we ask you to invite one or more of these children into your home. From Thursday, December 4th through the end of the week, we ask you to commit to making a sacrifice. Any child who is not placed by the end of next week will be dispersed again - perhaps to an orphanage in war-torn England or a children's home in New York.

This is your opportunity to help save a life. If you have dreamed of helping to change the world for the better, this is your chance. The Kaiser's Estate will be open according to the dates above for you to come to meet the children. For the safety of the children, the Kaiser's Estate will work with the County Sheriff's Department to interview each person who volunteers to foster. Please show your compassion and generosity next Thursday. Let nothing stand in the way of saving a life.

Chapter 4

"We can stay another hour, Virgil," Sheriff Tyson said. "But after that, I can't even see bringing any Deputies back out here tomorrow. This is already a touchy situation. There's got to be some laws being broken here. Lucky for you and the Kaiser, I haven't had time to think about what those might be."

"No county laws that I can think of," Virgil said. "Maybe some state, but I can't think of any either. Now, Federal...I don't know."

"Touchy," the Sheriff said. "The situation is touchy and the less I'm around it, the better. So I think today is all we're gonna be able to do. It's sour milk."

"Jeb's article said through the end of the week. We have to give it until tomorrow. "

"It doesn't matter what his article said. Based on today's turn out, I can't justify coming back tomorrow."

"I didn't think we'd find homes for all of them," Virgil said. "But I've gotta say. I'm shocked that no one came." He looked out across the lawn and towards the barn. "No one..."

"We'll give it another hour and then pack up, Virgil," Sheriff Tyson said.

Thank you for being willing to help," Virgil said. As he walked back towards the house, the Kaiser met him on the way.

"Not one?" he asked.

"Not one," Virgil said.

The normally verbose Kaiser seemed to be searching for words. "It was a good idea, Virgil. I would have sworn it would work."

"Me too," Virgil said. "Nellie would say it's the Lord teaching us to trust His plans."

"I thought we had learned that lesson many years ago," Nellie said as she walked up with Jeb.

"Sometimes there is no lesson to learn," the Kaiser said. "Sometimes, there is just disappointment."

"People are scared," Jeb said. "That's all. So are we, if you think about it. We're scared for the kids to go somewhere they don't know anyone. But they didn't know us when they got here. And now they do. There was never any chance that all of these kids would stay in this county. Or even in this state. It's a big thing to take on. It's a scary thing."

"I think we need to get used to scary things," Nellie said.

"I don't want to," Virgil said. "I want to run off anything that's scary. I want to make it more scared of me than I am of it."

"We're dealing with evil," Jeb said. "What made those kids have to come here in the first place is pure, unadulterated evil. And the only thing that scares evil is love."

"It's a naive mindset, son," Virgil said.

"I don't think so," Nellie said. "I think it's wise."

The Kaiser looked down towards his open gate, and then waved over to Sheriff Tyson and his deputies and called out to them. "I believe you all can go now, Sheriff. I am most grateful for your willingness to help. Get home to your families." The Kaiser then turned to the small group around him and said, "I have always thought the way Virgil thinks. But this past year, I tried something different. I tried what you just said, Jeb. But I...today I must admit that maybe love isn't enough. These children will certainly need more than that."

As the Kaiser started to walk away, he stopped and turned his head. The sound of gravel popping and then a car engine made everyone turn, including the Sheriff and the Deputies. At first there was nothing, but the guards had moved out of the road to make way for whoever it was.

An old blue pickup truck came through the gate, moving slowly up the lane to the yard where the Kaiser walked over to greet them. The driver was a black man with graying hair and a beard to match. As he talked to the Kaiser a woman got out of the truck followed by a young girl. "My goodness that's Abigail and her mother, Mabel," Nellie said. "Hi Mabel!" Nellie walked quickly to meet them.

"I hope I'm not late," Mabel said. "Mrs. Beaumont won't ever let me off early, and if she does, she docks me for a whole day."

The Kaiser and Mabel's husband walked up as she was talking. "Have y'all met my husband, Harold? This is Harold, y'all."

The World Comes To Mercy Creek

"Are we too late to help?" Harold asked slowly.

"You are not, Sir," the Kaiser said. "You are right on time. We just need to walk over here to our fine Sheriff and he has to assure me that he does not think you are an arch criminal putting together a criminal syndicate of grammar school children."

"Great day in the morning, Harold was fussing at me the whole way over here, telling me I'd made us late. He was talking about how he would have left me, but he reckoned it would look bad, a man without his own wife and kid coming here and filling his truck with children."

"Oh, Mabel," Nellie said. "You are a Godsend. You truly are."

"I ain't nothing special," Mabel said. "Now show me these children."

"Are you here for a girl or a boy?"

"Both," Mabel said. "We have room for two."

"To be honest with you, Mabel, no one else has come all day, so when my momma says you're a Godsend, she really means it," Jeb said.

"Keep in mind, people work for a living. Most of them aren't even off work yet. They'll come. Your article was well written, by the way," Mabel said.

"You think so?" Jeb asked.

"Well, it made my husband talk all week long about helping, and it made Mrs. Beaumont talk all week long to Chip about how glad she was that you got fired from the paper. So, anything that makes my husband happy and Mrs. Beaumont angry, is better than William Faulkner if you ask me," Mabel said.

Everyone laughed as they all walked together towards the building where the kids were still in their classes. A guard yelled out from the gate, and as they turned, they saw a stake body truck. It was Earl and Mellie, the Morrissey's neighbors from the mountain, and behind them, a black Ford car, and then another truck.

"I told you," Mabel said. "Some people still work for a living." She slapped Jeb's arm when she said it and laughed. "We got good neighbors in this county, don't we Jeb Morrissey?"

Over Mabel's shoulder Jeb saw cars coming up the hill in a long, slow moving line.

Chapter 5

That Sunday morning one of the roosters woke Virgil up.. This would not seem an odd occurrence, except for the fact that it had not happened for well over a year. Virgil was usually awake before dawn and the rooster often crowed his goodbye as Virgil left for the Kaiser's Estate. On that Sunday morning, though, Virgil slept well past dawn and he awoke knowing that every one of the children had a home, for as long as they needed one, at Mercy Creek and across the county. Virgil and Nellie had planned on taking in as many as four children, but by the end of the weekend, everyone already had a local home.

Ginny and Josh had taken in Agata. Ginny had formed a friendship with her over the past few months and she had announced, much to the surprise and delight of Virgil and Nellie and the rest of the family, that their home, wherever they ended up, would need to hold four.

"Let's leave early for church so we can enjoy this December sunshine," Nellie said.

Virgil looked towards Jeb, who was quietly eating a biscuit, and asked, "Why don't you come with us, son? The new preacher is a good one. I think you'd like him."

"I've got a busy day, Daddy," Jeb said without looking up. And then after a moment he looked at Nellie and said, "Sorry, Momma."

Nellie started to push the issue, but decided against it. "Should I expect you for Sunday dinner?" she asked.

"No ma'am," he said.

Nellie nodded and called up the stairs for Charlene to come on down. When she finally did, Charlene hugged Jeb and then ran out the door to the porch where Virgil and Nellie were waiting.

Jeb spent the morning reading past editions of The Herald. This had been his hometown newspaper since he was a child, and he remembered reading articles from it when he was barely old enough to read. This was not the same paper he remembered. He didn't have to look hard through each edition to find a favorable article about the Nazis or Hitler. One of the more recent articles, written by Chip, had been more of an editorial and at one point he had clearly said that it might be more in the interest of America if she joined Germany and Italy in the war against Great Britain. Jeb stopped reading it halfway through, and began to list in a notebook the items he would need in order to start his own newspaper.

When he looked at the clock and saw that it was after one o'clock, Jeb decided to head into town for lunch. First, he stopped by Joe and Emily's house, but it was locked up and no one answered the door. As Jeb walked back through the front yard to his car, he looked at the level ground where the stumps had been and remembered the day he dug them out. Esther had sat with him on the steps and asked him questions that made him think she cared about him, but she was just getting a lay of the land before she and Beth had tried to rob the Kaiser. He found himself wondering where Esther was, and when she would finally be caught. When she did, they would bring her back to Lyttle's Mill for trial, he supposed. As he got in his car and drove towards Main Street, he thought through whether or not he would visit her at the jail, and he had decided he wouldn't by the time he parked in front of the diner.

As he walked inside, Jeb realized the after-church crowds had beaten him there and every table was full. At the counter, a waitress pointed to an empty stool between two men he didn't know. He took a seat and ordered lemonade and a fried bologna sandwich. With his notebook open in front of him, he listened to the man to his left talk to a woman further down the counter.

"Oh yeah. It'll be a good one," the man said.

"Well that's news I like to hear," the woman replied.

"Yep. Those kids have been practicing the songs since September. And we even have live sheep and a horse and a goat. And oh, yeah, some chickens."

"Were there chickens in the manger?" she asked.

"I don't know. Who knows?"

"I'm just saying that sounds odd."

The man made a grunting sound and dismissed her concern. "Hey, did you hear about the Eatons?"

"I did. I'm glad you told them no. I agree with your decision."

"And it's not about those children being foreigners, neither. It's because the other kids worked hard all year, and it's not right, these new kids coming in at the last minute and getting to be a part of it."

"I had to move some of them out of our pew this morning. Well, I didn't. Bobby had Seth do it."

The man made the grunting sound again. "That's what deacons are for. Good for Seth."

"Here ya go, Jeb." Jeb looked up to see Shirley smiling at him. "And here's your lemonade," she said. "I liked that article. You're a good writer."

"Thank you, Shirley," Jeb said quickly. "Thanks alot."

"You write for the paper?" the man to Jeb's right asked.

"He used to," Shirley said. "Whatcha gonna do now, Jeb?"

"Well, I think I might--" Jeb looked around and lowered his voice. "I think I might start my own paper."

"Oh my gosh, Jeb. I think you *should* start your own paper. That's a tremendous idea. I don't like the Herald. They talk about other counties like they're better than us. My cousin Sophie won three blue ribbons at the fair for her pigs. Big deal, right? Well, I guess the Herald didn't think so, because they didn't even mention it. Not one article or mention of any of the stuff that happened at the fair," Shirley said. "Would your paper mention the fair, Jeb?"

"What's this about another paper?" the man next to him said. "Why does a small town like this need two newspapers?"

"Two newspapers?" a woman down the counter asked.

"Just an idea," Jeb said quickly. "I was just saying I had an idea."

"If you're starting a business, pick one that closed down during the Depression," the man to his right said. "We still don't have a hardware store, or a blacksmith."

"Mac sells hardware," a man at the end of the counter said.

"Yeah, but he would charge less if there was competition in town," the first man said. "I'm just asking why you would start something we already got when we don't have some stuff we need here?"

"It was just an idea," Jeb said again, taking a small bite out of his sandwich and chewing slowly.

"We need a shop that fixes electric lamps," a lady's voice called out. "My husband had to take ours all the way to Winchester. And the traffic there? Goodness gracious. Why don't you open a shop that fixes electric lamps?"

Jeb sipped his lemonade and took another bite of his sandwich.

The sound of noise from the street came in as the front door of the cafe was thrown open by a man who yelled, "Turn the radio on. Turn the radio on! The radio. Turn it on!"

"What?" someone in the diner asked.

More noise from the street.

"We've been attacked!" a man yelled in through the open door.

A waitress ran around the counter and turned on a small radio.

"What did he mean?" a young woman asked.

A small boy was crying.

"Quiet down!" a man yelled as he came in quickly from the kitchen. "Turn it up. Turn it up."

Another man yelled out, "Turn it up, please!"

"...by enemy planes, undoubtedly Japanese."

"Where?" someone yelled.

"Did they attack New York?" a man said. Then he spoke it louder. "Did the Japanese attack New York?" Several voices raised up telling him to be quiet.

"...just west of Honolulu, Hawaii. Pearl Harbor is located in a lagoon harbor on the island of Oahu. We cannot estimate yet how much damage has been done, but this has been a very severe attack."

Someone screamed and then the door opened with more street noise. Car horns and shouting from outside, made the radio hard to hear, so someone called out, "Turn it up!"

"Who attacked us?"

"The Japanese."

"How?"

"Why the hell would they do that?"

A different man's voice came on the radio and said, "*The Manager of this station would like, at this time, to make clear to our listeners that this broadcast is not a show. It is not a program. It is not an emergency drill. The Empire of Japan has attacked our nation using submarines and airplanes. This has been a deadly attack on our Naval base in Pearl Harbor. We are being assured that the skies and waters have been taken back under the control of the United States by the*

United States Navy. San Diego and San Francisco are in a state of emergency as declared by the Governor of California. The Governor of New York is expected to--"

Jeb stood up quickly and began to push through the crowd before he stopped and turned back to put money on the counter. As he made his way back to the front door, and out to the street, he stopped in shock as he saw traffic stopped in the street and crowds of people moving from stores and buildings onto sidewalks and spilling over into Main Street. To his right, Pete MacBatten called out to him. "Jeb! Jeb! It's happening."

Jeb turned and followed Pete and Pat into The Trading Post. All around him men were talking about War. "I'm joining up, Jeb," Pat said. "So is Pete."

"We knew it was close, we just didn't know it would be the Japs to do it. How stupid can they be? Messing with us? Us?" Pete shook his head and called over Jeb's shoulder. "Brian! Are you joining up? Me and Pat are."

Jeb turned to see Brian come in the door with his wife, Emily's sister Faith. She was crying and Brian looked like he was trying to console her. All around him men were talking about War. Across the store, Jeb saw Mac MacBatten standing by a radio. He was staring past everyone around him, as if his mind was somewhere far away.

Chapter 6

The white painted boards of the church glowed in the moonlight. For a moment, the building seemed to illuminate the area around it. As the outside lights were turned on, small groups of adults and children were silhouetted in the night as they made their way across the yard and up the steps of the building with the steeple reaching up into the darkness.

The first thing Reverend Rawls did after hearing the news was to spread the word that the church would be holding a special evening service for prayer for the country and for those who had lost their lives that morning. The second thing he did was call Reverend Spencer and ask for his help. Matthew Rawls had only been out of seminary for six months, and he was wise enough to know he needed someone wiser than himself to help these people who would be looking to him for guidance and help. Even though Reverend Spencer wasn't the pastor of the church and didn't pastor anywhere, he was loved and trusted by the community.

All across the town and the county and the state, and the nation, churches were filling with people seeking answers, or peace, or security, or maybe all three and more. Cars were lined up on the street to turn left into Lyttle's Mill Baptist Church or right into First Presbyterian. The parking lots of both churches were filled and there were no parking spaces empty anywhere in sight.

Virgil, Nellie, along with Charlene, parked in front of Joe and Emily's house and walked with them down a side street and up a few blocks to the church. As they neared the church, Nellie saw Jeb and called out his name. When he walked up, Nellie asked, "How long have you been here?"

"Since around three o'clock," he said. "After I found out, I didn't know where to go."

"You should have come by the house," Emily said.

"I stopped by around lunch time, but you guys weren't home," Jeb replied.

"We were at Emily's mom's house," Joe said. "It looks like we might need to move in there for a while."

"But none of that seems to matter now," Emily said. "All my worries seem so small after..." She didn't finish her sentence and no one spoke up to fill the silence as they walked inside together and found a pew halfway up on the right hand side of the church. As they sat down, Ginny and Josh, along with Agata came in and sat behind them. Nellie thought back to when they used to barely fill a pew. Now her family was stretching across two of them. Next to Jeb was an empty space and Nellie's mind went to Little Virgil.

Someone was playing piano softly and the church was surprisingly quiet to be filled with so many people. Reverend Rawls opened the service with a few words. His tone was somber and his voice was shaky. After Reverend Rawls prayed, he asked one of the Deacons to read the 23rd Psalm, and as he did, he stopped and took several moments to gather himself and try again. He had been a veteran of the Great War, and was having a difficult time not weeping through the whole service.

Next, Reverend Spencer stepped forward and began to pray for all of the young men who had died earlier that day, and then he prayed for all of the men who might soon be leaving to fight in the war. Jeb thought of his best friend Anthony and immediately felt ashamed and scared at the same time. Anthony had written that he would be stationed in Pearl Harbor, but Jeb hadn't even written him back yet. All afternoon and evening he sat wondering if Anthony was alive or if by some miracle he had made it. There had been many survivors. But there had also been so many dead. And the number of deaths were rising as the casualties succumbed to their injuries.

At this point in the service, Nellie began to cry softly. She looked down the pew and saw two of her boys who were of age to fight. Her third son, who was very close to the age to go was already gone from home, it seemed. Her heart ached that he had not come home to his family in a time like this. On the drive over, Virgil had said he would go to the Robertson's farm in the morning to talk to their youngest son and make amends. Virgil said he would do whatever he needed to do, even though he wasn't sure why Little Virgil was so upset. Nellie had said he probably wasn't sure either.

The World Comes To Mercy Creek

After that, a young girl stood up and sang an old hymn called "Wonderful Peace". As she sang, more and more people were pressing into the church until it was far beyond capacity. As men and women stood in the aisles and along the side and back, Virgil stood up to make room for any ladies who wanted to sit. Jeb did the same, followed by Joe and several other men across the congregation.

As they made their way to the back and found a place where they could stand together, Virgil and his boys bowed their heads as Reverend Rawls began to lead them in another prayer. This one was focused on all the countries which were already at war.

During the prayer, Virgil felt an arm around his shoulders and somehow, from feelings deep within him, he knew it was his youngest son. He opened his eyes and Little Virgil was there, leaning in and hugging him. "I wanna come home, Daddy. I'm so sorry. Can I just please come home?"

Virgil whispered "Of course," as quickly as he could as emotions threatened his ability to even speak. "Of course you can, son."

At the front of the church, singing started again. "A Mighty Fortress Is Our God".

Behind Little Virgil stood a thin young girl with long dark hair. She was hugging Jeb. Virgil recognized her as Vance Robertson's youngest daughter. Virgil pointed them to where Nellie was sitting with the rest of the family, and Little Virgil and Fern made their way up the side of the congregation as everyone continued to sing. When they got to Nellie, Little Virgil hugged her and leaned in to talk to her and she immediately began to cry as she pulled both of them to her tightly.

As the song finished, Reverend Spencer said, "Tonight, in our quiet little town, people are saying that the war has come to Mercy Creek and to Lyttle's Mill and to our county, as our nation has been invaded. And in reaction, many of our citizens will go forth into the world. Fathers, sons, and brothers will go forth in battle supported by mothers, daughters and sisters. And as our loved ones leave us and go to foreign fields and dark places, please help us to remind them and to reassure them, that they will never go so far from this land, or so far from the light, that we won't be waiting here with our arms outstretched and our voices ready to say, "Welcome back home."

Chapter 7

The sounds of New Year's Eve fireworks on the mountain were replaced with the echoes of hammers driving nails through boards at the Mercy Creek bridge as men and boys finished the roof just as the final snowflakes began to fall for the year of 1941.

Mac MacBatten moved swiftly from worker to worker, helping, supplying, and directing. Old men and young boys were spread across the bridge from end to end, side to side, and top to bottom. Different languages mingled as each man communicated in the best way he knew.

Leonid moved up and down a wooden ladder, carrying bundles of shingles and buckets of tools. He moved quickly and worked with intentionality as if trying to prove himself among his new countrymen, as he was acutely aware that they were now at war with his *former* countrymen. From time to time his eyes moved up the mountain to the ridgeline where he had stood just a few weeks earlier, digging a deep hole and burying the burnt remains of a uniform he had once worn with pride, but now found disgusting. His original intentions of coming to America were focused on finding ways to spread the message of his homeland among the youth of America, but the sounds and faces of the children up on the Estate throughout the past year made their way into a place within himself which was even deeper than the deepest parts of his heart.

All across the bridge, local men teamed up with boys who struggled to speak the language, but knew enough from Ginny's teachings to understand and to help. When Mac stood back and watched the progress all around him, it was not lost upon him that more than one bridge was being built among these workers.

This was the only construction on the mountain for several months after the attack on Pearl Harbor. The declarations of war by Japan and Germany caused the plans for the military facility to come

The World Comes To Mercy Creek

to a halt. This ceased the extension of any more roads and highways, which left the Beaumont's hotel virtually landlocked with only a temporary construction right of way and no highway leading in. Even if there were, the only reason for many visitors to come to the area was on hold. All the heavy equipment was long gone within a week of Pearl Harbor, leaving behind cleared and broken land and a creek that could barely be crossed in the winter or during rain storms.

Down below the bridge, Little Virgil and his father worked together to secure the braces that would make sure the bridge was sturdy and last for decades to come.

The two men moved from rock to rock, careful not to step down into the freezing mountain water. As his father walked off of a rock, Little Virgil stepped onto it, and in this way, they worked together to nail the lumber to the understructure of the bridge. When they were done, Little Virgil pointed out that they were in the perfect spot to see up to the top of the mountain, where Mercy Creek started.

They stood together for a long while, after the other workers had packed up and left. Neither one spoke for several minutes, until Little Virgil broke the silence. "I've always been amazed how that little spring at the top of the mountain becomes this creek. Then this creek becomes that big river," he said as he pointed to the Shenandoah. "If that spring tried to stay a spring, we wouldn't have the creek. And if all these creeks around here tried to stay creeks, we wouldn't have this river."

Virgil looked at his son and instead of speaking, decided to stay silent and just listen. A few cars moved slowly across the bridge. Their rumbling turned into the popping of gravel as they moved along down the road towards the highway.

"I guess sometimes we have to give ourselves up to be a part of something bigger than we could ever be on our own," Little Virgil said, as he dropped a stick into the water and watched it drift slowly away and into the darkness beyond the bridge.

The End

Acknowledgments

I want to start by thanking anyone who is reading this book. This is my second novel, and it wouldn't exist without you, because it was written at the encouragement of so many readers of my first novel. When I wrote My Life Was Mercy Creek, I never planned on a sequel, but I received so many notes and comments asking for one, that it became an easy decision when it was time to start my second novel. I missed Mercy Creek and the people there. Thank you for the opportunity to return and spend more time with them.

Thanks to my beta reader, Rebekah Dunlap. Thanks also to her husband, Jeremy, for helping me name the town of Lyttle's Mill. He wants no public acknowledgement so I take great joy in giving him what he didn't want.

Thanks to Dave Lloyd who has been my friend since the seventh grade. Any friendship depicted in my writing can trace its roots back to the loyal friendship I have been blessed to experience with Dave.

The art, design, and layout of the cover and the book are all the products of Chloe Tobin's mind and talents once again. She has been wonderful to work with, and I count myself lucky and blessed to watch her grow in her work as a graphic artist. She is a rising star and I can't wait to see the art she will create in the years to come.

The indie imprint which published this book is Independent Literature Brewing Company. My fellow book brewer and business partner, Jackson Tobin, has worked hard behind the scenes to make sure my books are available to as many readers as possible and I am so thankful for the work he is doing.

Thanks to Holly A. Dobrynski, owner and founder of The Pirate's Quill. She provided a listening ear and some guidance and advice when it came to the newspaper articles in the book. Holly will have a book of her own out soon and I can't wait to read it.

In my first novel, I referred to the area on the mountain above the Shenandoah River as "Mercy Creek". However, I only referred to the nearby town as... "town". For the sequel, I knew I needed to name the town so that readers wouldn't be confused as characters moved between town and the mountain. In naming the town, many readers suggested honoring someone from the area, and the easy answer was John Lyttle. Mr. Lyttle was a teacher for many years at Clarke County High School and most locals either have or have heard a story about his generosity and dedication to his friends, neighbors, and family. John Lyttle was my teacher for several classes, and I was blessed to attend church with him when I was younger. I hope his wife and daughters will accept this gesture of honor towards a beloved man, as we name the town, "Lyttle's Mill".

While Lyttle's Mill and Mercy Creek are fictional areas within a fictional county, and the inhabitants are fictional as well, there are several real and recognizable landmarks mentioned in the book such as the Shenandoah River, Winchester, and a few other nearby cities and towns. I must of course remind everyone that this is a work of fiction and all characters and stories are works of fiction from the mind of the author, but my inspiration flowed from my friends and neighbors of Clarke County and Berryville, Virginia.

Thanks to all the independent artisan shops and bookstores which have supported this book and so many other works of indie authors across the world. The heart and soul of the business side of books is often fueled by the support of independent sellers. I have felt that first hand.

The Morrissey family is largely inspired by my family. Thank you to my mom and dad, Jimmy and Sandra Queen. And thanks also to my brothers and sisters - Jimmy, David, Sandie, Jonathan and Rebekah. Each of you will of course recognize yourselves in some of these fictional characters because we share not just a family name, but also memories which were the seeds of these stories. I love each of you and I'm proud to be your brother.

My wife, Misty, has encouraged every letter of every word of every sentence I have written. I am more thankful for her than I can even begin to articulate. And to my kids, Jasilyn, Noah, Jacob, Caleb, and Charlotte: I hope you recognize yourself in every statement of hope and love you find within the pages of this book. I love all of you more than you can ever know and more than I can ever say.

Check Out The First Of
The Morrissey Family Novels

Order Your Copy Today!

Available Through These Retailers:
bookbrewers.com or Amazon.com

A coming of age story told from the point of view of a boy growing up in Virginia during the Great Depression. Set in 1933 and 1934, the stories of his family's struggles to survive are both heartbreaking and inspiring as we watch them go from the heights of peace and serenity to the depths of scarcity and hopelessness. Will they be able to rise together or will the brutal realities of the rural world they live in separate them and destroy their hopes and dreams?
My Life Was Mercy Creek is the debut, independently published novel of Virginia Author, Jason L. Queen.

INTRODUCING
THE PERFECT BEACH READ!

SUMMER BREW

a short-story compilation
presented by the book brewers
Coming May 2021

If you're reading this, you are already holding an independently published novel. Did you know that by supporting independent writers, **you** are actively contributing to the <u>variety</u> of print and other media available **everywhere** today?

www.bookbrewers.com

the book brewers want to know

Do you have a dream to see
<u>your story</u> in print?

Do you know that it is **never too late** to start writing?
Or to publish your work?

Get started at www.bookbrewers.com

Made in the USA
Columbia, SC
11 May 2021